The Dark Horse Stories

Leonard Holman

Acknowledgements

I would like to pay special thanks to my wife Dolores,
Sons Leonard and Earl and Daughter Donna Marie,
My grandchildren Emma and Saoirse,
Mayor of Limerick John Gilligan
And also my sponsors
For helping me to get this book published

Front and back cover photography by Dolores Holman

Table of Contents

Paddy the Reluctant Limerick Vampire
A Black Comedy

Paddy was getting restless in his coffin. He did not know how long he had been in there but, smelling his clothes, he knew it was a long time. Now, as he waited to get his strength back, he started thinking of the times he had left his coffin. There had only been two, the first time a fellow by the name of Patrick Sarsfield was blowing up trains and half of Limerick, upsetting the English. The second time a Civil War was going on. "Christ," he thought, "my timing is desperate."

"This will be my third time. I just hope it's more peaceful. I must be the only vampire in Ireland who never bit anyone. I'm a disgrace to the vampire clan. The last time I needed blood, I got it from a pig in Kildimo. Myself and my friend Maurice the Gummy vampire raided a farmhouse one winter night; the pig was very slippery and the only place I could stick my teeth in was his arse. Poor old Gummy tried to do it as well but the pig shit on him. Christ I hope he hasn't the same clothes on; there was a smell off him that night that would have knocked out a horse. When he was going back into his coffin, even he was holding his nose.

"Ah yes, I'm ready to go now," he thought, as he folded his hands. He left his coffin like a fog. When he had materialized to human form, he let his eyes get used to seeing in the dark again. Now he could hear children screaming and laughing in the distance. "I hope they're not at war still. Christ no war goes on that long. I could have sworn we were in the country the last time we went back in to our coffins. I must ask Gummy when he comes out."

Then he heard a noise coming from behind the big tree. "Is that you Gummy?"

"Yes!"

"What's wrong?"

"I'll tell you what's wrong, the roots of that tree are after growing around my coffin. As a matter of fact one came into the coffin and was about to go up my arse. I tell you I'm going to move my coffin from this place; it's not safe around here anymore. Where are you?"

"Over here."

"Paddy, how are you?"

"Not bad under the circumstances."

"Tell me did my teeth grow?" Gummy opened his mouth in front of Paddy.

"I'm afraid not."

"I can't understand it. They told me everything would grow; my hair and nails did, but not my teeth."

"Maybe you had a gum disease in your mouth."

"Sure, it's all the same what I had in my mouth; when you're a vampire everything is supposed to grow."

"Don't worry about it. I see you have the pig's shit on you still. No wonder the roots were coming into the coffin. Another year and you'd have been part of the tree."

"I tell you I'm moving from that spot."

"Are you ready to go and see how Limerick has changed?"

"Ready and able," Gummy answered as they walked down to the main gate.

"I don't remember these footpaths here, do you?" Paddy said.

"No. And it seems a lot cleaner then the last time. The old Celtic Cross over there, if I remember right, was broken and on the ground. Now look at it. It's as good as new. Maybe there's a festival coming up, what do you think?"

"I don't know, but the last time we went back into our coffins there was only the gate man's house, and now look. I wonder what all the lights are for."

"Well, why don't we go and find out?"

"It's so long since I flew and I'm ready to take off."

"Coming right behind you."

With that both of them started to run down the footpath; as they ran, they spread their hands, their bodies took the shape of bats, and they flew into the clear night sky.

Outside, a little girl was going from house to house for Halloween when she saw them.

"Look Mammy" she said, as she pointed up to the sky. "Two bats." But her mother was too busy speaking to a neighbour to look up.

"Oh they're lovely darling," she said as she winked to the neighbour. But the little girl kept watching the two bats as they circled over Garryowen.

Paddy was looking down on the houses and thinking, "This must be Garryowen. The last time I went through it there was only Goats Lane, a farmhouse, and the Pike. Now look at it." He flew on, taking in the new sights. "Well at least St. Johns and the Square are still there."

"Keep moving Paddy." They continued down Broad Street.

"Look at the Irishtown, all new."

"There are houses here as well. The gentry from t.
must have moved from Harts Stone Street to down. puntry
to talk to Gummy about all the changes. Need to r. Have
couple of minutes."
He circled St Mary's Church. "The graveyard will do jus
Time to land, Gummy." But Gummy came in too fast and
straight into a headstone.
"Are you all right?"
"What do you think?" Gummy called out. "Any chance of .
hand over here or are you too busy?"
Paddy walked over to where Gummy was laid out over the
grave.
"I think I'm dying," Gummy said.
"You can't die, you're dead already. Or have you forgotten?"
"Now that you've brought it up, I had."
"Had what?"
"Forgotten!"
"Look. There's a seat over there with a good view of Limerick.
Up you come. Christ, you'd want to change those clothes.
They'll smell you before they see you."
"Is that right? Anything else?"
"No."
They sat down on the seat and watched the cars coming in and
going out of the City. Now and then a light from a car would
shine into the graveyard and light up the place.
"I'll tell you something," Gummy said. "If Sarsfield had those
lights instead of lanterns, he would have beaten the English."
"I was with this woman one night down in Old Irishtown and it
was so dark I thought I was holding her hand, but it was the
fellow sitting next to her who's hand I was holding. I tell you I
had an awful lot of explaining to do. I bumped into him the
next night and, if looks could kill! And that was my last time as
a human down there."
"There was always a shower of lunatics hanging around. Well
what are we going to do now?"
"First get some new clothes, and then get some blood to put
some colour back into our cheeks."
"Speak for yourself, there's nothing wrong, with my cheeks. It's
a woman I need, a fine hefty woman. To tell you the truth any
kind of woman would do right now—even the toothless old bag
that used to go around Garryowen. That's how desperate I am.
How do you think I became a vampire? This one gave me the
eye one night and that was that. Where did it happen to you?"
Gummy asked.

"The Wa... ...ower by the Lax Weir. I went for a walk one
summe... ...ning, sat down by the Tower and fell asleep. When I
woke... ...his woman was sitting right in front of me. Now, at
the t... there were rumours going around of a woman
atta... ...g people, but I laughed it off. Soon we were in
con... ...sation and I said to her, "Is it not late to be out on your
ow...

"...n't you protect me?" she said with a laugh. "You are a
...ntleman, aren't you?"

...answered, "While you're in my company you need have no
fear. But now I must be going home."

"May I walk with you?" she said.

"Of course. But tell me, why this time of night?"

"Oh, I love the night and listening to the bat's. Can't you hear
them? Here, sit on this stone and listen."

So I did as I was told and, as I listened, she put her hands on
my head and I felt myself going into a beautiful trance. The
next thing I knew, she had moved my neck sideways and sunk
her teeth into my neck. The rest you know. Like you, I woke up
in a coffin and I'd become one of them. But I have never taken
human blood—only animals.

"But you know what, you still have the pig's shit on your
clothes. Time to move on, but this time we walk. There seems
to be a festival going on and I'd like to see the changes since
the last time. Then, there were barricades all over O'Connell
Street. I wonder what they've done with the soldier's barracks.
Maybe if we have the time we'll fly up that way."

"You can fly up there by yourself," Gummy said. "I have more
important things on my mind."

"Like what?"

"Like a woman. I'll hypnotize her with my eyes. Maybe I'll
hypnotize two—now that would be something. If that doesn't
put some life back into me, nothing will."

"Coming right behind you."

Jimmy O'Brien was drinking in his local when he got a phone
call. Sean, the barman, roared at him, telling him and the
whole of the bar that the voice of his sweet wife was on the
other end.

"Very funny," Jimmy said. "Give us the same again will you?"

"Coming up, oh master."

When he lifted up the phone his wife Mary said, "Did you tell
Sean to fill them up again?"

"I did not. As a matter of fact, I have my coat on and I was just
leaving. Another minute and I was gone."

'Well you'd better be home fast or your suitca. will be waiting for you in the hall. I mean it. I don't know what you see in that place anyway, but let me guess who's with you Paul, Tony, and, of course, your old Captain, the Basher imself. And you're talking about all the wankers who've joined the Club since all of you retired. There never was a second row like you, or a Captain like the Basher. And, of course, Paul and Tony should have played for Ireland. Am I right? But tell ne this, didn't Steven Holly play on that team as well? And now look at him. He takes his wife everywhere with him; foreign holidays three times a year."

"Will you leave me alone; he can't piss crooked with her. And, for your information, he never got on the first team. He wasn't good enough. It was men we needed that time, not little shits who kissed arse on the Committee."

"Is that right? So you won't be meeting the old boys tonight?"

"No, why?"

"Well, I was just speaking to Kathleen and she said the Basher was with you."

"No I haven't seen him since Saturday." Just then, the Basher's voice roared over. "Are you paying for them, or are you staying over there for the night? And give Mary my love."

"I thought you said you were on your own?"

"You won't believe this but, as sure as Jesus died, he's just after coming in the door."

"And what about the other two disciples?"

"Jesus, they're just coming as well. Isn't that a coincidence."

"There must be some form of telepathy between the lot of you. By the way I was speaking to one of the Neighbourhood Watch and she saw yourself and the Basher getting off the bus last week rotten drunk. She asked me to speak to you about it, because the two of you started singing dirty rugby songs outside the priests' house. I'm going down to apologise to the man right now and you can tell the Basher so is his wife. I'm ashamed to look at the neighbours now."

"Fuck the neighbours. You can tell the priest that we'd won a very important game, vital to the club. So myself, Basher, Paul, and Tony celebrated. Is there anything wrong with that?"

"No, only you've been celebrating for the last 25 years. You're even going to masses now for the dead members. And, between the lot of you, I'd say you didn't know one of them."

"Are you finished?"

"No, but you will be if you don't get home fast. I mean it, right?"

"Good-bye."

"I tell you I mean this time."

When he got back to the boys, Basher said, "What's up?"

"Some of the neighbour's didn't like our singing. One of them got onto the life about it. Fuck it, I told you not to sing outside the priest's house, especially his house. He's from Dublin and follows some club up there."

"Ah don't worry about it. Hey, Sean, how much do I owe you?" The Basher paid for them.

"You can get the next round. As the old saying goes, you might as well be hung for a sheep as a lamb," Basher said.

After a couple more drinks, Jimmy said "I'm off now."

"Don't forget Saturday—we're all meeting here at one o'clock. We'll have a couple of drinks and then well get a taxi out. Are you listening to me?" Basher said.

"That's great. But what am I going to tell the wife now?"

"Tell her you had to go back to work to do some overtime, I'll back you up."

"Don't bother. I'll think of something myself."

As Jimmy was leaving, the wide boys started shouting after him, "Sleep tight. Watch yourself when you get home and give Mary all our love."

"Very funny."

When he got outside, he thought, "It's such a lovely night, I'll walk down by the Court House."

At the graveyard side, he heard someone walking on leaves inside. As he looked up, two figures were clearing the graveyard wall. They gave him such a fright he let out a scream. When they landed on the road, they turned and looked at him. One said, "Thank you." Then they turned and walked towards the bridge. As Jimmy watched them walk away he thought, "I wonder what they were doing in there at this time of night? They must be working on the Church. I should have asked them their names. The way they cleared the wall they'd have been great for us in the lineout. Those two wankers we have now wouldn't catch a cold in Alaska if they walked around in the nude. Basher was right about them. They cost us the league last year.

"I'll get Mary a Chinese, maybe that will keep her quiet for a while. But I doubt it," as he walked towards City Hall.

Paddy and Gummy were now crossing the Bridge. "Look," Gummy said, 'a cannon. It's one they used against Sarsfield, I think."

"How would you know what kind of cannon they used?"

"Because I saw the train bringing them through Ballyneety.

Then your man blew them up."

"Well there's one that got away."

"Look there's a sign on the gate," Gummy said. "What does it say?"

"Read it yourself," Paddy said.

"I can't."

"Why?"

"Because I can't read. Now will you read the fucking thing?"

Paddy went over and read it.

"Well, what does it say?"

"It tells the time you can enter the building, and it's a Museum."

"What's that?"

"A place where they put old things."

"Like this?" Gummy said, as he pulled out a sovereign.

"My, aren't we rich."

"Well I never got around to spending it. Hadn't got the time, to tell you the truth. They were digging up a lot of graves back then. I had to keep moving every night; you wouldn't believe the places where I slept."

"Sure, I did it myself."

"I knew you were going to say that. Shall we continue?"

"Why not?" They passed Rutland Street and into Patrick Street. Gummy looked over to the other side and saw a suit in the window.

"Must have that." As he was crossing the road, a car came along and started to blow its horn.

"Must be some form of greeting," Gummy said. He waved back but a harsh voice came from inside it saying, "Get off the road. There are lights down there for crossing you fool," and then laughter.

"So I'm a fool," Gummy said, as he walked over to the car. But now other cars were starting to pile up and they started blowing as well. He hit the window, which was half down and said, "Did I hear you calling me a fool?"

Inside the car were two young men and two young women.

"Yes, that's right."

"Please step out onto the road."

Now the laughter had stopped and the driver had rolled the window back up. Then Gummy's hand came through and took the driver by the throat. "Now am I still a fool?"

"You're after breaking my window."

"If you don't apologise, I'll break your fucking neck." He put his other hand in and let them watch as the nails began to grow.

The girls in the back started screaming.

"Apologise to him."

"I'm sorry. I didn't mean anything."

"Again, but louder this time. Let my friend over there hear you."

"I'm sorry."

"Louder."

"I'm sorry."

Crowds had gathered now and were watching all of this. They started cheering Gummy on.

"The next time you insult someone, be prepared to die. Do you understand me?"

"Yes."

"Now get out of my sight. You make me sick, if that's possible."

As the car pulled away the driver was screaming, "See if you can see a guard. I'll have him up in court for this. No one does that to me."

But one of the girls was saying, "How did he do that with his nails? And the smell off him! Jesus I'm ready to get sick. I hope he's not going to the disco as well. He'll clear the place in seconds. And you keep your big mouth shut in future."

"I'm going up to Henry Street to report this."

"Well you can leave us out here. It was your own fault. You were showing off and you got what you deserved. Leave us out right here. Coming Maria?"

"Right behind you."

Paddy now joined Gummy on the other side. People were patting Gummy on the back and saying, "Fair play to you."

"Thank you my friends." But when they smelled Gummy, they moved off fast.

"Yes," Gummy said. "Tonight is my kind of night. But first, some new clothes. What do you think, Paddy?"

"Don't mind if I do. I'm in these since 1921. Tell me, did you notice anything about the young girls? They were wearing very little clothes—and on a cold night like this."

"Well, don't worry about it, just admire them. You know it's truc the most beautiful girls in the world are right here in Limerick."

"Amen to that! Shall we enter and get our new clothes?"

"Why not?"

With that, they were gone. The entered the cloths shop like a fog. Sean Whitmore was watching all of this from across the street; he was taking his dog, Spot, for a walk. It had been a week since he had signed himself out of St. Josephs Hospital—

mental stress and listening to too many people, that's what they told him. He needed another two weeks in there but he'd felt great until now. "It's all the wife's fault," he thought. "I was happy watching TV. Then I hear, 'can't you take poor Spot out?' 'Why don't you take him out?' I said back. 'But you could do with a little bit of air. I mean you were locked up for a week and they told me you needed at least two more weeks.'

"I knew she'd never shut up until I took him out. I should never have listened to her."

As he walked back over the Bridge, Spot started barking. He wanted to stay out longer. But Sean said, "Bark once more and I'll fuck you into the river and the wife with you. I wonder would I get away with it?"

Later Sean Whitmore signed himself back in, saying to Nurse Moore, "You wouldn't believe what I'm going to tell you."

"Of course I will."

Later she told Nurse Hourigan to increase his medicine. "He's seeing people disappear, now." And both started laughing.

Paddy and Gummy started going through the clothes.

"There are so many garments in here. A lot of money must be going around. What do you think, Paddy?"

"I agree with you."

They started to try on some coats but then Gummy saw the dress suits' and was over admiring them like a flash.

"Now here's my style—black and white. Well, most of them anyway."

He took off his old clothes and put on a pair of pants that were too small for him.

"Don't you think they're a bit small for you?" Paddy said.

"Not at all, they fit me like a glove." Then he put on the coat. It was also too small. Paddy said nothing.

"Well, have you picked out anything yet?"

"Yes. I like this tweed."

"Well, whatever suits you."

Gummy was at the mirror admiring himself.

"What are you looking in the mirror for? You can't see yourself in that, you're a vampire remember? No shadows, no reflections. Have you forgotten?"

"No I haven't forgotten, but I can remember what I used to look like can't I? Or have you a problem with that?"

"Sorry," Paddy said.

Gummy started to laugh and said, "Do you remember the time Sarsfield was looking for the smallest man in Limerick? He needed him for some special job."

"Yes I remember."

"Well, a couple of wide boys were drinking down in the old Irishtown that night and decided to play a little joke on him. They went up to Jimmy the Midget's house and told him Sarsfield needed him for a very important job. Now at the time Jimmy the midget was supposed to be the smallest man in Ireland, and when they had told him the story, he said he was willing to lay down his life for his country. So they filled him up with wine and brought him down to Sarsfield's Headquarters. They told him he'd have to go in alone as it was a secret mission and no one else was to know about it. 'Do you understand?' they asked him. 'Of course I fuckin' understand. Do you think I'm a fool?' 'Well of course not.'

"So Jimmy the Midget shook hands with every one of them and told them they may never see him again, just to pray for him and the success of the mission. 'Of course we will.'

"So Jimmy staggered over to where Sarsfield was staying and said to the guards, 'On the double, move it. Sarsfield put out a request for a brave man—well go in and tell him I'm out fuckin' here. As he collapsed back down the steps, the two guards looked at one another and one said, 'Will you wake him up or will I?'

"Toss for it." So they did.

"In you go," the guard on the left said. After a couple of minutes they heard Sarsfield screaming inside.

"I haven't slept in three days and you're waking me up, telling me Jimmy the Midget is outside drunk as a skunk and ready to go on a secret mission? What secret fuckin' mission? I don't know anything about this do you?"

"No sir."

"Is there something going on behind my back?"

"I don't know, sir."

"Bring him in. I want to hear about this secret mission."

After listening to the story, Sarsfield sent his best men out to catch the wide boys.

"Don't come back without them do you understand?"

"Yes sir."

"Good. I'll quieten them when I catch them." But he never caught them. The next, day the fighting started and most of them were killed. But not Sarsfield. Some of the men ended up in France."

"Ah the good old days. I'll tell you a better one. Remember Nora Ryan?"

"Of course I do. She lived just up from the square in the big house."

"Yes that's right. Well she was going out with one of Sarsfield's cavalry men. Now they'd been going out for some time, but in the meantime, he'd met one of the Hayes girls—not much to look at, but plenty of money."

"That's the grain people you're talking about isn't it?" Gummy said.

"The very people. Anyway, the day came when he had to choose one and guess which one he chose? The money, of course—he was no fool. Well anyway, down he went to Nora to tell her he couldn't see her anymore but that he hoped they could remain friends. Well, he left the building and, as he was just getting on his horse, a chamber pot full of piss broke off his head and covered him with it. And Nora was screaming from the top window, 'How's that for friends? And the next time you're passing you'll get the same fuckin' thing again and I won't give a fuck who you'll be with. You took my honour and promised me marriage.' As he walked away, a voice from the crowd said, 'Tell us was he any good in bed?' 'Who said that? If you're a man, step out and say it to my face.' 'You must be joking with the smell of piss coming off you.'

"Then one of the women shouted up, 'Nora, tell us, was he any good?' 'No! It was over before it started.' "Now the whole place was down on their knees laughing, and the cavalry man was shouting back. 'I came down from Dublin to defend this city.'

"Again the voice from the crowd came back, 'Who asked you to come down; did any one here ask this gentleman to come down here?' 'No,' the crowd said. 'Then we're all in agreement for you to fuck off back to where you came from and the sooner the better. Do you all agree?' 'Yes!' they roared back. 'I'll tell Sarsfield how you treated one of his men.'

"As he was just going into the square, another bucket of piss came down on him. 'Animals,' he screamed. 'If I had my way, I'd leave the lot of you to Cromwell and his men. They'd quieten you.' Then a stone hit the horses arse and he was gone like a flash down Old Irishtown.

"Nora was still looking out the window when a voice from the crowd said, 'I hope you wont be to lonely up there all by yourself.' 'It's yourself, Seamus. Why don't you come up and help me to get over him.'

"And of course he did. I heard later she took on half of Cromwell's troops and gave most of them the pox. She said she was doing it for Limerick and Ireland. "Now shall we go out and enjoy ourselves? We don't have much time left."

"Lead the way," Gummy said. When they got back out onto the street, crowds of young people were coming down Patrick Street. Some girls passed them and one said to Gummy, "I love your suit," and they all started laughing.

"Why thank you," Gummy said. Then he said to one of them, "I want to suck your blood."

"What? Did you hear that girls? He wants to suck my blood."

Now the girls had gathered around Gummy and one said, "And what do you want her to do?"

"What?" Gummy said.

"Well you don't want her standing up and doing nothing do you? Maybe she'll be lying down," another one said.

"Paddy, help me, get me away from these harlots."

Now the girls were roaring with laughter.

"Excuse me," Paddy said.

"He's not too bad either," the same one said. Paddy thought "I'll have to frighten them off." So he opened his mouth and started to let his vampire teeth grow. As they watched Paddy's teeth get longer one of them put her finger into his mouth and said, "Christ, they're good. They even feel like real teeth. Where did you buy them?"

"I did not buy them," Paddy said. "They're my real teeth."

"Yeah and these are false," and she grabbed her breasts. "Now where did you buy them?"

"I'm off," Gummy said, as he broke away from them.

"Coming." Paddy ran after him.

"Isn't that great? The only two vampires in Limerick and we're running away from harlots."

"How do you know we're the only ones in Limerick?" Gummy said. "The last time we where here, wasn't a woman attacking people up by the park and didn't she bite some of them?"

"Well yes, but they put it down to a madwoman."

"It was no mad woman who made us what we are. And maybe it was the same woman for both of us. Who knows? I curse the night I met her. I wish I was dead."

"You are," Paddy said.

"I'm dead alright but I can't lie down. Look, an eating house."

So they walked over and looked in the window. All makes of people where eating in there.

"I wish I could eat or drink something. It's nearly 300 years since I last ate or drank," Gummy said.

"Same here. But look at it another way, you won't put on any weight."

"Fuck the weight. I'd love to be back in old Irishtown with

plenty of drink around me. Maybe we'll go down there later. This is a new street. Let's go up it and have a look around."

As they walked people were singing and dancing; some form of music was coming from the tavern at the top of the street.

"Sweet Jesus, that could not be music, could it?" Gummy said.

"It looks that way."

"I'm going over to take a look. You know we're lucky in one way, that light doesn't bother us yet daytime does."

"How do you explain that? Paddy said.

"How the fuck should I know?

As they opened the tavern door and they looked in, they saw people dancing and talking.

"How can they hear one another?" Gummy roared.

"What?" said Paddy.

"Were you in the army?" one fellow asked as he passed them.

"What?" Gummy said.

"What year did you join up?"

"Join up what?"

"My Jesus, you could get £20,000, and don't take anything else."

"What's he talking about."

"I don't know. I think he's drunk. Let's get away from here."

As they moved down by the church, there were more people, and more singing, and more loud music.

"I'll go mad if I hear anymore of that shit," Gummy said.

"I know this place Paddy: it's the market. Remember it?"

"Of course I do. The neighbours out by Park used to sell cabbage and spuds in there."

"You used to buy them?"

"No. I used to rob them in the night. But I had to be very careful. Old Bull Flynn had a pitchfork and he swore that he'd ram it up the arse of anyone caught robbing his fields. And you can take it from me—he would have done it. He was one dangerous man so he was."

"I see the cobble stones and the pillars are still there. It's very clean, no horse's or pig's shit, and it looks as if it's been done up. Do you want to go in and take a look?"

"No. I can see all I want to from here. I think I'll spread my wings and fly a bit. Coming?"

"Why not?"

Gummy started his run first and Paddy followed him down Mungret Street.

Then Paddy heard a tear coming from Gummy's jacket. It was splitting up the back and, as he folded his legs, the arse of the pants went. As he watched Gummy change into a bat, a sleeve of the jacket and a leg of the pants were still hanging out.

Gummy was going straight for the nearest house. "He's going to hit it," Paddy thought, "and it's his own fault. I told him they were too small, but he knew it all."

But Gummy's luck was in. He got himself sorted out and cleared it by inches. They circled over the Irishtown, then went out by Clare Street and up into Rhebogue. After a while Gummy landed on the railway line and Paddy followed him down.

"Are you alright?" Paddy said.

"Why, what's wrong with me?"

"I thought you were going into the window back in Mungret Street."

"Not at all! I was just testing my wings, that's all."

Gummy looked over Rheboque. He said, "There are so many houses here and this used to be the country. Is there any country left, I wonder? Look. Lights everywhere, very few fields, no cattle or pigs—unless they're in the house too."

As they both were looking and thinking, a light shone on them.

"What's that?" as the light got nearer.

"Fuck it," Gummy said. "It's a train, jump fast."

As the driver of the train blew its horn, he let down the window and shouted at them.

"Stupid bastards, why don't you find somewhere else to drink? I'd better report this when I get back. One of these nights someone will get killed."

Gummy and Paddy had jumped down into a pool of water.

"That's all I need," Gummy said. "I was better off in my coffin, dreaming of the girls I'd had my way with. Not stuck in this fucking field up to my knob in water. I could kill myself.

"When are we going to die, Paddy? I mean really dead, as in finished."

"I wish I knew."

Then, thunder and lightening broke out over them.

"What can happen fucking next?" Gummy said, as the lightening got very bad.

"Better get out of here fast," Paddy said. "You don't want to be hit by lightening, do ya?"

"I don't give a fuck," Gummy said as the lightening hit him.

"This can't be happening to me," he was screaming, as another one hit him. Paddy had never seen anyone glow so much in all of his three hundred years.

"Here, give me your hand, I'll pull out of this place, it's not safe anymore. I thought the siege was bad but this takes the biscuit. Well, you're out now. There's a bridge over there, we can stand under it for a while. When they got over there, another man was standing in out of the rain as well.

"Good night," he said.

"It's a bad night," Paddy said.

"It'll be worse when I get home," he said. "I'm married to the biggest bitch in Limerick. I'm also drunk and wet and the door will be locked when I get home. Try and beat that! What happened to your friend over there, lightening hit him or what?"

"As a matter of fact, that's exactly what happened to him."

"Christ, you can tell a good one." And he staggered over to Gummy and said, "I used to have my hair like that in 1978. Also had pins all over my clothes. I was the best dressed punk in Limerick. Who was your group? Mine was the Undertones. Now who was yours? Let me guess, the Sex Pistols. Looking at you I know I'm right. I have a couple of cans here; we'll have a sing song and go down memory lane. What do you say?"

"Let me get out of here fast," said Gummy. And he started to walk towards the hop hill.

"Jesus, he's touchy," the drunk said. "My wife's maiden name is Maloney; he wouldn't be related to her by any chance would he? She's the same way; you can't piss crooked with her either. Will you drink a can with me?"

"I'm sorry but I have to go after my friend."

"Suit yourself," as the drunk opened a can and started singing at the top of his voice.

As Paddy was going after Gummy, he saw lights in some of the houses and he wondered what they'd do with the drunk.

When he got to Gummy he said, "Don't worry, everything will be all right."

"All right my arse. I thought the Jacobites and the Pike Men were bad but this place has gone fucking mad."

As they walked down the Hop Hill, they saw a plaque on a rock.

"What does that say?" Gummy asked.

"A church was here years ago. I don't remember a church here years ago do you?"

"Come to think of it, no."

They continued on down to the main road. When they got there they stopped to look at the traffic lights.

"Look," Gummy said. "It changes to different colours, wonder what that's for?"

As they crossed the road the lights changed again to green.

Gummy stopped to admire them. He said to Paddy, "I always loved that colour." By now cars were passing on both sides of him.

"Get off the road," they were yelling at him. And Gummy started roaring back, "Get off yourself, you fucking idiot."

"Wanker," another shouted.

"What's a wanker?" Gummy asked Paddy.

"Don't know. Maybe it's a name for people from the other side of town."

"Guess you're right." And Gummy roared back, "I'm no wanker. I'm from this side of the town. Fuck off back to where you came from yourself.

"I feel good after that; it's nice to let them know where you come from."

"Amen to that. Ready?"

"Yes."

As they started to walk away up by Pennywell, they saw a group of children around a dirty old car. One was writing in the dirt, "Wash me, please." Then the owner of the car came out and roared at them to get away from his car. As he looked to see what was written on it, he said to Paddy, "They want to go away and wash they're own fucking cars."

Gummy's finger was rubbing over the car when the man saw him.

"Going to a punk revival?" he asked. "Where's it on?"

"Down the road," Paddy said.

"How come I never heard anything about it?"

"Don't know." Then he stared to sing to Gummy, "*Don't fear the Reaper.*"

"Oh fuck," Gummy said. "Another one."

"I might go down there myself."

"Do that," Gummy roared back.

"I might see you down there and we'll have a drink"

"That would be nice," Paddy said.

And as he watched them walk away, "Christ, they never said where it was on, only down there, down fucking where? Those two never grew up," he thought. "Not like the wife Jenny and me."

"What do you make of the changes?" Gummy asked

"I don't know what to make of them, to tell you the truth. At least back then, if you took away Cromwell and his army, it wasn't too bad. I see there's some of the walls still standing."

"Well fuck me, so he didn't blow them all up. I always said they were mad down at this side of town and Cromwell must have met a couple of them."

"I'd say more than a couple." They both started to laugh.

As they turned to go into John's Square, a sign on the side of the hospital gate said, "Blood bank this way, please."

"Heaven has answered us—or hell; it depends on which way you look at it."

"You're speaking in riddles again."

"What's that place?"

"A hospital."

"And tell me, what happens in a hospital?"

"People die."

"Yes and some are healed. But what do they lose? Blood. And plenty of it. Now are you thinking what I'm thinking?"

"Lead the way, old boy."

"Certainly, old bean."

The porter, Jimmy Power, had worked at the hospital for the last 25 years. To the people in the pubs around the hospital, he was known as Dr. Maybe. If he knew someone who went in, he'd make it his business to go up and see him after the doctor had done his rounds. Then he'd pick up the charts and start humming to himself. Now if you did not know him too well, he'd put the fear of God into you. And some of the patients would be asking him whether they would be all right and his answer was always the same, "Maybe. But don't get your hopes up too high."

One unfortunate took Jimmy at his word, got out of his bed in a fit of depression, went straight across to the nearest pub and called a drink for everyone in the place. The pub was packed that night because there was a big match on the TV, but he kept calling a drink for everyone. In the end one of the people came down and asked him what he was celebrating. When he told them what Jimmy had read in the report, the whole pub started roaring laughing.

"Well," the man said, "you're a nice sort. "I only have weeks to live and all you can do is make a laugh out of it. But your time will come as well," he roared.

In the end they had to calm him down and tell him about Jimmy. When they had finished he screamed, "I'll kill the bastard," and ran out the door. As he was going back to his bed, the Matron caught him and called out, "Mr. Williams, if you're in here by any chance in the future, there will be no drinking, do you understand me?"

"Yes, but what do you mean Matron?"

"You should have been gone home hours ago."

"But I thought I was sick?"

"Who told you that?"

Just then Jimmy Power put his head in the door and said, "Everything all right Matron?"

"Yes, thank you Jimmy."

"You lousy bastard, Power. You just cost me a small fortune," he roared.

"How dare you speak to one of my staff like that, collect your things and leave this hospital immediately or I'll call the guards. Do I make myself clear?"

"Yes. But I'll see you again, Power, I promise you."

"Jimmy, do you know that man?" the Matron said.

"Never saw him before in my life," Jimmy said. "You know, when he came in he seemed a bit odd too."

"Perhaps it's the other hospital he should have been sent to. As if we're not crowded enough without getting lunatics as well."

"I could not agree with you more, Matron."

Later when the Matron had left the ward, Jimmy picked up another report, the man asked the same question, the answer was again, "Maybe, but we live in hope. I'll pray for you tonight." The man started crying and said, "Jesus, I only came in to get my appendix out; now I'll be going across the road in a box."

"Well, we all have to go sometime. Anyway, goodnight and sleep tight."

When Jimmy had left the ward the man took out his rosary beads and started praying. He also said a prayer for Jimmy, "One nice man," he thought.

Nurse Madison was walking down the corridor when she saw the fog going under the blood unit door.

"That bollocks Power forgot to close the window again, I suppose. He's up on the ward telling the whole place they're on they're last fucking legs but what's the use of complaining? He has the Matron wrapped around his finger. If you even looked at him you'd be suspended. Well I can't look for the window now; I'll find it later."

Meanwhile, inside Paddy and Gummy had changed back into human form and had started to look around.

"It's here somewhere, but where?"

After some minutes Gummy came to the fridge and opened it.

"Paddy," he said, "come over and feast your eyes on this!"

Paddy came over, took one look at it and said, "There's enough blood in here for a year. Shall we proceed?"

"Why not?"

"Is there anything we could drink the blood out of?"

"Hold it," Gummy said. And he came back with two jugs with writing on them.

"What does it say, Paddy?"

"For urine samples only."

"What's urine samples?" Gummy asked.

"Don't know, but it must be strong stuff, there's a right whiff off it."

"Fuck the whiff, just pour."

"Right away, sir."

"After gulping down the first drink, Gummy went over for another two. They went down as fast as the first two. Then Gummy left off a fart that made the chair he was sitting on vibrate.

"I've wanted to do that for a long time."

Then Paddy was at it. After a couple of minutes, both of them were farting. Paddy said "The colour is coming back to your cheeks."

"And yours the same."

"How come we never thought of coming here the last time? You know the answer was in front of us the whole time and look what happened to you, a pig shit on you."

"I don't want to talk about it."

He went over to a hanger with a doctor's pants and top on it. He took the off the dress suit, what was left of it, and put on the doctors uniform.

"Now they fit you perfectly," said Paddy.

"What will I do with these?"

"Leave them there. How about one for the road?"

"Why not? Christ, I feel great," Gummy said.

"And so do I."

As they drank the blood Paddy said, "What do you think about it?"

"It tastes very salty."

"I thought the first one had a tangy taste to it. You know, a bit strong."

"No, it's this one with me. Well anyway, here's mud in your eye."

"And yours too. And if you want to get your own back, piss against the wind," they both answered together.

When they had their fill, Gummy said, "Well, are you ready?"

"Ready and able!"

"Able for what?"

"Anything."

Just then, they heard a commotion outside the window.

"Something going on out there, let's listen."

Outside a woman was telling a child that everything would be all right.

"Now look, a doctor's coming."

"Well, what's wrong with her?" Dr. Neizeim asked.

"Well doctor, you won't believe this," she said. "A woman called her, and when she went over the woman bit her on the neck."

"What? Where did this happen"

"Up by the park."

"And how did she get away from this woman?"

"Some people heard the child scream."

"Have the police been notified?"

"I don't know doctor."

Dr. Neizeim called over a nurse and said, "Call the police straight away and tell them a woman outside the park has bitten a child. Which park?" the doctor asked.

"The Peoples' Park."

"Now," Dr. Neizeim knelt down by the little girl and said, "let's have a look at you."

"He moved the child's head from left to right. As he did this he saw two puncture marks on the child's neck.

"Nurse Madigan, have you made that call yet?"

"Yes, they'll be here in a minute."

"Take the child into the ward. Have her parents been notified?"

"I don't know, doctor."

The woman who brought down the child said she sent one of her friends up to tell them.

"Good. Did anyone else see this woman?"

"Yes."

"And where did she go to?"

"I don't know, one minute she was there and next she was gone."

"How do you mean gone?"

"It's as if she disappeared."

"There must be an opening by the bars."

"I don't know, doctor."

"Well, whoever she is, she has to be caught straight away before she does any real harm."

Nurse Madigan came back and said, "What do you make of it?"

"I think it's someone who is really sick and with Halloween and the full moon she either thinks she's a vampire or a werewolf. But whatever she thinks she is, she's dangerous and needs to be caught immediately."

"Here are the police now."

"Right, I'll see to them, you go back to the child. Maybe she'll say something, but I doubt it. All she wants now is her parents and they should be here soon."

Paddy and Gummy listened and said, "Are you thinking what I'm thinking? Our friend who made us vampires is on the prowl again. We have to do something fast before she makes more vampires. But why a child?"

"Maybe it's her idea of a sick joke. If you see a child in the night the last thing you'd think of is that she's a vampire. All she has to do is tell you she's lost, start crying, and the next thing you know, she's drinking you're blood. Let's get out of here fast and head for the park."

"Are we walking or flying," Gummy said."

"Flying. The faster we get there the better. She's not going to stop now. She needs blood and she won't care whose blood she gets. Ready?"

"Right behind you." As they again evaporated, the fog formed. When they got outside, St. John's Church was right in front of them.

"It's going to be tight, Paddy said. "We could go under the arch; there's plenty of room at the entrance side."

"We'll be seen," Gummy said. "It'll have to be here."

"Well, if you're willing to give it a go, so am I."

"Then let's do it."

As Paddy and then Gummy made a run, both of them took the form of bats.

"They just missed the main wall by inches," said Burns who was passing by, drunk.

Gay Boy saw them as well. "Now," said Gay Boy, who had been in the Army for years. And when he was drunk he'd tell you how he fought the Baloobas on his own. Now and then he got a little bit of help from the Army, but most of the time he had to fight them all on his own. And the more drink he drank, the more wars he'd tell you he'd been in, even the ones before he was born. He thought the Crusades only happened a couple of years ago and King Richard and he were great drinking buddies. And when the king had problems, he came to Gay Boy to sort them out.

"By Jesus," said Gay Boy, "Those hawks are big. They must be breeding in the church tower again. The last time it happened there wasn't a cat or dog safe. We had to shoot them. But Christ they were good and beautiful. These two hawks don't look that good, different breed I'd say. Wait until I tell the lads, this must be good for at least ten pints. I'll settle for nothing less," as he watched them fly up Gerald Griffin Street.

In Exchange Lane, Paddy and Gummy took human form once again and as they came out of the lane there was a crowd there. A woman came up to one of the Guards and said, "Did you get her yet?"

"No, but we're looking."

"Looking my arse, she's well gone. It would be more in your line to make the streets safe. It's even gone so bad now you have to watch yourself walking through O'Connell St. at night. And now even the children can't come out without being attacked."

The Guard said nothing and just walked away. Another woman said, "It's not his fault. He's only doing what he's told to do. Me, I blame the politicians, and their bullshit promises. All they can do is catch them. It's when they get them down to the Courthouse the case falls away. Their smart arse solicitors get them off and they're back on the streets that day. Their solicitors can then drive home with their big cars to their big houses in the suburbs while we in the housing schemes have to put up with it again. Isn't that right?" she said to another guard who had been listening. "No comment," he said.

"There's a future for you in the council," another woman said. They all started laughing. As Paddy and Gummy moved through the crowd, Paddy started getting a sensation through him.

"There's something wrong here," he thought. "I've had no human feelings since I became a vampire."

He turned to speak to Gummy, to ask him was he feeling the same thing. As he turned he looked straight into the face of the woman who had made him a vampire over 300 years ago.

"Well, well, we meet again. How long has it been? Let me guess. A lot of changes since that time don't you think?"

Paddy made a move towards her, but her hand was already around his throat.

"Everything alright over there?" one of the guards asked.

"Why yes, officer. I'm just fixing his shirt."

"All right, ladles and gentlemen, time to go home. There's no more we can do here tonight, so if you don't mind, go home?"

"Why, we don't mind at all," the vampire woman said back. "Do we?" she said to Paddy as she tightened her grip on his throat, and let Paddy see the nails starting to grow on her other hand.

"Do you want me to do the same with the hand on your throat? Well do you?"

Paddy shook his head. "The will to live is a great thing, even for a vampire, isn't it?" she said to Paddy. "Just nod your head. Nod."

Paddy did as he was told. Gummy had felt the same sensations as Paddy and went to the women who were standing by the bars.

"Ladies, forgive me for asking, but are any of you unattached?"

"What?" one of the women said.

"Well, are any of you free, as in do any of you ladies want a man?"

"Why are you available?"

"Well, now that you bring it up, I'm ready, willing, and able. As a matter of fact, I'm more ready than the last time."

"When was the last time?"

"The time Cromwell fucked up the City."

"Why, was he a councillor too?"

"You're making fun of me."

"How do you make that out?"

"Are you telling me you've never heard of Cromwell?"

"Of course I did, but the one we heard about has been dead a couple of hundred years."

"Well, that's the very same man."

"Christ if you haven't had a bit since then you must be really ready to go."

"Believe me I am and time is of the essence."

"You're a fast one. Did you ever think of getting in false teeth and combing your hair? What hospital are you out of anyway? It's not St. Joseph's, is it?" The women started to laugh again.

"Ladies, please go home," the guard said to them.

"Hold it a minute, we have a Romeo here with us."

"I don't care if you have Elvis Presley with you, move."

"Who's this Elvis Presley? Is he a general in our army or the English army?"

Then the women started to sing to him, "Are you lonesome tonight".

"Of course I'm lonesome, but if one of you would come away with me . . ."

The women kept on singing.

"All right," the guard said, "that's it, home. And I mean it this time." He asked Gummy what hospital he was out of.

"The one down the road."

"Well, would you mind going back there?"

As Gummy was looking at the guard, he saw Paddy going into the lane with a woman. "The lucky bastard. I always said it's the quiet ones you have to watch."

As he turned to go back to the other women, he thought to himself, "I've seen that walk before. That's impossible. But I did, now where?"

"Are you not gone yet?" the guard said to him.

"Just going."

Then it hit him—the Irishtown. "She's the bitch that made me a vampire. Sweet Jesus, Paddy's in trouble. I have to get into the lane fast or Paddy is dead." As he made his way through the crowd the other women were calling him, "Hey Romeo, we're over here."

Gummy knew he had to move fast. He got into the lane—no sign of them.

"She's in here with him, but where?" Gummy let his vampire senses take over now. He could hear the vampire saying, "Your stupid friend should be here any second."

The old ruined house! She's in there with him. He then evaporated into a mist and went in through the letter box. Sergeant John had been watching Gummy the whole time. He knew there was something strange about him, but when he watched him disappear he could not believe what he'd just seen.

"You've got to get a grip on yourself. You've been doing too much overtime and this blood pressure has you fucked up."

He knew if he called one of the men and told him what he had just seen, it'd be all over the station before the night was out and he'd be a laughing stock. Early retirement wasn't far away and he didn't want anything to get in the way of that. If they sent him for a medical, he was in deep trouble.

"Christ what am I going to do, the child was bitten by a woman, not a man."

He had read the case from years ago but it was a man who had just gone through the letter box. In tonight's case, as in the one years ago, it was a woman. Suppose there's a man working with her too? Christ, I can't walk away from this."

He went up to the old house, put his ear to the front door, and listened.

"They're in there all right, and whatever they are they're not human."

He had felt fear before in his life but nothing like this. He started to pray as he took out his truncheon and put on his flashlight. He then took a couple of steps back, ran at the door and kicked it in. As his light shone in the darkness he screamed "You're all under arrest, do you hear me?" Not a sound; but he knew they were in there.

The stairs were right in front of him and he stared to climb them. The cobwebs and dust left the sign of him but no one else. The stairs had not taken anyone in years and the weight of Sergeant Johns made them creak.

"Come out, I know you're in here. You're all under arrest," he shouted. As he climbed some more steps, the creaking was getting louder. Suddenly his leg went through one of the steps.

"That's all I need," he screamed as he left the truncheon and flashlight down. Then he looked up and saw a fog at the top of the stairs. As if it had a life of its own the fog started to come down the stairs towards him. Now it had two red eyes looking out of it.

"Sweet Jesus," sergeant Johns screamed, 'what's this?"

He had loved books all his life, especially horror and those dealing with vampires. He now knew what was coming down the stairs was a vampire. As the fog got nearer he hit out with his truncheon, but it was now on the ceiling and moving over him.

"Maybe it's escaping," he thought. But when it had reached the end of the stairs it came down from the ceiling and started to take shape. First a leg came out of it, then a hand, then another leg, and then another hand. It was as if it was dancing in front of him. Then a beautiful young woman stepped out of it and started climbing the stairs towards him. He threw his truncheon at her but she just moved her head and let it pass.

"Stupid man," she said. "Swords, crosses, and even holy water have been thrown at me but, as you can see, I'm still here."

He now knew he'd never get his leg out in time. He got hold of the banister and let himself down on the stairs. The vampire put her face against his and said, "You're a very stupid man. And worse, you now know what I am."

"You're a devil. You should be in hell where you belong," Sergeant Johns said.

"Is that right? I could make you one, too, did you ever think about that?"

"You follow children for blood."

"Anyone will do me, even you. But don't worry, if I took yours maybe there'd be another one like you. As you can see I can't take that chance."

Sergeant Johns started to pray and as he looked at the woman her face started to change. Her gums began to get bigger, and then her teeth. It was as if he was paralyzed; he could not move his hands. She then wrapped her body around him and started to caress his face with her hands and to lick his face. As he looked into the vampires eyes for the last time, she twisted his neck and broke it.

Gummy had gone through the letter box and, like a mist, went up the stairs.

"In here," a voice called out. As he went back to human form he went into one of the bedrooms and there she was, standing by an old fireplace, as beautiful as ever.

"Come to think of it, she's even more beautiful." And Paddy lay on an old mattress surrounded by empty wine bottles and other drinks.

"What did you do to him?" asked Gummy. "I just gave him what I should have years ago."

"What?" Gummy said and he collapsed. "You must be some ride."

"He'll be alright in a minute. He just wasn't used to it."

"What about me?" Gummy said. "I never got it either. You bit me before we even started."

"Well I wasn't in the mood that night."

"Is that right?"

"Yes, that's right."

"You seem to be in the mood now, judging by Paddy."

"That's right lover boy. I've been watching you with the women outside and I think you're ready too."

"I've been ready for the last 300 years but getting it was another thing."

But Gummy still had to ask her, "Why children? They harm no-one."

"When I was human I never harmed anyone either. Now do you want it or not?"

"Well, this should be some ride, two dead corpses. Talk about being rode to death."

"You still can't shut up can you? You were the same back in the Irishtown."

"I'm shutting up now," Gummy said as he watched her undress.

"I wonder," Gummy thought, "how many times she's taken off her clothes for innocent men. She has to die, she's like the plague. She destroys everyone she comes in contact with."

She had been reading Gummy's thoughts. "So I'm like the plague," she laughed. "I'll let you into a little secret, even when I was human I wanted to live forever and made it my business to seek out the Master. You might say I became a very good pupil, I even believe I surpassed my teacher. Now, it's time I finished the job I should have done years ago—kill you two morons."

"Jesus," Gummy screamed. "What kind of fucking idiot am I? I forgot she could read my mind."

She had him by the throat now and he could feel the nails starting to cut into his flesh. He pulled her body closer and with his loose hand grabbed her by the throat. He started to cut into her neck with his nails. With that, both of them broke away and, as Gummy tried to get some air, she hit him with a bottle across the face and then hit him again. Now he was on his knees. She broke the bottle on his head and, as he was trying to get up, she gave him a kick in the balls. Gummy let out a scream. He hadn't felt pain like that in years. He was now back down on his knees again. She flew across the room and, with her two feet, slapped into his face. As he hit the floor, all he could see was dust. It was everywhere now as she stood over him. She said, "Did you think I would have let you ride me? Or that prick on the mattress? It's time both of you went to sleep permanently."

Her teeth were down as she drew nearer to Gummy. Then he heard a voice saying, "Everything all right up there?"

"Saved," Gummy thought.

"Who's the bastard that's after saying that," she screamed as she evaporated into a fog. As Gummy was trying to get his senses back he could hear her speaking to someone outside the door. As he came out of the room he could see her leaving by the window. He went down to Sergeant Johns to see if he was still alive but as he looked down on him, he knew he was dead. Gummy moved his neck to see whether she had bitten him. "No. At least it's all over for him now."

He could hear people coming down the lane and a man's voice saying, "Sergeant Johns, where are you?"

"Better get Paddy out of here fast."

He raced back up the stairs, knelt over Paddy, slapped him on the face and said, "Wake up for fuck's sake or we're both dead. Wake up do you hear me?"

Paddy now started to come round. "Listen she's just after killing a policeman and a crowd is coming down the lane. Now get up, we have to move fast. We'll go out the window."

Paddy got to his feet, looked at Gummy, and said, "What happened to you?"

"I'll tell you after."

The crowd were at the door by this time and a man's voice was saying, "Sergeant, are you all right?" as he came up the stairs. After some seconds he shouted out to the crowd, "Someone run over to the priest's house and tell him to come over here fast. Mr. Ryan would you mind calling an ambulance?"

"I'll tell them to get here right away."

"There's no hurry; the Sergeant's dead."

As Paddy and Gummy went out the window Gummy's coat hit a pane of glass and knocked it out.

"Who's up there?" Guard O'Brien called. "There's someone in here," he said to the crowd. "I'm going up to take a look."

"Be careful," one of the women said. But he was already at the top of the stairs.

"All right, I know there's someone in here. Don't be afraid. All I want to do is ask you some questions."

He went from room to room but nothing. He then went into the last room; there was dust everywhere. He started coughing. He took his hanky out of his pocket and put it to his mouth. Now, as the dust settled, he looked at the window the glass had fallen from.

"Christ, there's broken glass everywhere."

He made his way to the window and looked down into the backyard. "Must've been a cat."

As he turned to walk away, he saw two big birds flying over the railway station.

"Well," he thought, "it couldn't have been one of them. One of them would have taken the window away with him."

"Well," the same woman shouted up the stairs, "what broke the glass?"

"Must've been a cat," O'Brien said. She then turned to the other women and said, "These old places should be knocked down. I remember Mrs. Scully some years ago was walking down Old Clare Street when a window from the top of an old house fell down on her. She was in Barringtons for weeks, cut all over. Sure didn't some of Patrick Street fall down as well, and the City Hall right across the road from it. And the road at the top of William Street collapsed. I tell you we're not safe in our own city. Shit! Here's Father Mitchell. He's up there Father."

"Thank you." The priest went up the stairs. He knelt down to give Sergeant Johns the last rites when he first felt the evil in the house. He could not concentrate on the prayers for the dead. He kept looking up the stairs the whole time. Something evil was here. Now, as he looked at Sergeant Johns, it was as if his face and eyes were trying to tell him something.

"What really happened to you Sergeant? You met evil didn't you?" he said as he closed his eyes. The ambulance men were at the bottom of the stairs.

"We'll take him away now father."

"I don't know. Maybe it would be best to wait until his superior comes."

"All right."

Father Mitchell went outside and took out a packet of cigarettes. He'd been trying to give up for the last week. He'd been told the best way to kill the longing was to keep a packet in your pocket at all times. But he already had them opened and had put one of them in his mouth. As he put the lighter to the cigarette he couldn't stop his hands shaking.

The women had been watching him and one came over and said, "Here, Father, let me light it for you."

Father Mitchell clasped his two hands together to try and stop the shaking.

"You'll be all right Father; the man's gone to Heaven."

He couldn't answer her, the cigarette was lit in his mouth but he was afraid to take it out in case he dropped it. He just leant against the front of the house and even outside he could feel the evil. He thought "What happened to the sergeant in there? What did he see?"

Then he turned his back on the crowd to take out the cigarette, but it was stuck to his lips. He went over to a car and rubbed his fingers across the top of it. The he put his wet fingers to his lips, got the cigarette out, and threw it away.

The woman had been watching him the whole time. She turned to her friends and said, "He's not well."

"He looked all right going in," one of them answered.

"Well he wasn't all right when he came out. Something happened in there."

"Will you leave us alone, all that happened in there was the Sergeant had a heart attack and that could have happened anywhere. Didn't my own father drop dead from one?"

"Where's the Romeo from the hospital."

"Gone. He went up the lane and must have gone through into Davis Street. I'm going home, anyone coming?"

"I am," one answered, "but I have to get some chips first. I was warned before I came out."

"Ah fuck him, you have him spoilt."

"That's a nice thing to say about your own brother."

"I don't care; he'd be better off if he got off his arse and looked for a job."

"I'll tell him you said that."

"Well it's true. Between the pains in his back and pains in his neck—he doesn't get pains in his arse though."

"Wait until he hears this."

"Fuck him."

As the women walked away, one said, "How's he in bed? Any pains in there?"

"No, he's fine in there, though he gets a bit stiff all right."

As they walked into Davis Street, you could hear the wife telling them about the other night and what they got up to.

Paddy and Gummy knew now it had to be tonight. If they didn't kill her no-one in Limerick would be safe. She seems to disappear when she wants to but she has to sleep like us. Where? Maybe she has a couple of hiding places and if one of them is discovered all she has to do is move on to another. They flew up the railway line and into Mount St. Laurence. "Now where is she hiding?" he said to himself. As they circled the graveyard there was no sign of her, so Paddy circled it again and as he flew over the old church he looked down underneath him and there she was coming at him fast. She hit Paddy and drove him up into the sky. He had heard the crack and he knew she had broken his wing. Now he was falling fast and if he hit one of the headstones his back or his head would be broken too.

"I've got to try to land on the church roof or I'm dead. Christ, where's Gummy? He's like a woman—when you need him, he's not there." He used the good wing to get him over the church roof. "I hope to Jesus I don't go through it." As he hit the roof, he bounced off and landed on the footpath. He turned himself back into human form as fast as he could and, as his wings changed into hands, he knew one would be useless. He then picked himself off the ground and was resting against the church when he heard her saying to him, "Well, well. I see you're having a bit of trouble." As he looked up, there she was, standing on one of the tombs.

"Break something did you?" she said as she jumped down onto the path. "I think you've outlived your life. What do you think yourself? It would be better off for all concerned if you and that fucking other idiot crossed over. What do you think about that?"

"If anyone needs to cross over it should be you."

"Maybe you're right, but who's going to put me over?"

"Me," came Gummy's voice from behind her as he hit her with an old iron cross. She let out a scream and leapt over the church.

"Are you all right?" Gummy asked Paddy.

"My hand is broken. I'm no good to you. You have to help me; she's too strong for me alone. Try and get her on the ground. Look out behind you!"

Gummy jumped up into the air as she came at him fast. She hit the church wall and let out another scream. Now smoke was coming off her hands and the side of her face.

"That's it," Paddy screamed. "The evil can't touch God's house."

"Christ," Gummy said, you're one ugly bitch."

"One who's going to kill you."

Gummy changed into bat form and flew as fast as he could straight up into the sky. He knew now all the running was no good. It was now or never.

"If I am to die tonight so what? I wish to fuck I'd died years ago with my friends and family, instead of having to walk around like a living corpse."

He looked down and there she was, coming at him fast. Smoke was coming out of her wings and face.

"Christ who's going to help me? Paddy can't fly. Think, Gummy, think fast. I'll have to get her down on the ground."

The same little girl who had seen them earlier that night was looking out her window. She'd had such a great time she could not sleep and now, as she watched the bats fight, she called out, "Mammy, come in quickly."

No-one answered her. "She must be asleep," she thought as she watched them herself. As they flew at one another, she thought, "I never knew they could fly so fast. Maybe they're eagles; they're big enough."

They were biting one another's wings, and as they fell from the sky, she thought, "I'm going back to bed. I'll tell Mammy in the morning."

Both of them hit the footpath so fast that they separated with the impact. Gummy was trying to get his senses back. He saw her coming for him.

"Get up or you're dead."

"Paddy come quick, for fuck's sake," he called out.

"Why are you calling him?" she said. "He's no good to you." As she lifted her hand she said, "Haven't you noticed? His wing or hand or whatever you call it is broken."

Gummy watched her as she hesitated to come to him. When he looked over his head, there was an old Celtic cross.

"Well, well, you can't touch me right now."

Gummy put his hand to the cross to lift himself upwards. It didn't affect him. He had always wondered why and had meant to ask Paddy about this. Now as he leant against the cross he said, "Tell me before you kill me, how is it that this affects you and not me? The same with the church."

"Why not?" she said. "Because I have killed and taken blood and will keep on killing. You and that other fucking idiot never killed anyone. You're a disgrace to vampires."

"Tell me," Gummy said. "How many are there in Ireland or Limerick."

"Always questions with you. You are one nosey bastard. In Limerick, as far as I know only me and the two of you. And, after tonight, just me."

Now she lifted herself from the ground and started circling towards Gummy. She was extending her arms and her nails and, as she circled, both of them were getting nearer to Gummy's throat. When they got too near, he ducked as she went for his throat and scraped the headstone. She let out a yell as smoke came from her nails. Gummy knew now he had drunk too much blood at the hospital and now, with her circling him the whole time, he felt sick.

Now she was right over him but with her eyes closed. Gummy called out for Paddy again. No answer. Had she killed him already? "No, impossible. She's been trying to do that to me since back at the church."

Gummy looked up the path to see how many crosses were on the way up. "That's my only hope, to try and make it back to the church. But, fuck it, there was nothing wrong with Paddy's legs, why isn't he here? Anyway, there are ten crosses on the way up."

Above him, the vampire said, "Christ, you keep forgetting I can read your mind. But why don't you give it a try? I'm a sporting girl."

"Christ," Gummy screamed, "will I never learn? You know I could wait until dawn then you would have to be gone."

"True, but so would you and it would only take a minute to kill you. No blood from you this time. Just your head off."

"Ah you're too decent," said Gummy. "So you're in this graveyard as well?"

"Now, you don't honestly expect me to answer that, do you? We ladies have our little secrets too."

With that Gummy made a run for it up the path as fast as he could. "Christ I'm going to make it," he thought. Then she lifted him off the ground and smashed him off the tree.

"Your time, I'm afraid, is up. Any last requests?"

"Yes, fuck yourself."

"And you do the same. No, I'll do it for you."

As she put her hands around Gummy's neck, he heard a scream and felt her hands flying off him. He opened his eyes and looked; she was down on her knees with Paddy driving a wooden stake through her. She jumped up, pushed Paddy away and tried to run back down the path. Paddy followed her and hit her in the back of the head with the old iron cross. She was screaming at Paddy, "Have mercy on me."

"I'll show you the same mercy you showed the people who had the misfortune to meet up with you."

With that he hit her on the neck and her head flew off.

Paddy roared back to Gummy, "Are you all right?"

"Yes, but if you don't mind me saying this, you nearly left it a bit late."

"I had to, she could easily have read my mind as well, so I had to wait my chance."

Gummy came down to where Paddy was standing and, as both of them looked down, her hair and her teeth were falling out.

"Another couple of seconds and all that will be left will be bones. Tell me if she had killed us, would we have gone the same way?"

"Yes. Anyway there's a barrel over there where the workmen have fires to keep warm. We'll put her body into the bottom of it and put some wood on top, so when they come in tomorrow morning, they'll each think the other one did it. They'll light it and no one will be any the wiser. How's that?"

"Great," Gummy said. "But there's one more thing for you to do."

"What's that, pray tell?"

"Kill me."

"What?" Paddy said.

"You heard me, I want to die. I can't go on any more."

"You're just a bit upset. A good night's sleep will do you good."

"Fuck it, Paddy, you're not listening to me. I want to sleep forever, not 50 or 100 years. I want to die. I can't take this life anymore."

"But there's so much to do."

"Not for me Paddy. I beg you, listen to me; I want to join my family."

"But you were happy tonight."

"But that's me, when I'm up I'm up, and when I'm down, I'm very down. There's no in between with me. As a friend, I beg you kill me."

"I can't. I'll be on my own. It's bad enough being in the coffin on your own, but then to wake up and have no one to talk to."

"Maybe you'll meet a woman when you come back the next time, but whatever was in me is gone. The last time, I felt it. But tonight I knew. You have to do it. I want peace, not this existence. As a friend I beg you. You know I can't kill myself."

"Can't you think about it?" Paddy said.

"I have, long and hard. The Limerick I knew is long gone. All for the better, but I don't belong here and neither do you come to think of it. Do me one last favour, will you put my bones on over hers? Then I can say I finally got on top of her."

"Look you're laughing again."

But Gummy knelt down and said, "Do it, Paddy. It's getting nearer to the dawn. Please."

Paddy picked up the iron cross, stood over Gummy, lifted it, and struck with all his might. As he watched Gummy's head fly off, he could have sworn there was a smile on his face. He then went up to where the timber lay in a pile, picked up a bit, came back and drove it into Gummy's bones.

"Just to make sure, my old friend."

He then turned and started to pick up the bones of the she-vampire. He brought them up and put them in the barrel.

"I suppose once you had feelings too, but I doubt it."

He then went back and picked up Gummy's bones and did what he had been asked.

"Farewell, my friend. I'll miss you."

He filled the barrel with timber and anything else that would burn as well.

"Well that's it. My job is done. Time to get some sleep." As he passed over where Gummy's coffin lay, he thought, "At least the roots of the tree won't be bothering Gummy anymore. Time to move. He went over to where his own coffin lay, let out a yawn and thought, "Now I have Limerick to myself. Wonder what it will be like when I awake the next time? But that's another day."

As he evaporated into his coffin and closed his eyes, for how long he did not know, overhead a star was falling from the sky and a long lost soul was finally making its way home.

The Waiting Game

He could feel the fear, hear the huffs and the deep breathing coming from the Confederate cavalry horses on the opposite side of the river. Many men from his company had already deserted; officers were screaming out orders every second from the dugout hole and, through the early morning mist, he watched their every move.

"I'd bet my last dollar they're about to charge," he thought. He saw them now taking their swords out. "I should have run away with the rest of them while I had the chance. Now it's too late."

Private John Russell, eighteen years of age, all the way from New York City, stuck in mud, his uniform filthy, wet and shaking with fear. "I don't want to die in this God-forsaken field. Mary, I should have listened to you," he shouted out.

"Shut up," a soldier screamed over at him. "They can hear you."

"Miss your momma, son?" another one asked him, and they all laughed a frightened laugh.

"I wish those men back home who told me to enlist straight away before the war is over were here in this stinking mud hole with me right now. They slapped me on the back and said I was doing the right thing. Where are they now? Sitting by the fire at home reading the latest news or, better still, wishing they were young men again. Bullshit. They're glad they're old. Now they can talk the talk."

Then he heard the bugler beginning to play the charge. And the next second they plunged into the river like an explosion. The cannon let loose; earth, men, horses, wagons, flew in pieces up in to the sky, behind, in front, and over him. Then the screams. He got back up and looked straight ahead again. Now they were at his side of the river. He took careful aim and waited for the order to fire. None came, so he fired at the nearest rider, knocking him off his horse. Then all hell broke loose.

He couldn't remember how long it lasted. But something had hit him on the head. When he regained consciousness, the first thing his nostrils picked up was the stench coming from the dead bodies lying next to him. Then the smell of smoke. Now he could hear voices—rebel voices—coming from somewhere very near. The smoke was making him sick; he tried holding his breath, but it was no good. The vomit came pouring out of his mouth. Throwing up on himself, he put both hands up in the air and tried to shout out, "Don't shoot. I surrender," as he threw up again.

"Well, well. Look what we've got over here boys. A live Yankee," one rebel soldier shouted out.

"Up you get, boy, slowly. And keep your hands where I can see them. Understand? Answer me, boy."

"Yes, Sir," John Russell replied.

"Good. Now walk over to me—but be careful, we don't want you to walk on some of your dead friends, do we, boys?"

Other soldiers now came towards him. He heard screams, men calling out for morphine. He glanced over and saw a torn canvas makeshift hospital.

"You hear that, Yankee? My friends are dying over there. How many did you kill? Answer me!" and he kicked the legs from under John Russell.

"I think I'll blow your brains out," he shouted down at him, as he put his gun to his head.

"Have mercy on me," John cried out. "I'm only eighteen."

"So was my brother, Jed. But he's dead—shot here today. Maybe it was you who shot him. How many of our boys did you kill?" he screamed down to John again. "Cat got your tongue? Answer me!" He hit him in the mouth with the barrel of his gun, breaking his jaw.

"What are you doing?" one of the soldiers shouted over at him.

"Well, now that you ask, I'm going to hang him from that tree over there. Does that bother you?" he asked the soldier.

"Yes," he replied. "He's a prisoner of war and should be treated as one."

"What are you, a Yankee sympathiser?" he shouted back at him.

"No but there's been enough blood shed here today. Leave the boy be."

"You heard him, boys. Our friends lying all over this field and he wants us to leave this Yankee alone. I'll tell you what I'll do. I put it to a vote; you soldiers are the jury. Now what do you all want to do with him?" he shouted out to them.

"Well come on, answer me. I'm waiting."

"Hang him!" they all shouted back.

"Or maybe I'll shoot him like a dog right here and now,' he said. No one replied.

"Let's hang him. I'll get a rope; just hold on a minute."

"Don't be long. We'll be pulling out soon. It wouldn't do to leave you behind—you could be caught. And they'd take down our friend here and string you up. And you," he pointed to the lone soldier, "keep your mouth shut or we'll take you down to the river and drown you. Understand?"

"Yes," he answered meekly. Turning to walk away, he said to John Russell, "I'll pray for your soul son."

"Please, in the name of God," he shouted out through his broken, bloody mouth. "Let me live, I beg you."

"No," they replied. And they all began to laugh.

"Got it," the soldier shouted now, walking back to them, holding up the rope and stepping over the corpses.

"Christ, there's some smell down by the river. Took it off a dead Yankee's horse. So we can hang him with one of his own."

"Right, you two, grab him. We're wasting time."

They got hold of him by his filthy wet uniform and started to drag him down to the tree.

"You're too slow," the leader shouted at them. "Get hold of a leg each, you two, and we'll carry him down."

"Where's the horse?" one soldier asked the leader.

"We don't need one. We'll put the rope around his neck and pull him up."

"But his hands," he said.

"Get a belt off one of the bodies. That will hold him."

When they got to the tree they dropped him down hard.

"Please," John said.

"Shut your damn Yankee mouth," the leader shouted down at him. "Here, give me that rope. I'll hang him myself," he said to the soldier. "Be my guest," he replied as he handed it to him.

He got hold of John by the hair, pulling him up. And as he did, he put the noose around his neck, throwing the rest over the nearest branch.

"Right, pull him up," he said to the men. "What's wrong with you? A couple of minutes ago you were all screaming to hang him. Well, boys, the time has come to do it."

With that the leader tied John's hands with the belt and said, "Right, let's get it over with."

They pulled the rope so hard his head smashed off the branch they were hanging him from. His legs began kicking out everywhere.

"Stay back, boys, or you could get a kick in the face," the leader said.

After some time the kicking stopped.

"Give it a twist—just in case," the leader said.

"He's dead, believe me," one of them replied.

"Then let go of the rope," the leader said.

They did. And the body of John Russell dropped down, in to the mud and wet.

"Let the rope stay where it is. A souvenir from us," the leader said.

"Good thinking," another soldier replied.

They heard shooting coming from the opposite hill.

"Time to move, boys," the leader said. "Time to get back to the other side of the river.

When the Union soldiers found John's body, one called out to their Sergeant, "Ritter, they hung one of our boys from the tree over there."

"Check to see if he has any identification on him," he answered. And remember, this was Americans who did this. So when we catch up with them, we'll hang some of them as well. Let's go now."

"Sergeant," said the one searching John's pocket. "It's not up to me—I just obey orders, like the rest of you. Cut the noose off we'll keep it, and when we catch some Johnny Rebs, we'll make our noose and knot just like this one, show it to them, and then hang them."

The fighting went on for the rest of the week. No mercy was given on either side. Two days later, Sergeant Ritter and his men came across a loose body of Rebels trying to get back into the woods. They attacked straight away and shot some of them dead; the rest surrendered.

"Well, boys, the war's over for you," Sergeant Ritter said to them.

"Is that right?" one answered him.

"Yes, that's right," Sergeant Ritter said. "And who might you be?"

"You could say I'm in charge of these men," he replied.

Dismounting, Sergeant Ritter opened one of his saddle bags, walked over to the leader and said, "Ever see this before?" holding the noose right in front of his face.

"Can't say I did. Where's the rest of it?" he asked.

"Back where you hung one of our boys," Sergeant Ritter said.

"Were you one of them?" the sergeant asked him.

"One of what?" he asked now, smiling straight back at the sergeant.

With that, the sergeant pushed the noose hard, right in to his face, drawing blood and knocking him to the ground.

"One of the scum that hanged him," he shouted down at him, as he lifted his boot and kicked him in the face. "You must have seen it. Answer me, Reb."

"Go to hell, you Yankee piece of shit," he shouted. And he spit the blood from his mouth straight up in to Sergeant Ritter's face. The sergeant said nothing, wiped his face, and then took out his revolver. He put it up to the other man's left eye and pulled the trigger. The back of his head exploded as pieces of his brain flew down in to the dew-wet morning ground.

"You!" he pointed to another confederate soldier. "Over here, now."

"I had nothing to do with the hanging; I tried to stop it," he shouted at the sergeant.

"So you were there," Sergeant Ritter said. "What about the rest, were they there as well? Tell me the truth and you'll live."

"All of them. They're the ones that hanged him," he said.

"God be praised. He led us to these murdering bastards. Justice is mine now, Lord," Sergeant Ritter shouted out.

"He's the one that went and got the rope and the belt," one said.

"He's lying. I tried to stop them," he said to the sergeant.

"Now just who is telling the truth here?" the sergeant asked. "Well?"

"Me, Sergeant," he replied. "I wanted to join the Yankee side so bad—that's where my heart belongs—but I couldn't, I was too deep south."

"Ever hear of a train or a horse?" the sergeant asked him. "You could even have walked. Let me guess you had no shoes or a horse, am I right soldier?"

"Yes, sir. You're right," he replied.

"Somehow I knew that was going to be your answer.

"Now that we have them, Sergeant, what do you propose to do with them?" one of his own soldiers asked.

"Shoot them. But not him." And he pointed to the informer.

They aimed there rifles at the prisoners, took aim, and fired. Two tried to make a run for the forest; some of the riders waited before they took out their swords and charged. When they caught up with them, they began to cut and play with their bodies, slicing their backs and then their faces. When they tired, they cut off their heads, putting them on the top of there swords. Then they made wagers to see who could throw their head the farthest. Bets were put on each head and after some time it was declared a draw.

Now Sergeant Ritter turned to the last prisoner and asked him, "What should I do with you?"

"Take me to your captain and I'll tell him everything. I know where they'll be waiting to ambush you," he pleaded, kneeling in front of Sergeant Ritter.

"Did our boy ask you for mercy before you hanged him? I want two ropes," he said to his men.

"Please don't hang me," the soldier begged.

"Don't worry I won't hang you," the sergeant answered.

"Thank you. I knew you were an honest man," the soldier replied.

"Spread him out, boys, and tie each rope to a leg. Now, my Johnny Reb, what's going to happen to you is simple—half of you will go this way, and the other half will go that way. You could say a part of you will be going home."

The soldier's bowels opened up with fright as the ropes tightened around each leg. Then two riders tied them tightly to their saddles.

"Ready, boys?" the sergeant asked them.

"Just waiting for the order," one replied.

"The rest of you get out of the way." The sergeant took off his hat—just like you'd see at any race meeting—lifted it over his head and, after some seconds, with the soldier screaming out for his mother, he brought it down. With that, both riders whipped their horses, each going the opposite way, as the soldier now frantically tried to untie the ropes.

They could hear the bones beginning to break, and then the tear as both legs tore away from the body; the top part was crawling around the ground, still begging for mercy. When the riders came back, one said, "I'd thought he'd be dead by now. Christ, look at all the blood pouring out of him." He began to crawl towards them with one of his hands reaching out, grabbing empty air.

"Does he know his legs are gone?" a soldier asked sergeant Ritter. "How do I know? Why don't you go over and ask him?"

"Put him out of his misery, Sergeant," one of the riders asked him.

"Sure, why not?" the sergeant replied. He asked the man for his sword, then walked over to the half dead man, waiting for his head to turn his way. When it did, he lifted the sword and cut off his head. Then he turned to his men and said, "I'd say he's dead now," and began to laugh.

None replied.

"Time to move on. Who knows, we might get some more before the day's out," he said to them. "Clean the blood off your swords." He handed the one he had borrowed back to its owner.

"Now mount up and let's go looking for some more fun."

Six weeks after the butchery of the confederate soldiers, Sergeant Ritter and his men were captured, some miles from Ebenezer Creek. No one knows their fate.

General Lee surrendered on April 9th, 1865. The war was now finally over, each side blaming the other for atrocities committed. Those who where blamed—not on the northern side, but on the southern side—were hunted down. Some they caught and hanged, most disappeared over the Rio Grande to Mexico to try and continue the fight from there. Yet more went back home and kept a low profile.

When the city's and towns had to be rebuild, there was good money to be made; with greed taking over, everyone became bosom friends. Those who could make a fast buck said, "The past is dead, long live the future." And America became one.

Culdrun

When Joan Archer's body was found in the river, the locals said it was suicide; she'd had suffered from nerves all her life. But one man knew the truth and now, 40 years later, he had come back from America, leaving two ex-wives and three grown-up children behind, to try and get to the bottom of it.

In the years he'd been away, he would now and then think back to that evening and remember the last two occasions he had seen her alive. The first time she had come running up the road, shouting to his mother "He's trying to kill me, Mrs. Coombs."

"Who?"

"I can't talk to you right now, young Liam is listening."

"I'll tell him to go away and then you can speak to me."

"I can't."

"Why?"

"Because I think he's following me." But when she looked around, there wasn't a sinner in sight.

"There's no one there, Joan."

"Maybe not to you, but to me, he's there."

"Can't you come in and have a cup of tea?"

"No thank you." And with that she was gone.

Later that evening, Alice Coombs told Liam to check that his father had locked the gate. "I don't want the cows going down to the river and getting stuck in the mud." Liam set off, putting on his coat and calling his dog, Daisy. When he got there, the gate was closed and he lingered for a while, throwing a stick for Daisy to fetch; she loved going after it and bringing it back— but trying to get her to let go of it was another matter. As he was trying to retrieve the stick from the dog, he saw Joan Archer running down by the side of the river; she stopped, pointed back at some trees and shouted "Leave me alone. I never did anything to you."

Liam watched her, thinking to himself, "The poor woman, she's shouting at nothing." But as she turned and ran down the path, Liam heard a voice say, "You're mine, Joan Archer, mine."

He went down on his knees and watched now in horror as a man walked out from behind the trees and started to follow her. Just then, Daisy dropped the stick and started to bark;

the man turned, put his hand across his face, and ran back into the trees.

Liam turned and ran towards home as fast as he could, with Daisy dropping and then picking up the stick and dropping it again right in front of him. "Get out of my way," he screamed, as he climbed over the gate and ran as if the hounds of hell were snapping at his heels. When he got back his father was home and he told his parents what he had seen.

"Listen," Liam, his mother said. "Earlier today you heard Joan tell me she was being followed, didn't you?"

"What are you trying to say, woman? Are you telling me he's made all this up?" Aiden Coombs asked. "Let him answer the question himself."

Again, Liam said that she was being followed. "He came out of the batch of trees down by the side of the river and shouted that she was his." When he was finished his father went into the kitchen and came back with his gun. "Where's the lamp?" he asked his wife. She went over to the cupboard and got it for him.

"I'll be back soon—hopefully with an answer," he said, putting on his hat and coat.

"Take Daisy with you," Alice said.

"No. If she saw her own shadow, she'd start barking."

"Well, be careful," she warned him.

"I will," he answered as he walked out the door.

"Can I go to bed now?" Liam asked his mother when his father had gone.

"No," she told him. "Stay where you are until your father comes back with an explanation."

As they waited, he watched his mother open first the door and then the window to look out anxiously, only to repeat it all a minute later. She must have done it a hundred times. She didn't sit down the whole time his father was gone.

When he did come back, he told his wife that Liam had been telling the truth. "There were footprints in the mud, right where he said he saw the man."

"Maybe they belong to someone out for an evening stroll earlier tonight?"

"No. They were just where Liam said the man followed Joan and then turned back when he heard the dog bark."

"We'd better tell the police," his mother said.

"Tell them what? That poor woman is sick, and he's just a boy." He turned to Liam. "Did you ever hear that voice or see that man before?"

"How do you mean?"

"Well, was he a local man?"

"I don't know."

"Fair enough. Go on up to bed; we can talk in the morning."

That night, Liam never left the window. He kept looking out toward the river, hoping to see someone or something.

The next day, they found Joan Archer's body. His father said that he had pointed out what looked like bruising around her neck and some scratches to the doctor, John Shepard. "Are you trying to tell me something?" was the doctor's reply.

"When we brought her back to the house, I said again that he should take a look at them. With that, he asked me what medical school had I graduated from.

"When he'd finished examining her, he said that she'd taken her own life and that was that, looking straight at me as he spoke. So maybe it was suicide. As for the cuts, maybe she got them from the weeds."

"That's it," his wife answered. "We'll pray for her tonight and leave it in God's hands."

And now, here he was, 40 years later, still thinking of the man who had run out from behind the trees. Whoever he was, he was either dead by now or in his seventies at least. He had to find out who he was, if only to put his mind at ease. His plan was to hire out the local hall, get a band to play, and invite all the local old folk. "If they ask what it's for, I'll tell them it's for being great neighbours when I was growing up."

First thing the next morning, he went to the priest's house to ask about hiring the hall.

"Well, it depends on what night you'll want it—we have the bingo and the local play group taking up nearly every night."

"Whatever night is free,' Liam said.

"Fair enough."

"And by the way, you're invited."

"I should hope so," Father Egan said. "I've been in this parish nearly 30 years, a lifetime for some people. Believe it or not, most of your old neighbours are still here—they refuse to die in this neck of the woods—and if I know them, they'll be delighted to come."

"When will you let me know father?"

"Give me a day or two."

"Fair enough."

Liam knew there was no need to advertise in the local paper— Father Egan would tell them from the pulpit. And right enough, he did. Two weeks later, they had their night and it cost Liam a fair amount. But money was no object; catching the killer was what mattered. The band played all the old music and kept everyone happy, but when he tried to bring up the subject of Joan Archer, he was met with silence. They either shook their heads saying they couldn't remember her, or they said to let the dead lie in peace. "Suppose she's not at peace?" Liam asked. But they just shook their heads again and walked away or got up to dance. Just before the last dance of the night, Liam got up onto the stage and thanked them all for coming.

Later, back in his parents' house, the phone rang. "Remember me?" a voice whispered.

"No, should I?" Liam asked.

"Well, try and remember this: 'Joan Archer, you're mine'." Liam froze, as he had all those years before.

"Yes, I remember you, you sick bastard."

"Don't say that. It was a good night tonight, but the food could have been better. See you soon. By the way, there's no way you can trace this call and don't bother trying to find out where I got the number.

"You know, I have fond memories of that night. I even followed you home, but that stupid dog of yours was barking. You thought it was the stick had him so excited. When he died, I knew you'd be heartbroken. Well, I'll let you in on a little secret—I poisoned him.

"And as for your stupid father, trying to play Sherlock Holmes, forget it. When you went away, I used to meet your precious father and have a nice chat with him. He always said that if you heard that voice again, you'd know it straight away. Well, my friend, you're hearing it now, but it doesn't sound familiar to you, does it?"

"I'll get you," Liam shouted into the phone.

"Never again." The voice was changing now into a woman saying "Oh please, Mr. Coombs, be gentle with me."

"May you rot in hell," Liam said and, with that, the phone went dead.

"Christ, I've never experienced anything like that before, not even in Vietnam. For an old man, his voice still sounds strong and, if I'm right, he's glad I'm back. This will get his blood flowing and his mind working again. Well, I'll do what we did with the snipers—play him at his own game and flush him out."

The next morning, Liam phoned an ex-army friend who had joined the FBI when he left the army. After listening to Liam telling the story, ending with the previous night's phone call, he asked Liam to give him a couple of days to work up a profile on him.

"When I have it done, I'll phone you. He reminds me of a case we had in Alabama 20 years ago. This guy set up his own church and then started killing his congregation. When we finally caught him and asked why he had done it, guess what his answer was? He wanted to bring them nearer to Jesus. Can you believe that? But here's the strange part: on the day of his own execution, he screamed that he wanted to live. This from the guy who thought nothing of taking someone else's life. He had to be dragged all the way to old Sparky.

"I believe this guy fits the same bill, for what it's worth. He's still in the community and, as they put the woman's death down to suicide, I'd look for more of them—women who got up and left without giving an address, that sort of thing. Because he didn't stop after her—that's if she was the first. His ego wouldn't let him stop. His victims are probably all women. For him it was—or still is—the thrill of the hunt; that's why he followed her. But I'll give this to the experts and get in touch with you when I have something.

"I'm not trying to frighten you, Liam, but I'd make sure my windows and doors are locked before I go to bed. What about a gun?" Santos Torres asked.

"It's not that easy over here," Liam replied.

"Well, if you can't get it one way, get it the other. You remember the old jungle trick—the one we used to do in the bars back in 'Nam? And swear them to secrecy. Are you listening or are you gone deaf?"

"I'm listening, believe me, you New Jersey piece of shit." They both laughed.

"God bless—and Liam, I mean it, watch your back; he's going to make contact with you again. This is like a dose of Viagra to him."

When Santos Torres had hung up, Liam made himself a pot of coffee and sat down with a pen and paper, writing down what he may or may not know about him.

"Number one. I don't believe he knows that I have army training. Maybe I'm wrong about that.

"Two. He may be good at frightening women and a little boy, but now he's dealing with an ex-soldier.

"Three. Like all killers, he's a coward, but a very clever one.

"Four. He has an advantage over me: he knows who I am but I don't have a clue who he is.

"Five. It's not his real voice that is speaking to me. I have to try and tape him the next time he calls.

"Six. Why didn't I keep my big mouth shut last night?

"Seven. Why did some people walk away when I brought up Joan Archer?

"Eight. You made a fool out of my father, winding him up with your soft talk. Well, my friend, I've dealt with people like you before. I'm going to speak to everyone in that age group, but I won't be as innocent as my father was. I'll listen very carefully to every little thing, and maybe the next time you speak to me your ego will try and test me that extra bit.

"I believe he will. To analyse this guy I need to find out whether he's married. Does he have children? Living with a sister or brother? No. He never married—she'd have found out a long time ago. You have to unwind after a killing and sometimes that can take a day or two."

When he had written it all down, he thought of Corporal Joe Schultz. A psycho if ever there was one; he killed for the sake of killing. Anything he saw, he shot. From the day he landed in 'Nam to the day he was killed, he was on a high. In the end, Liam was even afraid to turn his back on him.

He thought of a sunny day back in June of '66. They had been waiting for the Vietcong to cross a road in the iron triangle when Shultz appeared out of nowhere, putting a knife to Liam's throat and saying "Top of the morning, Lieutenant, and how do you feel today?"

"You crazy bastard," Liam whispered. "I could have you Court Martialled for this."

"But you won't, will you? I mean, back home, they're going to Canada and over to Europe, and even joining the Home Guard rather than come over here and serve their country. I hear they're burning their draft cards and even saying they're faggots. And here's little old me, doing all I can for Uncle Sam. You know when I get back I'm personally going to deal with those scum. And, Lieutenant, if you just look straight down, you'll see our Vietcong friends coming up the road. Got to get back to my position. It wouldn't do to say I deserted my post, would, it Lieutenant?" And with that he was gone without a sound.

"No prisoners that day or any day," Liam thought. "We killed them all. Later that night back in camp we wondered who was right—them or us. Or what the fuck were we doing over there.

"But we never did ask the questions. We just obeyed and either got killed or sent home when we were finished. Most of us were screwed up in one way or another and some great friends were left back there. Maybe Shultz was right. Had the Vietcong won and—just suppose—had invaded America, folks would have kissed ass and given them flowers and a lot of bullshit about free speech and then opened the gates for them.

"They were very lucky Schultz was killed, because if he had got back home he would have gone looking for some of those boys and shown them what the Vietcong would have done—just like he was going to do to them.

"Anyway, that's the past. It's now I should be thinking about. I heard someone say at the party that there's a dog's home somewhere in the city. They should have plenty of strays there; I'll try and get the same breed as Daisy. I read somewhere that after every Christmas pups that had been given as presents were gotten rid of the minute they started to grow. I could get lucky."

And he did the next day. But she needed to be trained; the first thing she did when he got her home was to leave her mark all over the place. Then she started at the curtains, but when she jumped up on the couch, she lay down, let out a sigh, and went straight to sleep. Only time would tell whether she would be any good.

Santos Torres got back to him some days later. "Well,' he asked, "what have you got?"

"Nothing much," he said. "Only what I've already told you. And I spoke to the Captain about it. He said everything that's been bottled up inside him all these years is ready to explode. So you could say that you're at the right place. Like me, he believes there have to have been more women who went missing or whose deaths were put down to suicide.

"By the way, I have a couple of weeks coming to me, would you mind if I paid you a visit?"

"I was hoping you'd say that. But what about Mary? Would she mind?" Liam asked.

"I don't think so. We're in the process of getting divorced."

"I'm sorry to hear that," Liam said.

"Too much time away from home makes Santos a dull boy. I'll tell you Liam, Vietnam fucked us all up. I even wake up in a sweat thinking I'm still in a hole waiting for Charley. But don't worry—I can still do my job.

"Well, do you still want me?"

"When can you be here?"

"I could catch a flight to Dublin and be there in, say, two days time."

"Two days it is, then. I'll be in the lounge waiting for you."

"Right. I'll get the bags packed and see you then. Before you hang up, is the adrenalin starting to pump again in you? Just like the old days?"

As Liam picked up the new Daisy, he wondered why he hadn't told Santos he too woke up in a sweat with the hair standing up on the back of his neck. It was just like those days, worrying about the boys stepping on landmines. The last days of Saigon, fighting street to street. Sweet Jesus, how did we come out of it?

"And why do I keep these things to myself? It must be the Lieutenant in me. No. He knows I'm the same way."

The next day Liam went looking for books about the history of the place. He bought one about strange occurrences that had happened down through the years. That night he read about the Druids burying their dead by the river, believing a sea god lived there. And how a mist would suddenly come out of nowhere.

"I remember it well, I went out one night with my father, rounding up the cattle. He was afraid they might take fright and walk down in to the river. He put a string with a bell on it around my neck, just in case I got lost as well. 'I'm not wearing that,' I said. 'It's the cows need the bells around their necks, not me.' 'Fair enough, then, you can stay home.'

" 'Wear it,' my mother said. 'He's going with you, Aiden. Now put your coat and hat on.' "

When they got to the field, Liam was glad he'd listened to his mother. "Where do you think they are?" he asked.

"I'd say they're sitting down somewhere in here." And with that, Liam fell over one, giving the cow and himself an awful fright. When he had picked himself up, he asked his father why the cow hadn't moved when he heard them coming.

"Maybe she's afraid that she'll walk into the river anyway. How should I know? I never asked one. Now shut up and use your ears."

Liam did use them there and later in Vietnam.

When he saw Santos coming through the door of the airport lounge, his first thought was that a bit of exercise wouldn't go astray.

"How are you, Liam?"

"Not too bad, and you?"

"Great."

"I see you've put on a bit of weight and the hair's waving you goodbye."

"Thank you," Santos said, "for those kind words. If you don't mind my saying, you don't look too good yourself." And with that they shook hands.

"Glad to have you aboard."

"Glad to be here, Liam. Have there been any other phone calls?"

"No."

"He's playing with your nerves. And how are they?"

"Not bad, but getting better. Drink?"

"Why not?"

Later, as they drove back to Liam's house, Santos said, "This won't be easy. He's been out there too long and he's good."

"So what'll we do first?" Liam asked.

"I need some sleep and in the morning you can take me down to where you saw him. It is still there, isn't it?"

"Yes. Nothing's changed except me."

"I'll also put a tap on your phone and then we wait and see. How many still have the number?" Santos asked.

"Don't know. I'd say the whole place, knowing my father," Liam replied.

Daisy couldn't stop barking when they went into the house.

"Want something to eat?"

"Why not?"

As Liam was getting the food, he looked down at Daisy's plate. There was dog food in it and some chocolate sweets. "Santos, come in here, will you?"

"What is it?"

"Take a look down there. I don't feed Daisy until around this time, and when I do she's jumping all over the place. And anyway, that's not my food. He's been in here."

"Are you sure?" Santos asked.

"Of course I'm sure. I never gave her any chocolate or put out any food."

"Jesus, he's one cool customer."

Liam went back into the sitting room and went over to Daisy. When he rubbed her neck, she just opened her eyes, wagged her tail, and then started to go to sleep.

"The bastard's poisoned her," Liam said. "Quick, start the car, there's a vet living about five miles from here."

As Santos took the keys from the table, Liam got a bag and put the contents of Daisy's plate into it. Then he lifted her up, saying, "Don't worry baby, we'll have you fixcd up in no time." When he had laid her in the back of the car, he said to Santos, "I'll drive. It won't do having you going down the wrong side of the road, and anyway you don't know where the vet lives, do you? She looks OK to me."

As they drove to the vet's house, Santos said, "I underestimated him. Don't be surprised if he's a serial killer. When we get back to your house, every bit of food or any drinks will have to be destroyed."

"Why?" Liam asked.

"I don't think Daisy or the food he gave her is poisoned, but he's letting you know he can get to you at any time. It's the old cat-and-mouse game, so we have to become the cat or we're dead."

When the vet had finished checking over Daisy, he said, "She's in perfect health, not a bother. Had the food been bad, she'd be sick already. And you want me to test it as well for what?"

"Anything."

"Fair enough. But it'll take a couple of days."

"I don't care how much it costs. How much do I owe you, Mr. Murphy?"

"I'll tell you that when I get the results back. Now, gentlemen, if you don't mind, it's bedtime for me. When you get to be as old as me you start nodding off very early."

"Tell me, did you enjoy yourself the night of the reunion, Mr. Murphy?"

"It was a grand night, Liam. And great to meet some of the old neighbours again. As for Daisy, she'll be fine in the morning."

"Goodnight then."

As Paul Murphy watched them drive away, he thought, "That was a stupid thing, leaving the food there. Well, what's done is done. But who was the man with him?" His eyes were going all over the place. "But that's the thrill of the game. Just need to be more careful."

As Liam drove home, Santos asked how long he had known the vet.

"As far back as I remember, why?"

"Well, he fits the bill and the age group."

"Will you give me a break, he's a pillar of society around here."

"Should that make him any different from . . . let's say the farmer that lives in there, or even the priest? If there's one thing I've learned from the FBI, it is that you check everyone out. And when you've done that, you do it all over again, but not the same way. Did you notice that, for a man who claimed to be sleepy, his eyes didn't look it? As a matter of fact, thy seemed to me to be taking everything in."

"That's what eyes are for," Liam answered.

"Any restaurants around here?"

"No, but there's a great fish and chip shop in Culdrun."

"It'll have to do."

"Do you know all the locks will have to be changed straight away? He let himself in."

"But where did he get the key from?" Liam asked.

"Either your father gave it to him, or he stole it while he was visiting him. But as I said, all the food will have to be destroyed."

"Not the tinned stuff?"

"Why not?" All he'd have to do is make a small hole and put drops of poison in. It's as simple as that."

"Fuck it. I only did the shopping two days ago, and now I have to throw it all out. Even the meat in the freezer?"

"Especially that."

Later, as they sat down to eat their fish and chips, Liam asked Santos to pass the salt. "I wouldn't if I were you. Anyway, they put some on back at the shop."

Liam started to laugh.

"What's so funny?" Santos asked.

"Well, this is getting more like Vietnam every second. You know, watch your back and dump the food you got from the village in case it's poisoned."

"You forgot one thing."

"What's that?"

"You were the lieutenant. It was you who told the sentry to keep his eyes open just in case they decided to pay us a visit during the night."

"He already has paid us a visit, or have you forgotten already? You're not going senile on me, are you Santos?"

"No, are you?"

"I don't know, to tell you the truth. I mean, right in the heart of Ireland, would anyone believe it?" Liam asked.

"Why not? A killer is a killer no matter what country he comes from. But a serial killer—he's different. He thinks he's a class act. And he's everyone's neighbour—says nothing but takes everything in. And your one has been doing it for years. I mean, he must know this house inside out. And he knows all those who went to America and England and how they're doing out there," Santos said.

"In that case, he knows I've done army service," Liam answered.

"Let's hope not, because if he does, he could go back to being your friendly neighbour again and until they drop off one by one he'll be watching you.

"Who's on first?" he asked.

"Me. I can't sleep. Too much thinking to do. You know, I still can't believe he came in here and fed Daisy."

"Well, that was his first mistake. There must be a place in Dublin somewhere we could get the bowl checked out for fingerprints. We can look up the papers or the telephone book and hopefully there'll be something on it. I can't ask the police, they'll want to know why. Also, just in case he does come back, he won't be walking like the old days. It's the sound of a car stopping or moving slowly down the hill with its engine switched off."

"Maybe I should sell up and go back with you," Liam said.

"You know that's not on. He needs to be caught no matter what, for the sake of the innocent people he's killed. I mean there are war criminals from the Second World War walking around with people still after them and it's only right."

"Maybe. But what about us?" Liam said. "We caught one or two as well, and we killed them."

"We had to," Santos answered. "If they had captured us—you know the rest. You saw what they did to some of the boys."

"Will I ever forget it? Listen, get some sleep. I want to think."

"Best news I've heard all day."

Later, as he drank his fifth cup of coffee, he thought back to the time when he had first heard the voice. Money was scarce then and a lot of people would go for walks just to kill a couple of hours. And there were usually some local fishermen out on the river too. Yet, on that evening, there was no one around. And it was one of those evenings you'd expect everyone to be out.

"I can't believe no one saw him. I mean, the poor woman was mad with fright, running down our road. And if she stopped to speak to my mother, she might have stopped to speak to someone else. She would have passed at least ten houses, five with young families in them. Surely some of them were playing in the field and if they were, they may have seen Joan Archer running down the road with her killer after her.

"But how to go about it? I made a balls of it at the reunion. I rushed in too fast. Fuck it. I was once one of them, but maybe I was too long in America. Maybe I was never one of them.

"Who do I start with? The kids I went to school with?"

Suddenly Daisy's ears went up and she started to bark. Liam slowly got up from the chair, switched off the lights, and watched as Daisy ran for the door. He picked up the poker from the fireplace, took the bolt off the door and went out, moving from side to side.

On the road outside, a car passed with its lights on full. As he watched it turn at Maloney's Cross, he thought, "It could have been him." Now Daisy was leaving her calling card on a piece of cloth. "So that's what you were barking about—you wanted to go outside. Christ, you're a clever dog. Two weeks ago, you didn't care where you went, you pissed all over the house. "Well, are you finished?" At that, Daisy wagged her tail, went back in, and made straight for the couch. "At least someone's happy," he said and sat back down.

Suddenly it hit him—the cloth outside the door, he'd seen it before.

"Jesus Christ, it's the same material as the dress Joan Archer was wearing the last time I saw her. He got back up again, went to the door, and opened it. Now, as he looked down at the cloth, he heard Santos' voice behind him.

"What's wrong?" he asked, now standing just inside the door.

"Between you and that dog, you'd wake the dead."

"Look, it's a piece of the dress Joan Archer wore on he night he killed her," Liam answered.

"How do you make that out?"

"Because it was so bright, and the flowers on it are the same."

"Maybe. But how many of those dresses were made back then? Now, if it had been Dior or some other designer label, I would take notice, but this was a dime-a-dozen dress."

"A car passed as well, with its lights full on."

"Christ, Liam, so were yours when we were coming back from the fish shop. I mean, it's not as if you were driving down route 66," Santos said.

"Maybe not, but this piece is going up to Dublin as well, and I swear it was him."

"Suppose you're wrong?" Santos asked.

"I'd bet my life on it."

"But Liam, we fucked up before."

"Santos, what's with you? Everything I say is wrong."

"Look, Liam, it's not that I'm just throwing questions in the air. If we make one mistake with this guy, we're dead. Now come back in. I'm not able for these cold nights."

When they were back inside, Liam turned and said, "Answer me straight, do you think I'm slipping?"

"What do you mean?" Santos asked.

"Please don't insult my intelligence. Do you think I left whatever I once had back in Vietnam? And as your once commanding officer, I want the truth, no bullshit."

"All right, you jumped in too fast and, until you step back and take a long look, he'll play you like a fiddle. Why don't you go and lie down. I'll stay here with Daisy."

"I guess you're right. A couple of hours in the sack won't do me any harm."

"Right, off you go."

"Yes, sir," Liam said as he turned and walked into his parents' bedroom.

Now alone, Santos opened a packet of cigarettes and put one in his mouth. "There goes another promise down the drain," he thought.

"Now, my friend, I know that was you and you're one sick bastard. And very clever as well. But you're also jumpy. So is Liam. For what it's worth, you've succeeded. They couldn't do it to him back in 'Nam, but you, my friend, have and if I hadn't seen it with my own eyes, I would never have believed it. He has become the child again.

"He must have gone through hell all these years, thinking of you. And then the phone call would have set him back.

"He knows now that night was a big mistake, and I believe it's playing on his mind—especially when you turned up.

"Well, my friend, you know a lot about Liam, but fuck all about me. And if my guess is right, I have you worried. It *was* you tonight. I'd bet my last dollar on it. And as for leaving the cloth, if we'd caught you, I suppose you'd have said you were out for a walk, as you do every night.

"You still want to kill him for the night he saw you. It seems you can't forget either and want to play games. But for how long? Well, my friend, it's time I stepped up a gear and instead of being the hunted, I'll become the hunter. We'll see how you like that."

The next day they went through the yellow pages, found what they were looking for and were told that would be no problem. They put the bowl and the contains in to a jiffy bag and decided not to send it from the local post office.

"People talk. No, it'll have to be the next town."

"Better safe then sorry then," Liam said. "Santos, you know, he's getting to me, don't you?"

"Yes, you can bolt the door and all the windows but you can't keep the fear out—especially when it's been in your head all these years. Then maybe its time you buried the devil," Santos replied.

"I'm going to give it my best shot."

"Now you're talking," Santos said.

"You know, I could die a very happy man if I had that bastard by the throat and watch as his life slowly slipped away."

"You've got to think positive, Liam. If you don't it'll be his hands around your neck."

"Don't worry, I'll come good on the day. I mean, it's not Saigon. And now that we're on that subject, there's something I want to say to you."

"Shoot."

"I want you to promise me something," Liam asked.

"That depends on what it is."

"If I die, or if, God forbid, he kills me—"

"What?"

"Please, let me finish. I want my body cremated and then bury half with my parents. Bring what's left to 'Nam, hire a helicopter and let the rest of me off over the Iron Triangle. That way, I'll have the best of both worlds—my parents here and the boys we left behind over there. It would be an order if we were still in the army."

Santos shook his head and that was the end of the conversation for the next thee weeks. Liam and Santos read up on everything about the place. They even let themselves be seen in the graveyard going over to headstones, writing down names of young women who were buried in there. Now and then some of the locals would stop to watch them. As they did, Liam would walk straight over the Joan Archer's grave, kneel down, and pray. When he was finished, he'd get back up and look out at them thinking, "Maybe he's one of you. If not, he'll soon know, won't he, boys?"

One evening, back in the house after supper, Liam asked Santos how it was possible for a guy like him to keep such a low profile all these years without anyone suspecting anything.

"Before I answer that one, how about some coffee?" Santos asked.

"On the way, Sergeant." As he was making it, the phone rang. Liam turned and looked at Santos, picked up the phone and said, "Yes?"

"No, not yes. But hi to you and your buddy. Well, are you getting anywhere with your enquiries?"

"Why?" Liam asked him.

"I walked out with your mother a couple of times and, believe it or not, I had my mind set to kill her one day, when your stupid, illiterate fuckin' father showed up and that finished that. It's my one regret in life, not killing her, but what can one do except kill another?" Then came the laugh.

"I know you think I'm sick," he said.

"I don't think it, I know it," Liam answered now, trying to keep himself calm.

"What about you and your friend? What did you do over in Vietnam? Me, I played with them before I sent them on their way. One-to-one personal service, you could call it. No enjoyment your way." Then he hung up.

"No goodbye this time," Liam said. "Did you get all that?"

"Most of it. How did he find out about me?" Santos asked.

"A word here and there, but done nicely."

"Now, where's the best place in Ireland to get the latest gossip or news?" Santos asked.

"The pub, of course," Liam answered.

"Right, then that's where we'll start."

Later that evening, they went down to Ryan's pub. When the owner saw them walking in, he walked over and said, "This is a nice surprise. We don't get many tourists in here."

"I'm from here, maybe you've forgotten," Liam answered.

"No, not at all. What are you boys drinking?"

"Whiskey for me," Santos said.

"And you, Liam?"

"The same."

"Coming right up."

When he brought the drinks, Liam asked how much he owed.

"On the house," Tim Ryan said. "That was a great night you gave. Any more coming up?"

"No."

"That's a pity."

When he had gone, Liam said "I think we should frame these drinks."

"Why?

"Because we're just after getting a drink from the meanest man in Ireland. His own father had a heart attack in here one night and, as he was being carried out, our friend there was still pulling pints."

"You're joking."

"Do I look it? If I said to him right now that I was thinking of selling up and moving back Stateside, I bet you anything he'd be back with an offer in five minutes flat. He'd be talking abut the cost of everything, and then how cheap you could buy a piece of land with a house on it around here."

Few came into the pub and, just as they were finishing their last drink, Tim Ryan came over and said "I'm bringing a band down from Dublin for next Saturday night. It'll be a great night and it won't cost you much to get in. You know, a cover charge like you have in America."

"We don't have that over there," Santos said.

"Are you sure?"

"Yes."

"Look at that bastard messing over there." And with that he was gone.

"I don't think he wanted to hear that."

Just then the door opened and in came the vet, Paul Murphy.

"Hello, boys. How are you? And Daisy?"

"Never better, Doc."

"Good. But from now on you can call me Mister Murphy, or Vet Murphy, but not doc. This is Ireland, not the US.

"Now that we're over that, can I buy you both a drink?"

"Why not?"

As he pulled over a stool, Santos thought to himself that Murphy must have been a strong man in his youth. Seeing himself being watched, Murphy said to Liam, "Your friend here doesn't say much."

"Sorry," Santos said. "Do you mind if I ask you a question?"

"Shoot," and he started to laugh.

"You must have been in every house in this town down through the years."

"Yes. And outside of it too."

"What do the other vets think about that?" Liam asked.

"I don't know. I never consulted them. These farmers wanted the best and so they came to me," the vet replied.

"You're a very modest man," Santos said.

"I'm just stating a fact. Ask anyone I dealt with. Good health, gentleman." When he had finished his drink, he said, "I think we have time for another," and, as he waited to be served, he asked Liam whether he was home for good.

"I don't know. A part of me wants to stay and another part wants to sell up and go back to America."

Now Tim Ryan came back down to them and asked "Did I hear someone say they were thinking of selling up?"

"You heard right," Liam said. "I'm going to put it on the internet."

"Why would you do that when you can sell it to a local and not to some foreigner—no offence to your friend here."

"None taken," Santos replied.

"I'd give you a good price. Mind you, I'm not a rich man, but I'm as honest as the day's long—your parents, if they were still alive, would tell you that. So why don't you come back in the morning and we can talk about it? Well, what do you say, Liam?"

"I'm caught for words," said Liam.

"He's speechless," Santos added.

"Well, hopefully, you'll be all right in the morning," Tim replied.

"I hope so."

When he had given them their drinks and gone back to serve other customers, Santos said, "That man has some ears."

"If this place was packed and you whispered that you were selling up, believe me, he'd hear you."

"He must have a sixth sense when it comes to property," Paul Murphy said.

After some drinks, the lights started to go on and off.

"Is there something wrong with the lights?" Santos asked.

"No. He's telling us there'll be no more drinks served. He'll shout it in a couple of minutes. I'm finished, and anyway, I don't want to get on the wrong side of Sergeant Barry." He shook hands with them and left.

"He has a strong pair of hands," Santos said.

"So would you if you'd had your hands up the arse of every animal you can think of for the last forty years. So you think the vet's our man?"

"No, but he's a suspect. He never married, yet he'd have been a prime catch."

"Maybe he's gay," Liam suggested.

"Maybe, but I don't think so. Also, he moved around a lot."

"So did the postman, the coalman, the bread man, and a hundred more I could think of. Are all you FBI the same?" Liam asked.

"Remember when we walked through a paddy field, why did we take our time?"

"Because they were mined," Liam replied.

"Then think like that from now on, if you want to die of old age. Whoever he is, now it's time to go home."

For the next couple of days, they went everywhere—even to a couple of neighbouring counties, but found nothing except a lot of empty houses, or old people living alone, their sons and daughters long gone.

"Why doesn't Tim Ryan buy some of those?" Santos asked.

"Because land can become dangerous."

"What do you mean by that?"

"Suppose there are two boys who live in that old house over there and it was left to the younger one."

"What if there were girls in the family as well?" Santos asked.

"They get nothing. It's as if they were never born, unless she was an only child, then she was lucky. Anyway, some of these houses became family feuds. Some would go as far as murder to get their names on the will. Anything goes with land. Blood means nothing. Nearly everyone left, including me, and I was an only child."

"But how is the house looking so well?" Santos asked.

"I paid one of the neighbours to look after it—not in money, in land. That's why it looks so great," Liam said.

"Well, our killer never left. I'd even say he had a field day with the young women and wives that were left behind. He also had the gift of the gab—charm the pants off them. You know, arrange to meet in some quiet place, and she's thinking he's thinking of her—you know in case some nosy neighbour sees them. But it was all for himself, keeping his exploits private. And, you said it yourself, back then if a woman was caught screwing around, she'd have been thrown out onto the road with nothing but the clothes she wore." He paused.

"I was speaking to three of the boys and they'd love to help you on this case."

"You mean come over here?" Liam asked.

"Sure."

"But what about their own work?"

"Most of us never take our vacations. Maybe that's why we're nearly all divorced. What'll I tell them?"

"Christ, if they all come over, the locals' think they've been invaded," Liam answered.

"No, they'll stay in Dublin and say the usual stuff about coming here to play some golf and look for ancestors," Santos said.

"No hard feelings, but what about the dark-skinned one?"

"Why not? Didn't one of your presidents come from my city of New York, and you can't tell me he was light skinned."

"Point taken," Liam said. "Now what do we do? This is your everyday work—I don't know how you do it."

"After 'Nam, everything's a picnic, believe me. You should have joined as well. Are you OK, Liam?"

"Just thinking about . . ."

"What?"

"Guess. I never wanted to hear bombs drop or men taking their last breath. I still can't believe we got out in one piece."

"Maybe because of what you saw as a boy—laugh all you like but Joan Archer never left you," Santos said.

"Haunted me, you mean."

"You're drifting again, Liam."

"When I think of the boys we left there . . . for fuckin' what?"

"Do you regret coming out of the army?" Santos asked.

"Don't know, to tell you the truth. If it hadn't been 'Nam, it would have been some other banana country. But it's all in the past and who gives a fuck about ex-soldiers?"

"Liam, it's time to come back to the living and catch this man."

"Drink?"

"Why not?"

Now, sitting at Ryan's bar, sipping whiskey. "You know, he could still walk away from this," Santos said.

"How do you make that out?"

"Well, there's his, age. His denial. And, as you said, a lot left and never came back. Never even wrote home. How many times did you tell the boys to do it? But we'll nail him."

"He's too full of bullshit. He believes that he's an artist and maybe now he wants the recognition. He thinks he deserves it."

"If I have my way, it'll be hell for him."

"Better make that phone call," Santos said.

And in the following week three Americans came down to Culdrun, walked around, played golf, and checked out their ancestors. And while they were going around, Liam had gotten no more phone calls, until one night after Tex Harris had given his report to Santos, it rang. They fell silent as Liam picked it up.

"Hello," Liam said. "Who am I speaking to?"

"Who the fuck do you think it is? Got to keep you on your toes, don't I?"

"I haven't heard from you in while," Liam said.

"How could you with your friends all over the fuckin' place? Do you think I'm a fool?" he asked.

"Far from it," Liam replied.

"Good answer. Now, I'm going to give you a clue. Ready?"

"Yes."

"There's a tree in the middle of Seamus Collins' field, do you know where it is?"

"Yes."

"Good. Now, somewhere around it, I buried a body. I forget her name. I don't really, but if I gave you that it would be too easy, wouldn't it?"

"You tell me," Liam answered.

"Got to go." With that the phone went dead.

Santos asked "How many people called Collins live around here, how many fields do they own, and how many trees are in each field? What do you three make of it?"

"Great," Tex said.

"How do you make that out?" Liam asked.

"Simple. We buy a metal detector, and go hunting. If anyone asks us what we're doing, what we're looking for, we tell them swords or anything that's old. All it will take is if she had a tooth filled, a watch, or even a buckle on a belt.

"Don't you think he's thought of that?" Santos asked.

"I guess so, but he did leave a piece of Joan Archer's dress. Just suppose that's all he takes. Remember, he's killing them, not robbing them. I think he's just made a big mistake, for what it's worth," Tex said.

"Time to head back to Dublin and buy one, then," Liam replied.

They all met two days later in the lounge of the old James Hotel having a drink.

"Who'll speak first?" Liam asked.

"Why don't you?" Joe Benedetti said.

"But you're the detectives, not me. Go on, Joe, we're all ears."

"Fair enough. First, the wife said that she'd leave me if I don't go home. She makes out we're screwing everything in skirts walking around Dublin."

"You wish," Santos said.

"He knows about us, which could drive him back to his normal self, if there is such a thing. But how did he find out? None of us said anything." They all agreed.

"I mean, how many Americans come over here every year, even to an out of the way place like Culdrun. Yet he figured us out. I say he's been watching your house the whole time and put two and two together. But does he know we're all FBI? And this is costing you a lot of money, Liam."

"Never mind, as long as it doesn't cost you your jobs. The twin towers and the terrorist threat?"

"Don't worry, they know where we are. You said your nearest neighbour lives a bit away from you, so what does that tell you?" Joe asked.

"That he's coming across the field," Liam answered.

"When the only thing Liam remembers from when he saw him going after Joan Archer is his height, which fits nearly everyone in Culdrun. But you were looking down, so he could have been some bit taller."

"What are you trying to say?" Liam asked him.

"Say if I was looking down on someone from a crane, he would look a lot smaller then he was. You said yourself the cows would go down to the river to get a drink. Now, with all the coming and going, there'd be plenty of mud,"

"You can say that again," Tex said. "I got stuck in it many times. Between the mud and the smell of shit, it would knock a horse out. And as they passed you they'd shit again. Then the flies would come. And the second you were free of the mud, you'd have to take your boots off and try and clean them. Now, you know why I joined the FBI—to keep myself clean and free of shit. Now here I am and you want me to go back into some fields?"

"You got it right, Tex. Better get a pair of boots," Santos said.

"Won't have to do that, he can have mine. Don't worry, I bought them recently, so I use my father's."

"What about the rest of us?" Joe asked.

"I think it'll be me and Tex for the fields," Liam said. "You city boys might get lost and that wouldn't do around Culdrun. Any more questions?"

"No," they replied.

"Then how about some more drinks?"

"Now you're talking," James "Alabama" Noonan said. "Time to chill out and find out everyone's little secrets."

"Very funny," Liam said.

And as the drinks flowed, Santos started to tell them about Vietnam and the pals they had left behind.

"One day a mission plane was shot down and landed right in the middle of an open field. Around it was forest and there, right in the middle waiting for us was Charley. Not a sound, but you knew they were there, the quietness and nothing moved."

"What did you do then?" Tex asked.

"I shot the pilot and blew up the plane," Liam said.

"You're joking."

"No. I had to. If they had captured him and the plane, he'd have told them everything after a couple of days. Too much of a risk. That's war for you. He was a young pilot and started to panic. He let off a flair gun, so everyone knew where we were. Had we gone in we'd have walked into an ambush. There was nothing else I could do."

"So you took him out," Tex said.

"I've already answered that. Remember, I was the commanding officer of the group and there were a lot like us doing the dirty work behind enemy lines."

"But he was one of us," Joe said.

"Yes, and if I was captured by them, Santos or any of my men would have shot me, and if they didn't and I had lived, I would have had them court marshalled for disobeying an order. It's all on the day. There were no rules. We killed them and they killed us. You have to have been there to understand."

"Even your own you killed. I don't believe what you just said. If that's the case, you were as bad as the SS," Tex said.

"That's right. While you were tucked up in your cosy bed, and mama reading you a bedtime story, Santos and the rest of us were making sure that you slept well because we didn't. And when you got up for your breakfast, you had no worries, but we had and we did it all for Uncle Sam. And we killed and yours truly gave the orders. But they were the cards we were dealt. I'd love to have been back in San Francisco wearing flowers in my hair. Instead we were stuck in paddy fields, afraid to look up in case we might lose our heads.

"What did we come back to but insults. And people spitting at us, wearing a 'love' T-shirt. I obeyed and I gave orders, just like the SS, we left a Corporal Shultz back there and his one wish in life was to get back home and meet these people and give them his point of view from a knife. They forgot that a lot of people there wanted us. Look what happened when we left. I had no choice. The pilot had to die."

"Listen, can we forget about Vietnam and concentrate on now and what we're all here for," Alabama Noonan said.

"That's fine by me," Liam said.

They drank in silence, looking at everything but each other.

"That was just the tip of the iceberg," Liam thought. "If I'd told them the whole story, they might have got up and walked away never to come back."

Later, in the toilet, Santos said, "Do you think you did the right thing, bringing up the past?"

"Christ, that's good, coming from you. It was you brought it up, not me."

"I'd keep it shut from now on."

"If I'd told them they were our orders, what answer would they have given? Well?" Liam asked.

"I don't even want to think about it," Santos replied. "Let's get back now that the air's cleared.

When they get back to the bar, Tex handed Liam a drink and said, "I apologise. I can't even imagine what all of you went through but, as you said, you had to do it. And to be honest with you, I don't understand. But then, I wasn't there, so who the fuck am I to speak about it."

"Well I'm glad you said it. Now, no more talk of the past; it's finished. Now it's time to catch him," Santos said.

"One question," Joe said.

"Shoot."

"Is there such a thing as time?"

"What do you mean?" Tex asked.

"Well, we know he killed years ago. Now, just suppose he stopped years ago. Like, if a killer gets off with murder, he can never be charged with that again. Does the same thing apply in Ireland?"

"He was never caught, I've already told you all this," Liam said.

"Sure you did, but when you saw Joan Archer running away from him you were only a boy and a lot of water has gone under the bridge since then. I mean, if we catch him, can he still be charged with murder?"

"I don't know," Liam said.

"Maybe not hers, but there are more," Santos said. "You told me once that they called the fifties the hungry years."

"Yes."

"Well, if that was the case, and our man stayed in Culdrun, he must have had money or a farm.

"It depends on the size of it."

"Suppose it was small?"

"He'd have left the wife to work it and head for England or America," Liam said.

"Leaving the wife alone and lonely. T.V. didn't come in until sixty one, I think you said. We know through our files that most serial killers are creatures of habit, and have the gift of the gab. They'd talk the knickers right off them. He even told you he used to have a talk with your parents. So why would he come around. He would never have tried anything while your father was there. I don't mean he was making a play for your mother," Santos said.

"Good. For a second, I thought that's what you were saying," Liam answered.

"He could have been a travelling salesman, going from house to house, selling anything from a nail to a door," Tex said. "They were all over Texas as well, and they would have known who had left and who stayed."

"But that could apply to the doctor and the vet," Santos replied. "I think he's our man. Those eyes of his are like a hawk's, they take in everything."

"So do ours," Tex said. "Maybe there's something different about him—like the Holmes case in New Jersey. There our friend would come back to see the body being driven away. On the fourth murder, we went back over our video and there he was, praying with the crowd. When we charged him, we asked him why he came back to pray. 'If I don't, who will?' was his answer.

"That case sounds like the one with the preacher you told me about," Liam said.

"That's right. When we went to his house, he had all the newspaper clippings of it and more cases like it. We should be looking for strange things that happened in and around Culdrun."

"That would be my job," Joe Benedetti said. "If there's one thing I'm good at, it's paperwork."

"Great, because the rest of us are useless at it," Santos said. "Now, everyone knows what they have to do. Maybe we should get one of the bombers to drop a daisy cutter and that would save a lot of time and expense."

"Very funny," Liam replied.

"Just joking."

"What's a daisy cutter," Tex asked.

"We'll tell you when you grow up," Liam said.

"Christ, we don't need 'Saturday Night Live' at all, we have comedians right here," Tex replied.

"I don't know about the rest of you, but I'm hitting the hay," Liam said.

"Must be your old age," Joe answered. "How are the old bones?"

"Goodnight," Liam answered, as he got up and walked out of the lounge.

Back in his room and lying on the bed, he thought, "Santos is right. It had to be someone like that. I even thought the same way years ago. But the Catholic in me and respect for those in higher places pushed it to the back of my mind. And so I kept it to myself. Even when bully Hayes used to come after me, I would have to make it to the fields fast. One day, I'd had enough of his bullying and waited for him with my Hurley. I told him to leave me alone or I'd hop this off his head. 'Do it,' he shouted at me, and I did." But it hadn't ended there.

Later, back at home, sitting down and having his tea, there was suddenly screaming and banging at the door. Liam looked out the window and there was bully Hayes with his head in bandages and his father and uncle beside him.

"Get your son out here fast," Pa Hayes was shouting.

"What the fuck did you do?" his father said to him.

"Don't use that kind of language in my house," his mother was shouting back at him. "Get out there and see what they want."

With that his father made a run for the door, nearly pulled it off its hinges, and said, "What's all the roaring about? Do you think I'm deaf?"

"Look what he did to my son. It's lucky he didn't kill him, and with a hurley as well," Pa Hayes shouted at my father.

"Keep the voice down, I'm right along side of you, not out on the road. I've been hearing stories about his bullying, but both of you pricks were the same when you were going to school."

"Who's saying that about my son?" Pa Hayes shouted as he put his face right up against Liam's father's.

"The whole fuckin' place, that's who. Now I'm going to go into my house. Then I'll be coming back out with my gun and if you're still on my property, I'll blow the balls off the two of you."

"I'll get the guards on you," said the father.

"I don't give a fuck who you get. But then, they're friends of yours, I've heard you were spotted coming out of the station at all hours of the night."

"Who told those lies?" Pa Hayes shouted back.

"The whole of Culdrun, that's who. Now fuck off from my door and tell your son to keep away from mine and everything will be fine."

"You're a hard man with that in your hands," Pa Hayes said.

"And so are you. That's why you brought your brother with you," Aiden Coombs replied. Then they walked back out on to the road, stopped in the middle, and said, "You can't do a thing now we're on public ground, so fuck yourself, Aiden Coombs."

"We'll see about that." He lifted the gun and fired over their heads and, like the son, you could hear their screams all over the place.

"My ears. I've gone deaf. You mad bastard," they shouted back at him. As he reloaded his rifle, they started running down the road.

"We'll be back with the guards."

"Good," Aiden shouted after them. "Tell them I'll have the tea ready."

When he finally came back in and started to calm down, he said to me, "Are you happy now? I'll be sent to prison. I could get a month over this."

"No you won't," my mother said. "And you want to do something with that tongue of yours. Get it blessed. That's if Father O'Shea would do it."

"If you don't mind my saying, it's over him that I'm talking like this. What do you mean I won't go to jail?"

"Here's what you do. You go up to the fields and shoot a couple of rabbits. That way, when they come back you can call them a pack of liars. And say the only thing you were shooting at were the rabbits. Now go."

"You're dead right," and he bent down and kissed her.

"Not in front of Liam, if you don't mind."

"You're the boss." And with that, he was gone.

Now up to that time, Liam had thought his father was the head of the house. "I believe he thought so too. Even when the guards had left, he turned to my mother and said, 'I fixed them, didn't I?' I looked at my mother as she walked back into the kitchen, throwing her eyes up in the air, and letting my father ramble on."

Two days later and back at home, the postman pulled up outside the gate and beeped his horn. Liam went out to meet him.

"Got a letter for you," Jim Ryan said, as he handed Liam the letter. "There's a lot of Yanks walking around Culdrun. Are they friends of yours?"

"Why do you ask that?"

"Well, you've been away for so long, you must have made friends with one or two."

"Maybe they're on holidays looking up their roots," Liam replied.

"No offence, Liam, but one is in the wrong country—Africa would be nearer home,' Jim answered.

"Maybe their mothers were Irish. It's been known for a white person to marry a black one," Liam said.

"Maybe, but I doubt it."

"Why?" Liam asked.

"Because I'd have heard about it, that's why," Jim replied.

"Suppose they don't want to talk about it?" Liam asked.

"No, they'd keep quiet about it, but say a relation who was keeping a grudge—and there's plenty of them around here, as you know yourself."

"Now," Liam said, 'what about a woman from around here that just packed up and left?"

"You mean like Madge Foley? She just up and left, yet the day before I was talking to her and not a word about her leaving and going to England."

"They were all doing it years ago," Liam answered.

"Yes, but I'm talking about last year. I suppose nothing changes. They can't wait to get out of here and then some can't wait to get back. Anyway, I'm off. I've a lot of driving to do. See you."

"Good luck, Jim." As he watched the van turn at the crossroad, he thought, "He never stopped. If that's the case, he must have his own graveyard somewhere around Culdrun. And I'd bet this farm that they're buried somewhere near his house. That way, he can look out his window and keep an eye on them. He's nuts."

"Yes, but like all nuts, very clever," Santos answered. "Were there many people with transport when you were growing up?"

"Not many," Liam answered.

"Do the gardai keep records of people who disappeared?"

"Don't know."

"Do you know any of them?"

"No. I mean, I salute them, but that's it."

"Why don't you make it your business to meet whoever is in charge."

"And ask him what?" Liam said.

"Tell him you're writing a book about Culdrun and its history," Santos replied.

"Not bad; not bad at all," Liam answered.

"Well, the sooner you do it, the better, just in case he kills again."

"On my way."

As he drove in to Culdrun, he thought, "How could he still be killing? All right, years ago, I could understand. But now, especially with the troubles, they'd be keeping tabs on the boys and it would be dangerous. Madge Ryan was a young woman, I think, and he's not a young man. Maybe she's in England, alive and well. It's all the one now," as he pulled up outside the station, locked his car and went in. He walked up to the desk, where a guard was writing out what looked to Liam like summonses.

"Can I help you," the young guard asked Liam.

"I'd like to speak to Sergeant Barry."

"He'll be back in a minute. Are you sure I can't help you?" Garda Ryan asked.

"No thanks. I'll wait."

"Are you from around here?" he asked.

"Yes, a couple of miles back up the road."

"Are your cattle gone missing—or the wife?" With that, he started to laugh.

"Why did you say that?" Liam asked.

"Just a joke. You can take one, can't you?" Garda Ryan asked.

"I hope so. But to put your mind at rest, I'm not married."

"So that leaves the cattle," and he burst out laughing again.

"You should be on a stage, not rotting away in a place like this," Liam said.

"Now you're the comedian."

Just then, Danny Barry walked in and came over to Liam.

"What brings you in here? Everything fine out on the farm?"

"Yes, no problems."

"Then what can I do for you?"

"Can I speak to you in private?" Liam asked.

"Of course, but it'll have to be outside."

When they got outside, Danny said, "Take a look at that thing there," pointing to a machine on the wall next to the door. "If anything happens here, the people have to speak into that and wait for us to arrive. The days of the local garda are gone. You're lucky you caught me. We were just about to close shop and go back to the main station—outback's, they call it. You'd wonder where the green tiger is. Anyway, what do you want, because I have a surprise for you too, which I forgot to phone you about. I think I'm going senile. But you first," Danny said.

"The ledgers and the old books that you have inside."

"You mean the ones that are covered in dust?"

"Yes."

"Like the history of Culdrun."

"Yes. Are you reading my mind, or what?" Liam asked.

"No." And with that he started to laugh.

"Did I say something funny? Or is it contagious with you and your colleague?" Liam asked him.

"No, and I apologise. But I know what you're about to say," Danny said.

"Tell me how you know that," Liam asked him.

"Because your friend has beaten you by a week."

"Which friend is that?" Liam asked.

"Now I know about the bet on who'll be the first with the history of Culdrun, so I promised him I wouldn't tell."

Liam froze as Danny Barry said "You'll have to do it the hard way, because I gave the lot to him. Must be some book he's writing."

"Danny, I beg you, please give me his name," Liam said.

"Now, we'll have none of that. All's fair in love and war. He told me you'd do this. Sure can't we have two books out on the place? Tell you what, I'll buy yours as well."

Now Garda Ryan came out and asked Danny whether he should close up.

"You might as well. Nothing ever happens around here. How're your friends—and isn't that cheating?"

"What do you mean by that?" Liam asked him.

"Well, he's doing his own research and I've seen your friends in the fields and the graveyard. Now that's not fair. You see, you went away and he stayed, so if I was a betting man, I'd put my money on him. Although now and then an outsider wins."

"Sergeant, the place is locked up," Garda Ryan said as he walked over to them. "I'll get the squad car and be back in a minute."

"Right. Jesus, I can't wait to read one of these books."

"Why won't you give me his name?" Liam asked him.

"Why should I?" he replied.

"Because strange things have happened around here down through the years and I believe that man you refuse to name is the cause of it all."

He looked at Liam and started to laugh. "By God, win at all costs, that's what America has done to you." The squad car pulled in and stopped beside them, and as he was getting in, he turned to Liam and said, "You tell a good one."

"When you're sixty, maybe," Liam answered.

"Anyway, we're off and when I see him I'll tell him what you tried to do to get his name off me."

As Liam watched the squad car drive away, he thought of the old saying that ignorance is bliss. "Where the fuck do I go from here?"

As he drove home, he tuned in to the local radio station to clear his head, singing along with the songs he knew. Then the news came on. "No bad news today, thank you" he thought. He was reaching down to change stations when the announcer said, "There is still no news on the disappearance of Tessa O'Gorman. What we do know is that she took her dog out for a walk, telling her sister that she would be back in an hour. Her sister then asked her to get a carton of milk, but she never made it to the shop. She was last seen turning down by the gate walk. She is aged thirty eight, five foot four tall, slim, and very dark. She was wearing a denim jacket and jeans, with a red jumper and white sneaker shoes. Anyone with any kind of information, please contact the guards at Dunagh; the number is 096 781 4556.

"And now for the death notices."

Liam pulled in to a side road and screamed out, "Danny Barry said nothing ever happens around here. What fuckin' way do they think? Unless, they're putting that down to suicide like some of the others." He turned off the radio and stopped outside an entrance to a long-deserted private road, got out of the car, and started to walk up and down.

"What in God's name is going on here? This guy killing right and left for years and he's pals with the sergeant. What next?"

Just then, a hand touched him on the shoulder. Liam let out a scream as he turned and looked into the face of Paul Murphy.

"Are you all right? Is there something bothering you?" he asked.

"No, just deep in thought. Where did you spring from?" Liam asked him.

"Nowhere, I was just out for a walk when I saw you pull in. Can't beat it. Clears the head. You should try it," he answered.

"Maybe I will."

"How are your guests getting along?" he asked Liam.

"What do you mean?" Liam asked him.

"We do get the occasional American looking at the castle, and some looking for their family tree, but now we're being invaded by them" he said.

"Well, that's progress for you. No use looking back. It's time to look ahead," Liam answered.

"True. But we do have to keep something from our past. But you've been away for so long, maybe it doesn't matter any more," he said.

"Everything that happens to my country matters. And also what happens to America. I love both."

"Do you? I find that strange. No, then again, you served in its army."

"Who told you that?" Liam asked.

"Your father. And your mother as well. And last but not least the man who delivered your letters.

"Got to keep moving; these roads can get very dangerous. A lot of young people are driving now. I remember a time when few had cars," he said.

"But you have to leave yourself out. When I was a child, you had a car," Liam said. "As you said yourself, the chosen few."

As Liam kept looking at him, he knew he was trying to hold in his temper. Then he said, "That's true, but then I needed it. I had to go out to calls anywhere in the country, day or night. Do you remember that too?" he asked Liam.

"Yes, I do."

"Good. Now, time to continue with my walk. By the way, give my regards to your house guest, Señor Torres, am I right?"

"No, you're not. It's not Señor, it's Mister Torres."

"Whatever, but he is Mexican."

"Wrong again. It's not your day, Vet."

"I told you I don't like being called that. You didn't learn much while you were away," he said.

"Oh, but I did. It gave me time to think."

"On what?"

"On people who went missing and still are. But you wouldn't know about that. Been too busy driving around helping people. You're good at that, aren't you?" Liam asked.

"Of course." He took one last look at Liam, and as he turned to walk away, he started to sing a song.

"He's one arrogant bastard," Liam thought. When he got back into his car, he looked into his front mirror and there was no sign of him. Then both of the side mirrors. Again nothing. Liam got back out of the car and climbed up onto the ditch, and there he was, on the opposite side of the field, closing the main gate. Parked along side it was his car. "I thought he said he walked."

When he got home, he told Santos. "You know, he believes he can't be caught."

"He must carry some weight around here. How much land does he own?" Santos asked.

"Your guess is as good as mine. I know all the land around his house, front and back, is his. And the back goes right down to the river," Liam said.

"Just suppose he fancied the farmer's wife and poisoned the cattle. That would leave the husband broke so that he would have to go to England, leaving the wife to look after the place. Now say she was from Dublin or any city, not knowing too much about farming and being lonely, who should start knocking on her door only the one and only friendly vet. And before long he's sleeping with her. Then he starts slowly to dominate her."

"In what way?" asked Liam.

"Maybe get her to pose for some pictures, that kind of thing."

"Christ, Santos, you're way off the mark. There's no woman in Culdrun would have done that sort of thing," Liam said.

"How do you know? The only one you knew was Joan Archer and you were looking at it from a child's point of view. Try the adult way. Think of that evening. It was her that was screaming, not him. And if someone had been passing, he was out for a walk when she started on him. Her nerves were bad all her life, everyone knew that. Why do you think the doctor put it down to suicide right away? As for your father, the same thing. Talk about land and livestock. But at the same time, watching your mother. No offence, but some were mothers too."

"True. But what about the priest? Their husbands? Brothers? Even cousins? Surely someone must have gone to the guards," Liam asked.

"Yes. And we have to find them. But don't mention the vet, just in case someone phones him and tells him we were talking about him. I think it's time to find the graveyard."

The next morning, bright and early, Paul Murphy opened his bedroom window and looked out at the morning dew rising from the field and began to breathe the fresh air. Suddenly, his eyes caught something moving in the field. He moved back from the window and tried to make out who it could be. He needed his glasses but they were downstairs. He rushed over to the wardrobe, opened it, put his hand in and reached to the top drawer, taking out a pair of binoculars. They had been given to him by the local hunt that he had allowed to cross his lands. He had no choice; they had given him a lot of business. Since then, they had been very useful. He could watch things from a safe distance. Now they call it stalking. What name will they give it next?

"Mind you, one surprised me. I had thought butter wouldn't melt in her mouth, until one night I crept up and saw what she was doing to her boyfriend. When I asked her to do the same to me, she laughed and told me to fuck off you sick bastard or I'll call the guards. Yes, you laughed and I waited. Not a week or a month, but two years. I even had your grave dug and ready for you. Then your neighbour told me and the whole of Culdrun that you were seeing farmer Downey behind your husband's back. 'Isn't she a slut, Mr. Murphy,' they said. 'Who am I to judge anyone,' I answered. 'You're too good of a man, that's what you are. But you can take it from me, if he finds out, he'll kill her.' 'God forbid.'

"I got back into my car and let out a roar of delight. Straight away, I put my plan into action. And with the help of these binoculars, I watched every move she made, right down to the nights she met him. And when everything was in place, one night she met me instead of him. Christ, did she plead for her life. I even had to gag her, just in case someone was out doing a bit of poaching and heard her screams. As I buried her, she was saying with her eyes that she would do anything I wanted. 'But you forget,' I said, 'or maybe it has slipped your mind,' as she now moved her head. 'Then please let me remind you. What was it again? Oh yes. You told me to fuck off.' And with that I put the shovel into the wettest and hardest of the mud and dropped it right over her face. Good memories."

He now walked back over to the window, put the binoculars to his eyes, and looked out. "So, I'm being invaded by the Yanks. Does that surprise me? No." He watched them go down into the brush. "Careful. Don't want you to disturb my babies. That's if they're in there. Now, time for breakfast. I have a lot to do today. Then call the guards and tell them there are trespassers on my land. 'And, as you know, there are old Druid stones in there. Do you think they're trying to steal them? Please come over fast. I'll be waiting.'"

"Well what do you think of this place?" Liam asked Santos.

"It's made for it," he answered as he looked down into it.

"Looks too dense to me; there are too many trees. And the ground is too hard for a man of his age," Liam said. "The ones he's killed in the last twenty years won't be here. They're somewhere else."

"I'm not saying that there are bodies here, but a look won't kill us."

"No," Liam replied.

"How many mass graves did we come across in 'Nam? Well?" Santos asked.

"A couple."

"And how did we find out about them?"

"People in the village told us," Liam replied.

"That's right. But if we weren't told, we'd have walked right over them. The same applies here, only no one's going to tell us, because no one knows."

"Santos, over here," Tex shouted. Both turned and walked over to where he was standing. "Take a look down there. See anything?"

They both looked and said "No."

"Look again," Tex said.

"At what?" Liam asked.

"The ground, it's starting to cave in."

"Some parts of it have been dug and not put back right," Tex answered.

"How do you make that out?' Santos asked.

"Look there." He pointed down. "Why isn't it caving in anywhere else?"

Suddenly, from behind, a voice said, "Gentlemen, do you know that you're on private property and are trespassing?

"What are you doing out here? Are you looking for something?" Paul Murphy asked.

"No. But what makes you think that?" Santos now asked him.

"Oh, I don't know. Call it a hunch."

He lifted up a shotgun and aimed it at them.

"Back in your country, I could shoot you for this. Also you have ruined my breakfast."

"We're sorry to hear that. But surely you don't mind us poking around," Tex said.

"Oh, but I do. There are old stones there and how do I know you're not trying to steal them?"

"Take our word for it," Tex replied.

"No. I tried to be nice to you. And, by the way, the one who is sneaking up on me, if he doesn't stop, I'll blow his fuckin' head off. My hearing is still good, and he wasn't in the army with you". He turned and faced Joe Benedetti. "No. He's too young and eager. The young always are. But if you move again, one more inch, you'll never see your pension."

He cocked the gun and aimed it at them.

"Hold it," Liam said. "There's no need for that."

"Oh, but I beg to differ. You have come on to my land looking for something. Now what could it be?" He turned and pointed the gun at Liam. "Answer me."

"All right, I'll tell you. Years ago, I lost my grandfather's watch somewhere in here and that's what we're looking for."

"At this time of the morning?" Paul Murphy said, as he started to laugh. "You can tell a good one."

"It's the truth," Liam answered him.

"I wish I could believe you. Now all of you, come out into the open where I can see you better. And no funny stuff." He continued to laugh. "This gun could go off accidentally and that wouldn't do—blood all over my fields, what would the cows think? Apart from my breakfast, I'm enjoying this. It's getting the blood flowing again."

"Why, was it stopped?" Santos asked him. "When was the last time it flowed?"

"You're not a vampire, by any chance, are you?" Tex asked, trying to draw him away from Santos.

"No. As for the last time it flowed, it was some years ago now." He put the gun up to Santos' face. "The rest of you, back off. Now, listen to me, you Mexican scumbag. You come into my country and walk all over my land, for what I don't know. I tried to be nice to you and this is the way you thank me."

"Oh, but you do know and I don't like what you just called me."

"You mean about being a Mexican piece of shit?"

"Yes, I'm an American with Mexican blood and proud of it."

"Of course you are. Just like that other piece of shit along side you. He's Irish American, or is it the other way around? Right now, I can't remember. But this is for all of you. Fuck off back to your own country—and that includes you, Liam Coombs—and leave us to get on with our boring lives."

"Beg to differ," Tex said. "I wouldn't say yours was boring, I'd say it was quite the opposite."

"Why, what do you know about me?" he shouted at Tex. "Answer me or I'll blow your fuckin' head off."

"And you'll be up for murder," Tex replied.

"At my age, who gives a fuck. Maybe I do a year or two and then again maybe I'll get off with it. You forget, you're on my land and land around here can cause a lot of trouble. Ask Liam. And with your name, you must come from Texas, right? Answer."

"Yes."

"Now see can I remember your history. A long time ago, wasn't that part of Mexico? And didn't a certain General, I think his name was Santa Anna, try to throw the lot of you out?"

"Yes, but a lot of the locals wanted us to stay," Tex replied.

"How do you know that?"

"I read it."

"Well, you can't believe everything you read."

"When it concerns my country, I do."

"Bullshit."

Sergeant Barry's voice could now be heard coming from the back of the vet's yard.

"What's going on out there?"

"Gentlemen, the posse has arrived. Trespassers," he called to the guard.

"I'm coming right over. And if that gun is loaded, take the bullets out of it right now. There'll be none of that shit in Culdrun."

"Fair enough," Paul Murphy replied.

"Don't ever put a gun in my face again or insult my ancestors. And it's you who's a piece of shit," Santos shouted at him.

"Why, does it bother you?" he shouted back.

"It'll bother you more the next time. I'll ram it up your arse. Understand?" Santos replied.

With that Paul Murphy started to laugh.

"Keep it up, but make sure your dentures don't fall out." Santos now started to laugh.

When Sergeant Barry saw Liam, he asked "What are you doing out here at this time of the morning?"

"I'll tell you. I believe we are standing in a graveyard."

"Of course we are. Who do you think put the stones there in

the first place?" Sergeant Barry answered.

"Who are you talking about?" Liam asked.

"The Druids, of course. Who are *you* talking about?"

"The women who have gone missing down through the years here in Culdrun and the surrounding counties. How old are you?" Liam asked Paul Murphy.

"What kind of a question is that to ask?" Sergeant Barry said.

"I don't mind answering. I'm seventy next birthday."

"Then you should check out the last fifty straight away, Sergeant."

"Give me a break will you, Liam. I know all this bullshit about your book, but just because the vet was one step ahead of you, that doesn't give you a reason to harass him. I thought you were better than that." Then he turned to the vet and said, "When you're finished with the record book, will you please give it to him and stop all this bullshit. You're worse than a pair of children."

"Certainly, but there will be some places crossed off."

"Fuck it, Vet, I only gave you a loan of it. That's public property. Well, I'll have to take it back. If the Superintendent hears about this, I'll be demoted."

"I was just joking," the vet answered.

"I don't care. I should never have given it to you in the first place. And, as for the rest of you, I don't want to get another call saying you're on his land again. Not unless he invites you. Now, as you lot go out the way you came in, the vet and I will go back to his house and he'll give the book back to me and I'll put it in its rightful place.

"Just look what's after happening here, two old neighbours falling out over whose book will come out first. Anyway, the past is dead. It's today both of you should be writing about. Now shake hands and we'll forget about this. Come on, we're not leaving until you do."

Liam walked up to where the vet was standing and put his hand out. And if looks could kill they were now coming from the vet.

"Come on, Vet, you're a bit long in the tooth for all this shit," the Sergeant said. The vet grabbed Liam's hand and started to squeeze hard. Now back in 'Nam, between patrols, to kill time they used to play arm wrestling and Liam had been ready for the vet's grip. Now, as he squeezed his hand back, he asked him "How does it feel to be getting it instead of giving it?"

Next thing, the vet started shouting. "My fingers, he's trying to break them," as he tried to pull his hand away.

"That's enough, Liam. Let go of his hand," the Sergeant said. And after one final squeeze, he let go. "That was for Joan Archer and all of the others. Do you hear me, you piece of shit?" he shouted at the vet.

"Arrest him, Sergeant," the vet said.

"For what?"

"Intimidation and trespassing."

"Why do you want to do that?" the Sergeant asked him.

"All right, then. Get them off my property now or I'll report you to your superiors. I have friends in high places. Just remember that, Sergeant."

"Are you threatening me, Vet?"

"No. Just letting you know you're not far off the pension, and you're in a nice quiet place. I'd say a move at your time of life would be upsetting. And of course for your lovely wife as well. Especially her garden. I don't think she'd like leaving that."

"You know, Murphy, I thought I knew you, but now I see another side of you that I don't like."

"Is that right, Sergeant? Well, I don't give a fuck what you like or don't like. Just do your job and get them off my property."

Turning to the others, he said, "Gentlemen, if you don't mind, you have to get out of this fuckin' field before the vet gets a heart attack."

'Not vet, *Mister* Murphy," he screamed.

"Whatever," the Sergeant answered. "But maybe I'll come back and see what's down there that you're so touchy about. Now it's time to hand me back the book. Your house, please."

And as they walked back, the vet turned to see whether Liam and his friends were leaving as well.

"Let's go. We found the place," Liam said.

"Wrong. I'd say we found one of them," Santos replied. "He must own a lot of land around here. How could we go about finding just how much he owns?"

"The Land Commission or the County Council. But I don't think they'll tell you," Liam answered.

"So what do we do, then?" Tex asked.

"We do it the old-fashioned way. We knock door-to-door. Not where we see the new houses, but the old ones that are falling down. I'd say it's from them he bought the land before they took the boat."

The next morning, bright and early, Sergeant Barry came knocking at Liam's front door. When he opened it and saw who was there, he thought, "So, he's bringing charges against me."

To the Sergeant, he said, "Come in and have a cup of coffee. No use standing out there in the cold." As they walked back in, Daisy started to growl at the Sergeant.

"Take no notice of her, she's just showing off," Liam said. "Sit down and I'll get you the coffee."

When he had given it to the Sergeant, he said, "Penny for them. You're miles away."

"He's bringing no charges against you. Pity. Just a while ago I went back to the field to check it out and, you're not going to believe this, I was stopped by security guards and no way would they let me in. They said I'd have to ask Vet Murphy for his permission. *Me*, a policeman. I'm still in shock. At first I thought it was a joke, but no, they told me they had been hired to keep watch on the old stones and when their shift is finished, two more will take over from them. So I asked them if they'd be sleeping at the vet's house, no, they answered. All they're allowed to use is the kitchen and the outside toilet. The rest of the rooms are locked. He also told them to keep an eye out for you and, of course, your friends.

"Now, I'm thinking, what the fuck is in the field if he's paying good money to keep you out of it. I know those stones have been there donkeys years and no one's ever touched them. Next you appear and there are security guards working around the clock and they're as bewildered as me. When they came down they thought it was a building site they were going to and when he showed them the field, they thought he was mad."

"He is," Liam replied.

"So anyway, they phoned their boss and he told them that's it. And he's paid up for the next six months. What do you make of all this?"

"My guess is, he knows I don't have much money unless I sell this place."

"What do you mean by that—talk straight for fuck's sake, will you," the Sergeant said.

"All right, here goes. Of the people that are here with me, one is ex-army and the rest are FBI on leave. All are married or have ex-wives to support and, as you can guess, that costs money."

"Just what are you looking for? I know now it's not the book."

"No, there never was a book. They're here to try and bring a serial killer to justice and maybe he's Ireland's first."

"And who is he?" the Sergeant asked.

"Our mutual friend Murphy."

"For Christ's sake man—have you taken leave of your senses?" the Sergeant asked as he got up from his chair.

"I wish I had, Sergeant, but you have the proof."

"And how have I that?"

"The book you took back yesterday—it's written in it."

"Liam, he's an old man."

"I know that—but he wasn't fifty years ago when he started off. And, like all good serial killers, he learned as he went along and opened his own graveyard. Santos believes that as he got older he opened another one somewhere in the county, but the question is, where?"

"You're serious? You believe all this shit?"

"Sergeant, I've seen it with my own eyes." He then told him about Joan Archer. When he had finished, the Sergeant said, "But she's buried in Culdrun cemetery and not in that field. I was told by one of the boys that buried her that they had to tell the priest that she'd died from a stroke and not suicide. If he had found out she'd have been buried in the small plot at the back of it and not with her own."

"And what if my dog hadn't barked?" Liam asked. "Some weeks ago I got a call saying that he could have poisoned her. Now, for her to let a stranger near, and to eat what he gave her . . . No, Sergeant, it was him; I'd stake my life on it."

"What about all the guards that have come and gone since then?" he asked Liam.

"Different times. But there were always killers who made it their time and I believe we have the king one right here in dear old Culdrun."

"May I ask who you are speaking about?" said a voice coming from right behind them. The Sergeant got such a fright he dropped the coffee on to the floor. Its contents came splashing back onto his shoes and pants. He let out a scream. Liam jumped up and, standing right behind him was vet Murphy.

"I hope you don't mind my coming in like this, but the door was open."

"Now that you're in, what do you want?" Liam asked.

"I just came over to tell you that from now on security will be watching that field, so no more trespassing. Got that? Or do you want a letter from my solicitor as well?"

"Go fuck yourself," Liam shouted at him.

"No, you fuck yourself. Now goodbye and have a nice day. Oh, by the way, Sergeant, that goes for you as well." And with that he turned and walked back out the door.

"Now do you understand me, Sergeant? When you set foot in the house Daisy growled at you. Yet when he walked in— nothing not a sound."

"Where's the toilet?" the Sergeant asked.

"Down the hall, second door on the right. I can give you a loan of a pair of my pants, although they might be a bit tight on you."

"Very funny," the sergeant said as he walked down to dry himself off.

Liam turned to Daisy and said, "What kind of a guard dog are you? When I tell you to sit, what do you do? You shit all over the place. Well, there'll be no more of it—it's outside for you from now on."

When Sergeant Barry came back, he said, "I'm sorry about your floor."

"Don't worry about it, that stupid dog baptised it a month ago."

"Jesus, with what you were telling me and him coming in like that, I nearly baptised it as well."

"Don't worry, he'll do nothing to you," Liam said.

"How do you make that out?" the Sergeant asked.

"You'd put up too much of a fight."

"For fuck's sake, I'd put him away with my hands tied behind my back and down on my knees as well with my eyes closed." He started laughing.

"But how did he come in without making a noise?" Liam asked.

"Maybe we were talking too loud," the Sergeant said.

"No. Years of practice, that's how," Liam answered.

"Listen, while I was drying myself, a name came into my head."

"Whose?" asked Liam.

"Tom Kelly, that's who. He was stationed here years ago. He lives in Cork now and maybe it would be worth your while to go and have a talk with him. I have his address back at the station."

"Have you his phone number? It would save a lot of time," Liam asked.

"No. But I don't think he'd talk over the phone to a stranger."

"What age is he?" Liam asked.

"About seventy five. And if anyone knows anything, it'd be him. The next time I'm passing, I'll bring the book with me and you and your friends can have a good look at it."

"That would be great," Liam said.

"I'll phone you when I have it done," he replied.

"Fair enough."

The next day, Liam's phone rang. When he picked it up, it was Sergeant Barry. "Good news," he said. "I told Tom Kelly what you told me and believe it or not, he's mad to meet you. And the sooner the better."

"That's just great. When?" Liam asked.

"That's up to yourselves. I also had to ask his permission to give you his phone number. So get pen and paper ready and I'll give it to you."

"One second."

When he had the phone number written down, the Sergeant said, "I have the book in the boot of the squad car and when I have the time, I'll drop it out.

"Someone stole some of John Stokes' cattle and left the gate open in the other field. The cattle from that field are walking and shitting all over the place, so be careful driving, just in case they're on the road as well.

"I'd say it was some of the little bastards from the town that opened the gate—too much time on their hands. These school holidays are too long. They should all be fucked into the army like they do in America."

"But why would they steal cattle? And has any of them a truck big enough?"

"No. All they have is cars ready for the scrap heap."

"Maybe none were stolen," Liam said.

"Well, he says that they were and, him being the owner, I have to take his word for it. So I have to wait and see. Have to hang up, Liam. Guess who's about to walk in the door?"

And as he was slowly putting the phone down, he heard the voice of Vet Murphy asking, "Any news on the whereabouts of my friend's cattle?"

When it went dead, Liam wondered why he would be so interested in Mr. Stokes' cattle. Maybe, with him being the vet, Stokes had asked him to drop in find out what was going on. But if that was the case, all he had to do was phone up.

The next day Liam and Santos were knocking on a door on the outskirts of Cork. A woman of about forty opened it and said, "You must be Liam Coombs and Santos Torres?" She put her hand out. "My name is Nora . Please come in." They were shown in to the front room.

"My father's in the back garden. I'll go and get him."

When she was gone, they started to look at the pictures hanging on the walls.

"This man believes in framing his past. And I thought we Yanks had that corner of the market sown up," Santos said. They were all there from his boyhood to his passing out and down to his retirement.

"Well, do you see anything that would be of any interest to you? Don't mind me, I'm Tom Kelly. I hope you're both hungry; my daughter is making sandwiches with my own vegetables. A habit I picked up in Culdrun. How is everyone up there?"

"Well."

"Not everyone?"

"You know why we're here?" asked Santos.

"I know. My daughter told me. How are you?" He put out his hand.

"Very fine, Sir." Santos replied.

"No 'sir' in here; Tom will do fine. Now, which one of you speaks first?"

So Liam told him about Joan Archer and what had happened since.

"And now lets hear from Santos and what he makes of all this," Tom Kelly said.

"Here goes. I'd bet my last dollar he's our man. He has all the hallmarks—the vanity, the arrogance, letting you know he knows what you're thinking."

"Go on," Tom said.

"What baffles me is how he's gotten away with it for so long."

"Finished?"

"Yes."

"Well, it's like this. You'd find it hard to believe the power held by the Church, doctors, and politicians years ago. Yet, way above all of them was the man who could save their livestock. Remember, this was and still is farming country. He was like a God. And, believe me, he thought he was one too."

"You knew him?"

"Yes I did, Liam. You don't remember me, do you?"

"No."

"But I remember you as a child. And I also knew some of the women who went missing. I'll tell you a short story. Poaching was big business back then—salmon, I'm talking about. The hotels and guesthouses couldn't get enough of them and, when the season started, the locals would get out their nets and down they'd go to their own patch."

"Tom, if you don't mind me saying, what's that got to do with Vet Murphy?" Liam asked.

"Please let me finish. One night we caught a poacher. Now, he knew the least he would get would be six months, so he said, 'You'd be surprised who my buyers are. Now, just suppose I let it slip, where would that leave me?' 'When you're finished I'll let you know,' I answered. 'There's a certain gentleman who likes to give a party now and then for the horse jumping people,' he said.

"Now, one night he caught a big one, and the following night he walked to this man's house—not by the road, but through the fields, which he knew like the back of his hand. After going some distance, he had to sit down and rest. Now, the great thing about poachers is their hearing—well, most of the time. It was in the middle of the field that he sat down for a rest and to look around, just to make sure he wasn't being followed. He had left the fish down on the grass and opened the bag for a last look. 'You're a big and heavy one, aren't you?' he said, when suddenly he heard someone breathing right behind him. Then his cap was knocked off his head and a voice said into his ear, 'Will Purcell, what are you doing in my field at this time of night?'

"He told me he jumped up off the ground with the fright he got. But when he turned and saw who it was he said, 'Jesus Christ, where did you come out of? It was you I was going to see.' 'Could you not wait until the morning,' he asked. 'Are you mad or what?' Will shouted at him. 'No, I don't think so,' he replied, as he came around and looked down at the fish. He put his hand in his pocket and took out a five-pound note, old money, and handed it to Will. 'I don't have any change,' Will said. 'Keep it, but don't tell anyone, understand?' 'Of course,' Will replied. That was good money back then. And with that he lifted the bag, threw it over his shoulder, and disappeared into the night."

"Let me guess who that man was,' Liam said. "Vet Murphy."

'I don't think it was that hard, was it?" Tom asked.

"No."

"Come over and take a look at this photo, will you please?" When they went over, he asked them whether they recognised anyone in it. Tom was being presented with a decanter set, and right behind him was Vet Murphy.

"What was that for?" Santos asked Tom.

"For taking a child out of the river. His mother also disappeared."

"And what became of him?" Liam asked.

"Off to an orphanage. After that, I don't know. What I'm trying to say is, when Will Purcell got back home, he took out the money, just to make sure it *was* five pounds he'd given him. And as he looked at it, there was fresh blood on it. And when he was getting undressed, there was blood on his jacket where Murphy had put his hand. He worked out that the vet was poaching as well, but had to buy his fish to keep up appearances. About a year later, I went back to the night of the rescue and it was the same night that the child's mother went missing. Now, take a look at this photo, you see the child looking up at him? And if that's not fright on his face, I don't know what is."

"Do you think he saw something, Tom?" Santo asked.

"The night she went missing, no. But the other nights that he called, yes. I remember reading somewhere that people like him start off by watching or taking underwear off the line—back in those days, everything was hung out to dry, so if anything went missing she'd have known. And maybe she knew it was him. A woman on her own with a four-year-old child, living in a house where the nearest neighbour was a mile away, no street lights, no phones, no nothing. Just thinking about it would frighten you."

"Did you do anything about it?" Liam asked.

"Not much. He was a drinking friend of my boss, so I kept my mouth shut."

"You know, if this happened back in America, they'd call it a cover up and heads would have rolled," Santos said.

"Well, I can assure you, it wasn't. But now and then, when the husband left, the first thing that the wife would do was bolt the door, put the children into care, and head for the bright lights. Most ended up walking the streets, some met another man and started all over again. That was Ireland for you. Saints and scholars all over the place, so we were told, and we swallowed it, hook, line, and sinker."

"How many were stationed there in your time?" Santos asked.

"Four," he replied.

"And not one of you thought something was going on around there? Back home, I could understand him getting away with this for a long time, but not here—as you say yourself, a place where everyone knew each other. And yet he's still killing to this day."

"Impossible," Tom answered.

"Why's that?" Liam asked him.

"Well, for one thing, we're a modern force now."

"You mean, where once there were four men, now you have to speak into a recorder set into the wall to make an appointment?" Liam asked.

"All right I'll give you that, but you're forgetting one thing."

"What's that?" asked Santos.

"His age. He'd be no match for a young woman," he replied.

"I beg to differ. If you saw photos of some serial killers, and then saw photos of the people they had killed, you'd think it was a mistake. But killing is a drug to them, and most don't care who they kill—men, women, children, even babies. It's all the one to them, as long as they kill—and, of course, not being caught."

Tom Kelly walked back over to the chair and sat down. Then he said, "We've never had serial killers like that here."

"I don't believe that for one second. This guy is an expert and he wasn't the first here in Ireland. They're in every country. Russia had one going from station to station, picking up strays, taking them into a forest, cutting their hearts out and eating them. When he was finished he'd get back on the train and go home to his family," Santos said.

"Well, there was none of that in Culdrun," Tom replied, as he got back up off the chair.

"But there was and still is," Santos said. "And it's going on within a radius of two hundred miles and, as a vet, he would know every land or boreen. Have I got that right?"

"Carry on," Tom said

"And, as you said, he'd be welcome in every house."

"But you forget one thing," Tom said. "Most were married or had children."

"That was better for him. They had to keep quiet. But I think some called his bluff, and those, he killed. I'd say there are some women still living in Culdrun who know the truth."

"Out of the question. We'd have heard of it," Tom said.

"Maybe. But I do know that no matter what country they come from, women love to talk. One could have told a neighbour before she disappeared."

"Let's just say you're right. But what about the other guards in the other counties, are you saying that they were as stupid as us?" Tom asked Santos.

"Cool down. I'm not calling anyone stupid," Santos replied.

"Maybe we weren't up to your FBI, but we did our best, believe me." Then the door opened and Mary came in with a pot of coffee and a tray of sandwiches.

"Everything all right in here?" she asked as she looked at her father.

"Fine," he answered.

"I hope you're all hungry."

"Believe me, we are. And your timing was perfect," Liam said.

She walked over to the photos. "Well, come on, eat up. You too, Dad."

As Tom started to pour out the coffee, Mary said, "He used to give me the creeps, the way he'd sneak up on you."

"Who are you talking about, Mary?" her father asked.

"The vet, Murphy, that's who I'm talking about." The second she mentioned his name, her father's hand started to shake as he put the pot of coffee back down on the table.

"Why did he frighten you?" Santos asked her.

"Well, sometimes, when Dad was working nights, he used to call around. And always the right time. Years later, I thought back on something that happened one night. I was in the kitchen as Dad was going out the door and I heard something scratching at the window. I looked up, and there he was smiling down at me. I let out a scream and Mama gave me a slap in the face. I remember you asking her what I had done wrong. Then Mama started to scream at you 'Go out and do your job and I'll do mine here'. And out you went, Dad. Later, I saw her opening the door and in he came with his sick smile."

"Is he still alive?" she asked Liam.

"Yes"

"I suppose only the good die young and creeps like him live forever. Anyway, that's enough of that," as she walked back out the door.

Then Santos said to Tom, "You can throw me out if you like, but did you know about this?"

"No. I loved her more than anything."

"And you had no idea he was coming to your house?"

"No. That's as God's my witness. And Nora never said anything. In a country place, neighbours would come and go nearly every night. Do you find that strange?" Tom asked Santos.

"Yes."

"Why?"

"Because what I'm saying is that he thinks he's above everyone else and still does. So what was he like all those years ago?"

"Guess you're right," Tom replied. "One winter's night, I was cycling into the station when I thought I saw someone standing in the middle of the road. When I got to the spot—nothing. Then I looked around one last time, just to make sure, got back on the bike and started to cycle away when I heard a stick break. I don't mind saying it now, but it put the hair on my head standing—or what was left of it," he smiled.

"What did you do then?" Liam asked.

"Kept going. But someone was there. The stick was broken, not by walking on it, but by their hands."

Then Santos said, "Tom, are you lying?"

"What do you mean" he asked.

"You knew, or guessed, she was seeing someone."

Now Tom started to cry. "Yes."

"But you didn't know who with?"

"No," he replied. "Do you know what that can do to you in a place like Culdrun?"

"No. But I can guess.

"Where's your wife now, Tom?" Santos asked him.

"I don't know, and that's the truth. She left as well."

Santos turned and looked at Liam. Then Tom said, "Are you saying he killed her as well?"

"We don't know. Has she ever tried to contact you or Mary down through the years?"

"No. Not even a line or a phone call. Can I come back with you?"

"For what?" Liam asked him.

"To catch him. What kind of a question is that?" Tom asked Liam.

"Listen to me, please. This very moment, he has security watching one of his fields, and if you suddenly appeared, you could jeopardise our work. Sure, we're slow, but he's worried now and starting to show his true colours."

"I could say I only came back for one last look around," Tom said.

"What do you mean by that?" Santos asked.

"I'm dying. I got the news last week. At the most, there's six months left in me. Cancer."

"But what about your treatment?" Liam asked.

"I'm taking all kinds of pills right now and they're doing the job. And as for the chemotherapy, what will that do? Maybe give me another month. Anyway, I don't want Mary to see me as a skeleton."

"You haven't told her?" Santos asked.

"No. I don't want her upset. What security firm did he employ?"

"Why?' Liam asked.

"Because some of them were started by former colleagues of mine."

"No. He's their client and they could phone him up and tell him you were asking questions about him."

Then Tom took a picture from a drawer. "Look. That's when we first moved to Culdrun," he said as he passed the picture to Liam. He looked at it and then passed it to Santos.

"You know, Tom, I think I remember you now, cycling by our house. Who took the photo?" Liam asked.

"I'll give you one guess," Tom replied.

"Christ," Santos said. "He was one fast worker. No offence, Tom."

"Even after what she did to me, I still loved her. There's no fool like an old one."

"But, Tom, you were a young man when all of this started."

"Maybe coming from Dublin to Culdrun drove her up the wall. She hated the place."

"Then why did you stay there?" Liam asked him.

"At that time, wives stayed with their husbands. Well, most. And my job had a good pension."

"But why did you live outside the village when you could have stayed in the house next to the station?" Liam asked him.

"I was very jealous of her. I used to watch my colleagues around her and I didn't like it."

"You thought it was one of them," Santos said.

"Yes."

"And you did nothing when he or someone broke the stick. Why didn't you turn and go back?" Santos asked.

"I've already answered that. And this was Ireland, not New York."

"It still boils down to the same thing," Santos replied.

"Gentlemen, I'm getting a bit tired and, if you don't mind, I think it's time to call it a day." He stood back up. "And when we meet again, I hope I'll have some answers for you."

"Fair enough," Liam said.

"And not a word to Mary." With that he opened the door and shouted down the hall to Mary, "Come here and say goodbye. They're going away."

"Coming."

When they got back in the car, Liam asked Santos, "What do you think of him getting on board?"

"Could be good, but I doubt it."

. . .

Tex had been watching the field every day since the run-in with Vet Murphy. The security men took their break at the same time, but not to the house, to their van. When they needed to go to the toilet, it was behind some bushes. He must have told them to stay in the field, even if they had to take a crap. Tough job. And, as Tex watched them walk down by the river, he thought, it's time I did the same. He then took one last look, and there was the vet, standing by the van, keeping an eye on them.

"He wants his pound of flesh," Tex thought. Then he turned and looked straight up at Tex, pointing in his direction. "It's impossible. His eyesight couldn't be that good at his age. I'll have to be more careful from now on. It was raining yesterday morning, maybe I left some footprints in the mud." Then the vet lifted his hand, put his finger to his throat and moved it slowly across it. "Try it, you bastard," Tex wanted to shout out. Just then someone tapped him on the shoulder. "Christ," Tex said, "You're after frightening the crap out of me," turning, thinking it was one of the boys. Suddenly he felt something moving slowly across his throat. For a second he wondered what it was, but when he put his hand up, he felt his hot blood gushing down his coat. Now, looking at his murderer, he thought, "It can't be."

Then he tried to shout out, but no sound came. Nothing. He reached out and tried to grab him by the pants, but he stepped back and said, "Please, no blood on my boots. I'm rather fond of them. Been with me through thick and thin. Now, what am I going to do with you? But I don't want you worrying about anything. I'm going to give you a decent burial. I'm afraid you won't have many visitors, as you can guess. All my corpses love a nice quiet spot and I've just the right one for you. Now to finish this business. I'm getting a bit cold."

He then bent down and picked up a cane, twisting the head off it, and taking out a sword. Tex tried to crawl away, putting his bloody hands on the mud stones and the root of a nearby tree. Anything to leave a clue. Then his head was pulled back and the murderer sliced through what was left of his neck.

As blood started to gush out, he said, "I'll have to get someone to plough the field first thing in the morning." He now got hold of Tex by the legs and hid him under some bushes. "I'll have to get rid of him fast. He was what you call a foot soldier and we know who's giving the orders. But I'll deal with him in due course." Then he bent down and took hold of the end of Tex's coat and started to clean his sword and knife.

"Now for your head. Don't want one part of you here and the other part over there. What would one of the security men say if he found you? He might get a heart attack," and he started to laugh.

. . .

Back home, Liam was sitting down, then getting up, walking over to the window, pulling back the curtains, and looking up and down the road.

"Are you trying to put my nerves at me?" Santos asked.

"Tex should be back by now," Liam replied.

"Don't worry about him. He's well able to look after himself."

"Has he his mobile with him?" Liam asked.

"Are you crazy? He goes nowhere without it and that includes bed."

"Give him a ring, will you," Liam said. "Maybe he's on to something."

"But if I do that and the security man hears it, then it's goodbye to our surveillance. Let's give him another hour, then it'll be getting dark and he'll be wasting his time out there."

So they sat and waited. As the hour slowly dragged by, they heard no footsteps, and no sound of the gate opening. Nothing.

"Call him, Alabama," Liam said.

Alabama, who had his mobile already in his hand, hit Tex's number and waited.

"It's ringing, but he's not answering."

"Try again," Liam said.

"The same."

"Get your coats on. It's time we paid a visit to the security men."

When they got there, the boys were in the van, watching the highlights of a soccer match. Liam knocked at the driver's window. The driver looked up and asked, "What do you want?"

Liam replied, "We're looking for a friend of ours."

"Well, he's not in here. You're not hiding anyone, are you Paul?" he asked his colleague.

"Not that I remember, but I'll take a look just in case." He turned his head and laughed. "No. Nothing. And you lot are trespassing." He let down the window. "Are you trying to get us sacked from our handy job?" he asked Liam.

"Have you two been here all day?" Liam asked him.

"Why?"

"I've already answered that."

They both now got out of the van. The one who had been sitting in the driver's seat said to Liam, "We were brought in here to keep you and your friends out of this field and here you are. What is it with you and the stones over there?" he asked.

"Is that what you were told by the vet?"

"Yes, and he's paying our wages, so we listen very carefully to him."

"Our friend who is missing is a diabetic and he forgot his medicine. We're afraid he could go into a coma or worse."

"I'm sorry to hear that. And I know how you feel, my own brother is one as well and he does the same. But we've seen no one."

"What about the other boys?" Liam asked.

"No. The only thing that happened today was that the vet sneaked up on them and started screaming like a raving lunatic."

"What did they do wrong?" Santos asked.

"Only that he caught them sitting in the van again. He sacked them and said he was bringing in a new security firm. Then they said that it was raining. 'I can see that,' he replied, 'but if I can be out in it, so can you, especially as I'm paying your wages.' So, one word led to another and he reported them and now they've gone to the union. So this could be our last night here."

"Do you mind if we take a look?" Santos asked him.

"Are you mad? If he sees the lights, he'll be on the phone straight away to our boss and he's not too happy now."

"Tony, if your brother was out there, would you have asked?" the other security man said.

"Fair enough, but I'll have to go with you, just in case."

"Whenever you're ready."

"Right, boys," Liam said. "Keep an eye out for anything."

"I thought it was your friend you were looking for?" Tony asked Liam.

"It is, but mud and grass can say a lot."

Then Tony turned to Santos and asked whether he was an Indian.

"Afraid not. Why do you ask that?"

"Well, in all the cowboy films I've seen, the Indian would find anything, even a needle in a haystack. Although, if he saw this fuckin' place, he'd be on the first plane back to the reservation." He started to laugh.

"Spread out," Liam said. "And if you don't mind we talk only when we have to."

They moved slowly across the ground. Joe Benedetti would bend down now and then and rub his hand against the grass. Then Liam would ask, "Anything?"

"No."

"We'll move to the stones. I'd say that's where Tex set up his camp."

"Tell me," Santos asked Tony. "When you're finished your shift, where do you meet the other boys?"

"Back there. The first day we started, I drove into his yard. Next thing, he came running out of the house and told us never drive into the yard again, as the neighbours would see the van with our sign on it. Then he told us to go where we are now. But I think he wants us there so he can keep an eye on us— you know value for money and all that shit."

"Is he always shouting at you?" Santos asked him.

"That's the strange thing."

"What do you mean?" Santos said.

"When he came over to us in the yard, his teeth were black, his hair grey, the collar of his shirt filthy, and he could have done with a wash. Later, he came back and apologised, but now his teeth were pure white, his clothes perfect, the hair black, and not a bit of dirt on him. Later, when I told it to Tom, he said he'd just cleaned himself up. Me, I think I was speaking to a brother or a twin."

Now all the men had stopped and were looking at the security man. He put his hands up in the air and asked whether the vet was related to one of them.

"No," Liam replied. "But how do you make out you were speaking to another person?"

"Where I was brought up, the next-door neighbours were twins and if you met them, now and then you'd think you were talking to the same person. They even had the teachers in the school fooled."

"Then how did you know which one was which?" Santos asked.

"Simple—the way they laughed. And one had a very bad temper. The other was quiet. And I'd bet my wages there are two of them living in that house."

"What do your colleagues think?" Joe asked.

"They think I've lost the plot."

"How do you mean?" Santos asked him.

"Gone round the twist like Chubby Checker. Forget it."

They now came to the wooded part of the field.

"Where would be the best vantage point?" Santos asked.

"Here," Alabama replied. "He could see everything from here."

"Are you saying that you were spying on us as well?" Tony asked them.

"Yes," Liam answered. "But not over these stones. I have two in mine as well. As do other farms."

"Then why has he security watching his?"

"That's what we're trying to find out."

Then Alabama said, "Over here." When they got over to him he said, "Look down there. There are some stones missing."

"Oh fuck. There goes my job," Tony said.

"And bark has been cut from this tree. Something was dragged and then dumped down here. Then whoever it was walked back that way. Not towards the vet's house, but yours, Liam."

"Could it have been Tex?" Liam asked.

"Maybe. Let's get back to the house. There's no more we can do here."

When they got back and checked it out, everything seemed to be in order.

"Someone was here," Santos said. "He came through the back door. No mud or anything, so he left his boots or shoes outside. No fear in Daisy, but he was here. You've a great watchdog in her, Liam."

"What do we do now?" Joe asked.

"Christ, if we were back in 'Nam, we'd report it straight away. But, here, who'd believe us? I mean, Tex was—I mean, *is* a big man, aged, what, thirty five? And the vet is seventy. If we told Sergeant Barry what we think, we'd be laughed out of Culdrun."

"Tex is dead," Santos said. "And we're looking in the wrong place. Sure, they're going through the motions. And I believe they're hoping we'll get a search warrant and dig up a part of the field to find nothing. Then we'd be told to stop harassing the vet or we'd be in trouble.

"I'd say they used it but not in a long time. Look at the growth of the trees and everything else around there."

"But even if you're right, there'd have to be bones still down there. We have to bring in the cops," Joe said.

"Give me a minute, please," Liam said. Then his mobile started to ring and, when he saw whose number came up he said, "It's Tex. You gave us one hell of a fright."

"Is that right? Well, I hope it's one of many. I just found it by the side of the road and your number happened to be on it. Do you believe me?" the voice said.

"No, you sick bastard," Liam screamed back. "Listen to me and listen good. And try to stay calm."

"I'm not deaf," the voice said. "Your friend has gone back to his wife and family. That's if he has one. But, of course, he has her number on his phone as well. Is the rest of that shit listening to me as well?"

"You'll pay for this," Santos screamed.

"I don't think so."

Liam put his finger up to his mouth, telling Santos to cool down.

"Has the cat got his tongue, or did you stop him from interrupting our little conversation?"

"Go to hell, you sick bastard," Santos again shouted.

"Not yet. Not before you and your tin soldiers are gone back home. Coming over here, trying to catch me. How many do you think tried that or even guessed it?" he asked.

Liam wanted to scream back that they knew he was a twin and

that that was how he'd gotten away with it all these years. He held off, waiting till the right time came.

"Got to go. Hope you find your friend. Who knows what tomorrow will bring," he said.

"I'll get you if it's the last thing I do," Liam shouted.

"You know, it just might be," he replied. And with that the mobile went dead.

"What did you make of that?" Alabama asked.

"He scared the shit out of me."

"Where was he phoning from?" Joe asked.

"Where do you think?" Liam shouted back at him.

"The sooner I'm out of this place the better. And I thought New York was bad. You can keep the country; it's the city for me from now on," Joe replied.

Santos said, "We could go straight down to the house, kick in the door, and start looking. But I think we'd be wasting our time."

"I think you're right. This field is only a smoke screen," Liam replied.

At the same time, in another field some miles away, Tex's head and body were about to be buried.

"I'm just after having a chat with your friends. I'm afraid they don't have a clue where you are, but I do, don't I?" He covered the head first. "Never liked people staring up at me. Not even ones with no body."

When he was nearly finished, he took the mobile out of his pocket and said, "I nearly forgot about this," and threw it into the grave, saying, "You might need it more than me. You know, just in case you get lost or lose your way from wherever you are. But for now, you're right here and here you stay," and he started to laugh out loud.

Mick Maloney had drunk a fair bit; he'd been at it since tea time and he was well over the limit. He had left his car back at the pub and started to walk back home, taking all the shortcuts. When he first heard it, he thought it was his imagination. Then he thought it was an owl, coming from an old barn building on the opposite side of the field. Then he heard it again. "That's a human; I'll swear on it. Wonder who's in there at this time of night?"

As he looked across, he saw a light move around inside it. Could be a couple of young lads from the village acting the bollocks, or taking drugs. He followed the light with his eyes, now moving, now stopping, now being put down. Then the sound of the doors creaking and then being locked. Then the torch being picked up again, as it moved around, checking the building. Then it was switched off and he heard someone walking over to the old boreen.

When he got home, he found his wife, Nora, in the kitchen. She turned to him and said, "I didn't hear the sound of the car driving in. Please don't tell me you've crashed it or that the guards stopped you?"

"What makes you say that? I left it safe and well back in the village."

"You mean you left it outside Regan's pub," she said.

"Yes, like all good citizens of Ireland," he answered.

"How do you know what they do? I suppose they all phone you up. Do you know you have to be in work at eight o'clock tomorrow morning? How are you going to get there now?" she asked.

"Don't worry about it, I'll be there."

"You could have been killed, walking that road at this time of night, with all those young fellows flying around the place in their new fast cars. If one had hit you, do you think he would have stopped? If you'd wanted a drink that bad, I could have driven you in tomorrow night when I was going to bingo. But, no, you had to do it tonight. Well, your dinner is in the oven and you can heat it up yourself."

She turned and looked at him. ""What's bothering you now," she asked him.

"There was someone over in the old barn," he said.

"How do you know?" she asked.

"Because I took the short way home and I saw a light shining inside and outside it. And I heard someone laughing," he said.

"Maybe it was a courting couple?" she asked.

"No. There was only one," he said.

"Are you saying that someone was on his own in an old barn that should have been knocked down years ago and was laughing to himself at this time of night?"

"Yes. I think it was a local hiding drugs and could have sampled some of it himself. You know, a halfway house. That's what they're doing all over the country, so why should Culdrun be any different? Will I phone the Sergeant up and tell him? Answer me, woman. I'm waiting. Now, what's wrong with you, Nora?"

"Christ, you won't believe me, but years ago, in my parents' old house, I could see the barn clearly from my bedroom window and I'd stare out at it every night, hoping to see a ghost or the banshee. I never saw one, but I did see lights, just like you did tonight."

"Nora, that was years ago, and whoever owned the place was working late. There was no drugs back then."

"Then let me finish, will you please."

"Who am I to stop you?" he answered.

"The next morning, I told my father. He told the owner and that was it—no more lights.

"But six months later a house went up for sale. My father wanted it and he put in a bid but it wasn't enough. That same night a knock came to our door and who was standing there only the owner of the house. He and my father went into the kitchen and, when they came out, there was a smile on my father's face. When the owner left, my father turned to us and said, 'We'll move in the morning or next week'. The deal was, swap ours for his. My father tried to give him some money as well, but he wouldn't hear of it.

"The very day we moved, the bulldozer came and knocked down our old house. I thought it was the land he wanted, but my father said the land we got with the new house was better. But both were happy with the deal and that was that. And he's still a gentleman to this very day. Do you think I should call him first?"

"Who?" Mick Maloney asked.

"The vet Murphy. It's him who owns the land."

. . .

Liam was tossing and turning in his bed, thinking of what he was going to tell Tex's wife and his parents. "I should be well used to this, having done it so many times before. But you never do. Maybe he's still out there alive. Who am I kidding? He's dead."

Then he thought back on a village near the iron triangle. They were told it was a Vietcong stronghold and to check it out. As they slowly moved through the paddy fields, mortars started to explode all around them. Next thing, parts of bodies were flying past.

And then, as fast as it started, it stopped. When they finally got in to the village, they had the people rounded up and asked them where the Vietcong had gone; they all shook their heads. Next a sniper shot one of Liam's men and they ducked for any cover they could find. Some of the villagers ran for the river. In the confusion, they shot some of them

Some minutes later, another shot rang out, but this time, he missed. They hadn't a clue where he was shooting from. Then they heard the sound of leaves being pushed gently in the grass just ahead of them. Santos, who was the nearest, let fly with a grenade. Nothing. Another shot, but now this time from behind them. But now one of the boys had seen his head disappear back into the ground.

"They're under the fuckin' ground," he shouted out.

With that all hell broke loose.

"I've heard about this shit," Marvin from Harlem screamed out.

"What did you hear?" Liam shouted back.

"That they're right underneath us, and we're sitting' fuckin' ducks. There have to be tunnels all over this fuckin' place."

"Start digging the ground with your bayonets. We have to find the entrances, and fast," Liam ordered all of the men. "But be careful. It could be booby trapped."

As they got closer, Indian Joe shouted out "Cover me," and slowly moved to where the head had disappeared, with his flamethrower burning up everything in his path.

"One of you get up here fast. I've found it. And bring some grenades. I'll give those bastards something to remember us by."

Liam ordered them to stay where they were, just in case they tried to make their escape through the paddi fields. And, sure enough, out came teenagers—boys and girls—from the village first.

"What do we do now?" Santos asked. "They're going to use them as a shield. What do we do?"

"Try and pick them off," Liam replied.

"What if we can't?" Santos asked.

"Then kill the whole fuckin' lot," Mick Finn answered.

With that they let loose. They turned and tried to make it to the paddy field with its cover.

When it was all over, nothing moved, not even the livestock. Liam never bothered to count how many they killed that day. Their loss was four killed and seven wounded. When the chopper came, they burned the village. Some wouldn't come out of their shacks, so they burned them down around them. All on Liam's orders. That's what war does to you. You become a killing machine, as Joe Shultz used to say. There's a killer in each of us, waiting to get out and it's all on the day.

Liam thought, "If my parents could have seen it—the boy who stayed up nights when a calf was about to be born, who cried when one got hurt—they'd turn in their graves. But that was war and that was the way we had to fight. No mercy. No nothing.

"Try to explain to people stateside that this had to be done.

They'd look at you as if you were a madman. Then, maybe I was. But if they'd seen what the Vietcong did to our boys when they captured them, they'd have sung a different song.

"You can smile now, Vet Murphy, you and your sick brother, but you'll pay. Just like they did."

. . .

Mick Maloney got up fine and early the next morning, making sure he didn't wake Nora up. The head was bad enough without listening to her as well. When he came into the kitchen, his sandwiches were already made and left on the table. Fair play to her. With that, he opened and closed the door gently.

Now, making his way down the road he was deciding whether to go in and check the barn or not—just to see whether someone was hiding drugs or acting the bollocks. Suppose they found out it was me reported it, they'd burn me out. No. I'll do as Nora said. I'll keep my mouth shut.

As he got nearer to the village, a car pulled up and offered him a lift. When he opened the passenger door and got in, Santos said, "Nice morning for a walk."

"Your Liam Coombs' American friend, am I right?"

"Yes."

"Well, you're a Godsend. I had to leave my car in the village last night."

"Break down?" Santos asked.

"No. Too many drinks. I had to walk home. When are you going back to America? The whole village is wondering," Mick asked.

"Don't know really," Santos replied. "I hear all of you can't wait to see the back of us."

"And you're great walkers, too. There's not a field you haven't walked on, so I hear," Mick said. "And no one wants to see the back of you except Vet Murphy. I hear he's hired security to keep you off his land."

With that, Santos started laughing and asked, "Why would he do that? We're only tourists, out enjoying a walk and minding our own business, taking in the country, you could say.

"Well, here we are. Which one is your car? It seems more than you left their cars here last night."

"That one up there."

As they passed the garda station, Mick was wondering what he should do.

"Something bothering you?" Santos asked.

"Tell me," Mick asked, "were you or any of your friends out walking last night?"

"Not that I know, of. Why?"

Mick told him the whole story. When he had finished, he looked at Santos and asked whether he was all right.

"Yes. I'm fine."

"If you don't mind me saying, you don't look that good to me. Now, what I told you is between you and me, right, Yank?"

"Right, Irish."

As they shook hands, Mick said, "We have to have a drink before you go back."

"Fair enough," Santos replied.

As he watched Mick get into his car and drive away, he started to cry. After a couple of minutes, he took out his mobile and phoned Liam.

"I think I know where Tex is. A neighbour of yours stumbled on it last night. We've found his graveyard."

"Are you sure" Liam asked.

"I have that feeling. The one that puts the hair on your neck standing."

"What else are you thinking?" Liam asked.

"I tell you," Santos shouted down the phone. "I'm thinking of going out to their house and killing those two sick bastards."

"Listen to me. Cool down. It was a million to one you picking him up and him telling you. Santos, we're going to do this our way. They won't walk, I promise you. A couple of hours won't make a difference. I've waited forty years. I beg you, Santos, don't fuck it up."

"OK. I'm coming back."

"We'll be here waiting."

As he put his mobile back in his pocket, there was a tap on the window. He looked up and standing outside was the young Guard O'Brien and Vet Murphy.

"Please lower the window,' the guard said. When he had done so, he looked straight up at the vet.

"Is there anything wrong? We were watching you from the station window and you looked very upset."

"Oh God. Don't let me blow it," Santos thought as his hands tightened around the steering wheel. Then he said, "Not that it's any of your damn business, but my wife is about to divorce me."

"Listen, don't worry about it," Garda O'Brien said. "There's plenty more fish in the sea. You just caught the wrong one. Am I right, Vet Murphy?"

"You're on the ball. I couldn't have said it better. And of course there's plenty of young and not so young women here and in the surrounding counties."

"Then how come you never married," Santos asked the vet. "I'd say you'd make a fine catch."

With that, Garda O'Brien started to laugh.

"Maybe normal sex was no turn on for you, was it Vet?"

If looks could kill! He threw them now at Garda O'Brien.

"Sorry, just joking."

Then he bent down and whispered in the window, "The hunt is best. Then it's all over for the ladies. And now and then a man who gets to nosy . . . get my drift, Yank? And don't try to get out of the car. I have one of the best witnesses right here alongside of me. Am I right, Garda O'Brien?"

"What's that? I didn't hear what you just said."

"I said breakfast is on me."

"That's very nice of you. What about yourself?" Garda O'Brien asked Santos.

"No. I'm afraid I'd be bad company right now."

"I suppose you would. But keep the chin up. She might change her mind. I hope you keep the house. My father always said, make sure you keep a roof over your head. Then maybe she will."

"Who?"

"Your dear departed wife. Just joking." He turned and walked away to join the vet. Then the vet turned, lifted his hand, and put his finger up.

"And up yours too," Santos said as the two walked into Ryan's restaurant.

When he got back to the house, they were all standing around a map that had pins stuck in parts of it.

"Are you OK," Liam asked him.

"I'm fine."

"The coffee's just been made. Go in and get some."

"I don't need it. I just want to know what the plans are."

"Right. Here goes. First, he doesn't know what you've been told. And the man who told you will tell others, so it has to be tonight, just in case one of them walks into Regan's pub and says what he's been told. Everyone knows who owns what around here. Any questions?" Liam asked.

"I have." Alabama said. "How could two nuts walk around here with a free hand all these years? I can't understand it. It's as if everyone closed their doors and said that as long as it didn't happen to them, well and good."

"Well, tonight is payback night," Santos said.

Then the phone rang. Santos picked it up and a female voice

asked could she please speak to Liam.

"It's for you, he said as he handed the phone to Liam.

"Hello, this is Liam speaking. Who is this?"

"Mary Kelly, Superintendent Kelly's daughter."

"How are you?" Liam asked.

"My father died last night."

"I'm sorry to hear that," Liam said.

"Thank you. But I phoned up because I was wondering about the conversation you and your friend had with my father."

"May I ask why?" Liam said.

"The second that you left the house, he went straight up to the attic and brought down everything he had about Culdrun and started to write down names of people who had gone missing down through the years. But what I can't understand is that he put my mother's name right at the top. Now he told me that she just walked out on us. Why? It even got so bad, he stopped taking his medicine. This morning I was cleaning out the fire, just to stop my brain from driving me mad, when I found all of his tablets and a note saying that all his files were to be given to you.

"God forbid, but I think he committed suicide." She started to cry. "He was all I had. What did you say to him?" she asked.

"I told him what he had guessed for years."

"What was that," Mary asked.

"I can't answer that right now. But tomorrow you'll have the whole truth. I promise you that. I'll phone you myself."

"But why can't you tell me now?" she asked.

"If I told you, I don't think you'd believe me.

"Fair enough. But I'll have relations staying with me and I don't have a mobile, so when you phone ask for me. I'll be waiting."

"I'll see you at the funeral, if that's all right with you," Liam said.

"He'd have wanted you to be there," she replied. "I'll put the files away, just in case one of the relatives gets nosy."

"But you read them, didn't you, Mary?"

"Yes."

"What did you make of them?"

"I don't know. To tell you the truth, I find it all strange, to say the least," she said.

"Why?"

"When you read them you'll understand. I don't think my father ever got over my mother and maybe it did something to his mind," she said.

"No, there was nothing wrong with his mind, believe me. It's all fact, not fiction, and it happened right here in Culdrun."

"Was my mother one of his victims?"

"Yes," Liam answered.

"I don't know what to think or to say. It's all too weird to understand," Mary said.

"Well, I'll have the proof for you first thing in the morning. And, hopefully, you'll be able to bury your mother as well as your father."

"That would be nice. Goodbye, then. I'll see you at the funeral. And be careful," she said to Liam.

When he had put the phone back down, he said to Santos, "Tom Kelly is dead."

"I'm sorry to hear that. But didn't he say he had a couple of months left?"

"I think he finished it himself. He left us his files. When I go to the funeral, I'll collect them. And don't say he must have known as well."

"Fair enough," said Santos.

"Now. Back to business. It's tonight we need to concentrate on now. Have a look at the map and tell me what way you'd go about it. Any of you feel free to speak. The more the merrier. But the thing is, we have to nail both of them, not one. Now is payback time. There are some shovels in the back; we have torches. Is there anything else we might need?" Liam asked.

"No, that covers everything. Is the barn out of the way?" Joe asked.

"Yes. If it's the one I'm thinking of it is. You could drive past it and never know it was there. Only for Santos giving Mick Maloney a lift, we'd still be in the dark. If we park by the side of the road, we'll be spotted straight away. The neighbours would all know that's the vet's land, and they all have his phone number. So our best bet is the boreen."

"And what would that be?" Joe asked.

"A side or little road. While you two dig, we'll have to be watching your backs, just in case Mick Maloney did phone him. Or maybe he still thinks it's the other field we're interested in. Let's hope so."

"When we find the bodies—and I think we will—what do we do then?" Alabama asked Liam.

"We phone the guards. Why?" Liam asked him in reply.

"Because we could do to them what they've been doing all these years. Make them disappear. The cops would be looking for one, not two, and after a while, they'd be history—just like the people they murdered."

"Fair enough. But are we forgetting Tex?" Liam asked.

"No one's forgetting him. He's right in front of us and so are those two sick bastards. I'm a law officer, but I'd gladly take them out," Santos said.

"Don't you think that's crossed my mind as well?" Liam replied. Just then a robin flew in through the open window and landed on top of the book case.

"My, you're a cheeky one, and a robin too. Someone must have forgotten to tell you that Christmas is still some time away. Now, out you go the way you came in." said Joe.

"Leave him," Liam said. "He'll go back out when he's good and ready. Just don't stand in his way."

"What do you mean by that?" asked Joe.

"He's telling me I'm a dead man and now that you've told me, I thank you."

With that, the bird flew around the room and then back out the way he had come in.

"That's one cheeky little fellow. The next time—that's if he comes back—I'll have a biscuit for him."

"He won't be back, he's delivered his message," Liam answered.

"Which is?" Santos asked.

"What I've already told you. Do you want me to spell it out for you?"

"I thought you were joking," Alabama said.

"Do I look like I am?"

"For fuck's sake, Liam, are you losing your marbles or what? Hundreds of birds fly in to people's homes every day and are they all going to die too? Maybe all this is getting on top of you. Why don't you look on the bright side—this will all be over tomorrow and you'll become famous—the ex-lieutenant who came back home to solve a forty-year-old mystery and instead caught two serial killers in dear old Ireland, the land of saints and scholars. And twin killers, who just happen to have their own graveyard. God forbid—what's next?" Santos asked.

"All right, I get the message. But just in case, I want you to sell this place and give my share to Tex's widow," Liam said.

"Are you forgetting something? What about your own ex-wives and your children?"

"They're well looked after and I already have it written down. Now you're the main man and this place will make good money."

"Liam, you've got to think positive and not talk bullshit."

He got up and walked over to the top drawer, took out the will, and walked back over to Santos. "Just take it and shut fuckin' up. I'm getting a pain in my head from all this. Just promise me you'll do it. I'm waiting."

"I promise. And the other thing as well."

"Thanks. That's after taking a load off my mind. Now, we wait."

Time dragged by slowly. No one spoke. Either they were looking out the window or getting some sleep.

"Gentlemen," Alabama said, "I think we're being watched. Now, no sudden movements. Just say something, one of you."

"Where?" Joe asked.

"Behind the tree that's just inside the field. Now I could be wrong, but I don't think so."

"But it's dark out there," Joe said.

"All right, it's a cow, if that makes you happy," Alabama replied.

"There's nothing in that field and we all need to cool down. But I'm going to get up and walk into the kitchen and then out the back door. Give me a couple of minutes and then follow me. Make sure you're armed and you're the last one, Alabama. When we're all gone, keep talking to yourself. It's you he'll be watching. Again, give us a couple of minutes and then follow us," Liam said.

"Watch your back," Santos said.

"I'll be fine." He got up and walked into the kitchen. Then the click of the back door.

"I'll go next," said Santos. "Count to twenty and follow us."

"Right," they replied.

"Will I turn off the light, Alabama?" asked Joe.

"Leave the fuckin' thing on. What do you want to do that for?"

"Maybe he'll think we're having an early night," Joe said.

"Grant me patience, Jesus."

He now went out the back door.

Liam climbed over the back wall carefully. He knew now what ex-soldiers meant when the said it was better than sex. "I knew all along, but I never admitted it. Although the ex-wives would love to remind me. I tried to explain it to both of them as honestly as I could and their thanks was that they both took me to the cleaners.

"Now, which way to go in without making any noise? There are two ways in, both by gates. The nearest one is ready to collapse, so it'll have to be the other."

Now Santos was beside him.

"Remember when you asked whether the blood was starting to flow and I said no? Well, I lied," Liam said.

"I knew that. But did you ever think what we could have been if there'd been no 'Nam?" Santos asked.

"A shower of boring, middle-aged pricks." They both started to laugh gently.

"It'll have to be the other gate. Ready?"

As they moved slowly back up the road, passing the house, Liam looked in. There was Alabama, talking to himself.

"If my guess is right, he knows we're on to him," he whispered to Santos. "Make for the gate."

As they moved towards it, they heard a whimpering behind them. Both turned and pointed their guns; there, looking up and wagging her tail, was Daisy.

"That's a good girl. Now go back home," Liam whispered at her. Then she heard Alabama coming up behind them. First she started to growl, then to bark.

"That fucks it. Let's go," Liam said. With that they both cleared the gate at the same time. The second they hit the ground, they went separate ways with Daisy following Liam and barking all the way. When they reached the tree—nothing.

"Fuck it, he's gone," Santos said. "Look down here," and he shone the light on the ground.

"What?" said Liam.

"Can't you smell? Someone has just put out a cigarette. He has to still be here."

The Daisy started to bark and ran straight into the darkness.

"Come on, let's follow her."

"But where is she?" Alabama asked.

"This way," Liam answered, as they heard her snapping at someone. Then they heard a shriek and then something being thrown onto the ground. When they found her and shone the light down on her, blood was coming from her throat.

"The bastard has cut her throat." Then Liam shouted into the darkness, "I'll get you."

Then a stone landed about a metre from them. Then another.

"So you want to play games as well. I'm ready and I'm coming for you."

"Calm down, Liam. You're letting him get to you," Alabama said.

"I don't give a fuck." And he moved in the direction he thought the stone had come from.

Liam knew the field like the back of his hand and made for the dry part.

"Santos is right," he thought. "We can't bring back the dead, but we can help those two in joining them."

"Where are you?" Liam shouted out.

Then a voice whispered from behind him, "I've dreamed of this day—do forgive me, I mean night," as he stuck the knife into Liam's back. "Who's the piece of shit? Please tell me before I slit your throat as well. Just like I wanted to do it to your dear, departed mother. But if I couldn't have the mother, then the son will do. Mind you, I'm getting a bit old for all this."

He grabbed Liam by his hair and pulled back his head. As he did so, Liam turned, lifted his gun, and drove it into the other man's mouth, breaking his rotten teeth and saying, "Smile," as he pulled the trigger. His head jerked back with the impact, blood shooting out of his mouth. Letting go of Liam's hair, he put the hand holding the knife up to his mouth and then dropped it as the other hand caught it, still moving backwards. Then he stopped and started walking back towards Liam.

"No way, Jose," Liam shouted, as he emptied the gun into him. As he dropped to his knees, he still tried to knife Liam again, cutting his hand. Then he let out a gurgling sound and collapsed. Dead.

Liam got back up slowly, the pain now shooting through his body. He stood in front of the body and gave it a hard kick. "Just to be sure," he said to himself.

Then the rest came running up and looked down at the body. "What kept you?" he asked them.

"This damned fog. Which one is he and do you think anyone heard the shots?" asked Santos.

"I don't know and I don't care."

"It's not the vet. What do we do now?" asked Joe.

"We keep to the plan and head straight for the barn."

"What about him?" Santos asked.

"Fuck him. He's going nowhere. Hopefully, the foxes will shit on him. Give me a hand, will you?" Lam asked.

"You're not that old that you can't help yourself," Santos answered.

"Please." And as Santos put his arm around him, he felt the blood.

"He came up behind me."

Joe came over with the knife covered in blood.

"He was one silent bastard," Liam said.

"Fuck it, why didn't you shout out?" Santos said.

"For what? I got him didn't I?"

"Yes, and he got you too. We have to get you to a hospital fast."

"I'm going nowhere, only to the barn. When we're finished, then I'll gladly go to the hospital."

"OK. If that's what you want. Now let's get out of here, just in case someone does show up."

When they got to the barn, Liam said, "Turn on all your lights, it doesn't matter now. Who has the clippers?"

"Me," Alabama answered.

"Then cut the lock."

"Yes, Sir."

As they pushed in the door, the hinges made a wailing sound. Liam turned and said to Santos, "What do you smell?"

"Death," he answered.

"Remember the camp we went into in '68? The one by the river?"

"Will I ever forget it? We could see no bodies, yet the smell of death was everywhere."

Then Joe said, "Not to interrupt you, but come over here."

When they got there, Joe, who was standing beside a chest of drawers, said, "Take a look in there."

Santos put his hand down and pulled open the top drawer. Inside it were women's clothes, going back years. Santos now took out a pair of suspenders.

"Good old New York. They bring back many happy memories. They're old, yet they don't look or feel it."

"My guess is they'd take them home and wash them but couldn't hang them out. So he'd have a dryer or maybe both were into wearing them. When we get him, we'll ask him. There must be more in here. Don't say it."

"What?" Santos asked.

"How did they get away with it? But when this shit hits the fan, there'll be reporters swarming all over the place. I have to sit down. I'll be over there by the window."

"Are you OK?" Santos asked him.

"To tell you the truth, I think my legs are starting to go from under me."

"Here, Joe. Give me a hand."

"Coming."

As they walked him over, he asked, "How many do you think are under us?"

"Who knows?" Joe replied.

Now, sitting on the window ledge and watching them, he thought there had to be someone else in it with them. It's too weird to have been able to go on for so long.

Now, Alabama's mobile rang. "It's just a text from the wife.

"She's not leaving you, is she?" Joe asked.

"Why?"

"Well, she must be one frustrated woman by now. That's if

she's as good as you say she is."

"Very funny. Now look what you're after making me do. I'm after hitting Tex's number by mistake. Will you leave me alone? I'm bad enough without you and your stupid comments."

As Alabama was about to turn off his mobile, another started to ring from somewhere inside the barn. With that they started to flash their lights all over the place.

"Who's mobile is it?" Liam asked.

"Not any of ours."

"Then there's someone else in here."

They took out their guns, and went into a shooting position.

"Hold it," Santos said. "Hit Tex's number again."

"What?"

"Do as you're asked."

He did and they waited. Then it started to ring again.

"Sweet Jesus, did they bury him alive?"

"Shut fuckin' up and keep ringing. The rest of you, keep quiet," Liam shouted from the window ledge.

They moved to the corner of the barn.

"It's coming from down here," Joe said.

"Get the shovels and start digging. He could still be alive," Joe shouted over. Now, as he watched, he prayed he was dead when they put him down there. After digging for some minutes, they found his mobile first, then his head.

"Sweet Jesus," Alabama shouted, as they both jumped back out of the hole in horror.

"The bastard cut his head off."

"At least we found him," Santos said. "Now we can bring him back home with us when we're finished here."

There was a bang as the door of the barn closed. Liam was the first to shoot and then the rest followed suit.

"When you're finished shooting," Vet Murphy shouted in, "Maybe there are a couple of questions you'd like to ask me. You know, your last request, that kind of thing.

"You can see the windows are of the old style. There must have been a lot of small men walking around back then, right Liam?"

"Go fuck yourself," Liam shouted out.

"No, my friend, you fuck yourself. Now I have to wait for my twin to come. Did you know I had one, Mister Coombs?"

"Of course I knew you had one," Liam shouted back. "And 'had' is the right word. I blew his sick fuckin' brains out an hour ago. Now he's over in Halpin's field, spread out and up to his eyes in shit. You could say shit to shit—you know, instead of dust to dust, old bean."

The vet started to scream. As he did, Liam shouted, "Make for the door now." With that they ran as fast as they could.

"Why did you kill him? He wouldn't harm a fly," the vet shouted in.

"No, just women, the cowardly bastard."

The vet started to laugh.

"You love swearing, don't you Liam? But I suppose with your background, you're used to it."

Then they heard another voice outside, saying, "Is that you vet Murphy?"

"Yes, and who are you?" he asked.

"I'm Mick Maloney. I forgot to phone you and tell you I saw a light down here last night. So, when I saw more tonight, I decided to take a look myself to see what's going on."

"That's very kind of you,' the vet said.

"Hi, Mick. It's me, Santos. Ask the vet to let us out, will you please?"

"Why has he you locked in there?" Mick asked Santos.

"Because he's a killer. Don't go near him. Remember the light your wife saw as a child?"

"Yes."

"Well, that was the vet with his sick twin burying one of your wife's neighbours. That's why he sold the house so cheap to her parents. To get them out of the way. Are you armed?"

"I have my hurley with me," Mick shouted.

"Don't let the vet near you," Santos shouted back.

"He's alongside me now."

"Yes, I am. And what can I give a good neighbour? Or a nosey one?"

"What's that you said, Vet?" Mick asked him.

"I said you should have minded your own fuckin' business and kept your big mouth shut," as he slipped behind him and cut his throat. Those inside could hear someone gasping for breath, and then the body hitting the ground hard.

"How are you going to explain that to his wife?" Santos shouted out.

"Why explain it? I'll kill her as well. My twin and I have been doing it for many years. Now, enough of this small talk, time is of the essence. Tell me, Yank, do you like a barbecue?"

"Not really. Why do you ask?" Santos said.

"Pity. Because you're about to have one. Only instead of chicken and hamburgers, it'll be you and your friends."

"And how are you going to sweep that under the counter?" Santos asked him.

"I'll tell them I haven't been here in years and was just about to come down and take a look at it as a builder was very interested in it."

"Suppose they want his name?" Joe shouted out.

"My god man, at my age, I'll tell them names come and go. You know, Alzheimer's. Who would doubt me?"

"I would," Sergeant Barry answered, as his light shone on the Vet's face. "You're under arrest. Now, open the door and let them out."

"Keep your distance from him," Santos shouted out.

"Don't listen to them," the vet replied, as he walked up to the door. "By the way, Sergeant, I forgot to tell you, there's a body over there. He had a heart attack, I think. I tried to help him, but I was too late. Pity."

Sergeant Barry now turned and tried to see if there was anything he could do. As he did, the vet made his move.

"Sergeant," he said. "Be a good man and take the light off my face."

"Shut fuckin' up," the Sergeant replied.

"Certainly," he said, as he took a gun out of his pocket.

"Did you ever see an animal killed by one of these? Answer me, you piece of shit."

"No, damn you."

"Not a pretty sight. Even worse when it's human. Now what am I going to do with you? Got it. I'll let you go. Why don't you run away? The darkness will hide you. And I'm too old to follow."

"Don't listen to him, Sergeant," Liam shouted out.

"That's nice, coming from the prick who started all this. Couldn't leave it alone, could you, Liam? Now, what age are you, Sergeant?" the vet asked.

"Thirty eight," he replied.

"Now do as I say, or you'll never reach thirty nine, understand?"

"Yes."

"Now kneel down and stay there," as he put the gun to his head.

"If I pulled this trigger, your head would go all over the place. Even up on me."

As Santos and Liam tried to keep him talking, Joe was picking away at one of the windows.

"Could you move a bit faster?" Alabama whispered.

"Don't worry, I'm nearly there. This one took the brunt of the bad weather down through the years."

"Thank God for that," Alabama replied.

"You in there, you've gone very quiet. Cat got your tongues?" the vet shouted in.

"I suppose you've found the body of your dear, departed friend. Or maybe someone else. But don't worry, there's plenty in there. One for each of you," and he started laughing. "But I can't take the praise for him. My twin was the man that gutted him. That was his style. Mine was more refined."

"Answer me this," Santos asked.

"Of course I will. We'll call it your last request. And your friends' as well. What is it?"

"Are you a cross dresser?"

"In plain English, what the fuck is that?"

"Do you like wearing women's clothes? I mean their underwear, things like that," Santos shouted back.

"How dare you, Yank. You are one sick bastard."

"That coming from you, who murders innocent women. Must be a while since you looked into the mirror. Did you enjoy washing their clothes? Answer me, you piece of shit."

"Fuck yourself," the vet replied. "Now, I must ask Sergeant Barry to do something."

"Like you asked Sergeant Kelly's wife?" Liam said.

"Oh yes. I'd forgotten about her. Now I remember, she wanted me to run away with her. Me, with that piece of shit. Then she said she'd tell everyone about us. Can you believe it? So she had to go as well. Maybe she's listening in there. I think the suspenders belonged to her. I can't swear to it, but I'm nearly certain.

"Now, Sergeant, if you don't mind, move over to that barrel. That's a good man. And when you get there, knock it over. Not towards me, mind you, but in the direction of the door."

"No," came the reply. "And you're under arrest." He shone his light back on the vet's face.

"Don't do that,' the vet said.

"You're coming with me." He started to get back up. The vet put the gun to his head and fired. As the bolt tore through his head, inside they could hear the sergeant's screams.

"He's after killing him. How long more over there?" Santos asked.

"Done," thank God.

Joe pulled the window back. "Who's the lightest?"

"Me," Alabama whispered.

"Get your ass over here fast. Where's your gun?" Liam asked him.

"In my holster."

"Then take it out and take the safety catch off and put it in your fuckin' hand."

"Sorry."

"The second he hits the ground, out you go."

"What about you?" Santos asked.

"I'm right behind you."

Now the vet shouted in, "Did he think that I'd let him live?"

"But now you have to light it yourself," Liam shouted back.

"You mean that you want me to walk over to the door, stand right outside it, and strike a match?"

"Why, is there another way?" Liam again shouted out.

"Of course. There's my old reliable lighter. My twin wanted to burn down this place some time ago. He said too many houses were being built around the place, so he brought out petrol, just in case someone got nosey. Great man for thinking ahead. I'll be sad to see it go. But then, I look on the bright side, because you'll be gone too."

Liam now heard the lighter hitting against the door. Then the smell of smoke. "I'd better get out of here fast." As he got off the window sill, his legs went from under him. The movement and the feeling in his legs were gone.

"The knife must have cut something. Now think fast."

The smoke was starting to come in under the door. "My legs are gone, but my hands are all right. I can crawl."

Making his way to the other window, he heard Santos say, "Liam where are you?"

"I'm on the ground."

"Why, what's wrong with you?"

"My legs are after giving out." The roof slates now started to crack with the heat.

"I'm coming in."

"Don't. I'll make it," as he watched him come back through the window.

He ran over to Liam. "Give me your hands, I'll drag you over."

Liam lifted them up, Santos grabbed them and started to pull Liam towards the window as part of the roof collapsed down into the barn. "I think we'll just about make it," Santos said.

"Did you get him?" Liam asked.

"No. I'd say he's long gone. Before he went, he threw the two bodies into the fire. He'll have to make for his house. We'll nail him there. There's nowhere else left for him. Now, what about you?"

At the window, Santos was about to lift him up when, suddenly, a hand with a gun came through it, pointed at

Liam's head.

"Guess who? Don't make a move for your gun or I blow this prick's head off," he said to Santos. "Now, Liam, we have some unfinished business to attend to."

With that Liam tried to push the gun away, shouting at Santos, "Kill the piece of shit." The vet looked surprised and then smiled as he put the gun to one of Liam's eyes and fired. Then, he turned to Santos with a pleading look, and for a second Santos thought he was going to give himself up. He fired the first shot, hitting him in the head. The remaining bullets he put into his body as he collapsed back outside on to the ground.

Now the others came running. When they saw the two bodies, Joe shouted in "Are you OK in there?"

"Get Liam's body and pull it away fast as it's blocking me." With that, Alabama lifted his body and put it over his shoulder, saying, "It's clear now."

As Santos jumped out, the roof collapsed. "That was close," he thought, as he looked down at the vet.

"Will I throw him back into the barn and let him burn?" Joe asked.

"No. That would be an insult to the people buried in there. Let Holy Ireland see its own home-grown serial killers." He walked over to Joe and Alabama and said, "Tidy Liam up. We don't want him looking like that when they come, do we?"

. . .

By the following week, it was world news and they were asked on to every talk show. Santos was asked about the first time he had met Liam and their time in Vietnam. Now, tiring of answering the same questions, he turned to the presenter and said, "When Liam and I came back nobody here wanted to speak to us. It was as if we had started the war. Now everyone wants to know about him. It's strange what a couple of years can do.

Back in Ireland, from the two sites, they dug up fifteen bodies. Again, the same question, how did they get away with it? The politicians were using it by promising it will never happen again. They hope. Or not while they're in government.

And no one knew he had a twin. Santos and the boys thought that was strange; all they had to do was look up their birth certificates. "But that's not our problem any more. Some even wanted to know why they had carried and used their guns and thought they should be brought to trial. But that got thrown out some months later.

When it had all quietened down, they came back to Ireland,

drove straight to Culdrun cemetery, and buried half of Liam's ashes with his parents. His ex-wives and children made no objection to it.

They went to a Dublin estate agent and put the farm up for sale, giving him all the papers. They then got the next plane out. Two more changes and they landed at Dallas airport. They then went straight out to Tex's grave. The day they buried him the government had stayed away. Probably they didn't know how to handle it.

Then they drove to Tex's house and told his wife about his share of the farm and everything else. She just cried and nodded.

And finally, one week later, they were back in Vietnam, flying over the Iron Triangle. Then Santos said to the helicopter pilot, "One more time. Just for old time's sake." And as he flew back over it, Santos took out the urn, opened the side door and turned it upside down, letting Liam's ashes finally go back to a place where, if truth be known, he had never really come out of.

As they watched Liam's ashes disappear down into the trees and fields below, Santos started to sing Liam's favourite song. The only one he sang when he got drunk in the bars of Saigon, *The Eve of Destruction*. And as he sang, he thought, someone must have known. They had to have known.

The Betrayal of Edwin Homes

1919 had been a bad year for the movement in Limerick. Between shootings and some volunteers being locked up, nothing had gone right for them.

Edwin Homes, a local volunteer, wanted more than anything to spend Christmas day with his family. But at twenty eight he was already a wanted man with a price on his head. There was terror everywhere, and a fear of betrayal. In the past six months three of his friends had been shot dead; he knew the information had to be coming from the inside, but whoever was giving it out was covering his tracks very well. They had questioned a few they thought might be the informers but had had no success in finding the source of the leak. He had learned to trust very few people. His commander had told him to watch his back at all times and never to go back home the same way he had come.

Now, stopping at the Guinness store, he could hear Christmas songs coming from one of the barges. "At least someone's happy," he thought. "Now, which way to go?" He knew going back to his own house was out of the question tonight. Tomorrow, I'll move early; so it will have to be a safe house for tonight."

Slowly, he walked past the barges. When he got to the main gate, he stopped again, carefully looking up and down Clare Street. Not a sign of anyone. Suddenly a noise came from the singing barge. Watching from behind the main gate, he could see one of the men coming up from below and shouting back down, "Someone just passed here."

"What do you want us to do about it?" a voice answered from below.

"Whoever he is, if he runs in to the military he's a dead man."

"Well that's his problem, not ours. Will you close the hatch? The snow's coming in."

"Right," he answered. And with that, he went back down.

As Edwin looked at the way he just come, his footprints were there for all to see. This was the first Christmas it had snowed in years. "Just my luck," he thought. "Mind you the place is looking great."

He took the revolver out of his overcoat pocket, opened it, and put it inside his pants. "Better safe then sorry," he thought.

"Anyway, here goes."

He ran across the road; stopping momentarily outside the fish shop. "Must keep going," he thought, as he ran up to the corner of Broad Street, where he turned and looked back at the way he had come.

"I'm a dead man if I keep on this street. I have to get off it fast."

As he moved across the road in to Watergate, a lamp went on in one of the houses. A woman pulled the curtain back and looked out at him; she blessed herself and closed them again.

"I'm getting nervous and making too much noise. I'll have to calm down. Maybe the new snow that's falling will cover my tracks."

He was walking down by the back of the Tivoli, and realized now that it had been a big mistake to try and get home.

"Well, it's a bit late now. I'll just have to get on with it. God, I'm freezing. And my fingers are stuck together. I can't go up High Street; the place will be crawling with them. Better to go up to the old graveyard and think something out. My father used to say to me, 'you're one of those who'll have to learn the hard way.' And he was right."

Now, inside the graveyard, he knew the exact spot from where he could see almost everything. As a child, he used to play hide and seek in there. And now, as a man, he was doing the same thing. Only now it was kill or be killed. He looked over at a house that had a light on still.

"I could knock at their door. But with the tracks I'm leaving, they'd know exactly where I am. Why did I ever think otherwise? My best bet is to get back up to Plassey and stay in the cousin's hut."

As he walked back out, the noise of his footsteps on the snow could be heard a mile away.

"Well, there's nothing I can do about it."

More curtains were pulled back. Making his way in to the Long Can, he thought back to the time when the ghost of a woman had supposedly been seen there. Kids dared each other to walk it. You hid your fear. When my turn came, I started off with a slow walk. When I got to the middle it was fast and near the top I was running as if my life depended on it. Just like now. And I'm making so much noise the whole place can hear me.

He turned into Penny Well and again, not a sign of anyone.

"Thank God for that. I suppose if there was no curfew I'd have been spotted long ago."

Throwing caution out the window, he took the revolver out and knocked off the safety catch. He had to make Rhebogue fast.

"If I've been seen by an informer, he'd have to walk to give anyone the information. Unless he had a telephone—and if he had the whole place would know about it, so that's out."

Running across the Dublin Road—still nothing—he made his way up Rhebogue Hill. He turned halfway up. "Christ," he thought, "it's so peaceful. And the church is looking beautiful." He remembered the first time he had gone to Midnight Mass. "It was a night just like this. I was with my father and aunt. I found a stick and started to write my name in the snow. Then my father took it off me, saying, 'Do you want to let the whole place know you're going to mass?' 'So what about it?' my aunt answered back. 'He's doing nothing only going to mass. Some of your friends would want to go before they kick the bucket and start screaming for the nearest priest.' With that the two of them kept it up all the way down to the main door of the church and as we were going in my father, thinking he'd have the last word, said to me, 'That's the last time you come with me.' 'Good,' my aunt replied. 'I'll take him from now on.' But that was long ago and, I suppose, far away." Turning, he started to hum *Silent Night.*

Suddenly he heard the clicks and then the order to fire. He lifted and aimed his revolver but could see no one. Then the noise. And then he felt the pain as the bullets tore in to his body. For a second he thought he was flying; when he hit the ground what he had just been looking at was now upside down. He tried to lift his revolver but there were no feelings in his hand. He tried to get back up but he couldn't move. He heard footsteps walking down towards him and a voice asking, "Well, is that him or not?"

"Yes, sir. It's him."

"Good man. You've done an excellent job."

One walked down to him while the other stayed back.

"That voice—I know it well. Think! Oh Jesus, it can't be. He was my friend."

Now an auxiliary man was looking down at him.

"Well, Edwin old boy, we finally got you. It took time and money but now, it's over—for you, anyway."

"Clever," he thought. "They came in from the Dublin Road side—no footprints. Nothing. He pointed his gun and took aim. In the last seconds of his life Edwin Homes thought, "All I wanted to do was come home for just one day. That wasn't asking for too much. Or was it?"

The Visit

James O'Shea sat looking out the window of his country house. It was September and the winter was setting in. Far away he saw the lights of the city and thought, "When I was young I loved the night life, the singing and dancing and being with the woman of my life". That was long ago and she died some years ago. She never got over the deaths of her twins, who only lived for half an hour, babies James and Louise. But she always believed in her heart that both of them looked at her and reached out for her before they died.

That was impossible yet she believed it was so. She never got over their deaths. I went to work and forgot about her, rarely coming home—any excuse would do. She, alone in the house, started to drink and slowly lost her mind. The doctors told me that she would be better off in a home where she would be looked after. At the time money was no object, business was booming. I was making money left, right, and centre. I had met another woman on a casual basis and that suited me fine until one night one of our so-called friends told her about me and that finished her. That night after a combination of pills and drink her heart stopped. May God forgive me, Louise; I still love and miss you. Just then the nurse, Mrs. Ryan came in.

Nurse Ryan: All right, James, have you taken your tablets?

James O'Shea: Yes I have, but what are they doing for me only stopping the pain of the cancer that's killing me.

Nurse Ryan: That's no way to talk. There are cures being found every day.

James O'Shea: Maybe there is, but it will be too late for me.

Nurse Ryan: Now that's enough of that. All you want is positive thinking. That can move mountains.

James O'Shea: Maybe it can, but I don't care anymore. I've had it with all the relations coming out of the woodwork. But when I'm gone they will be in for a big surprise.

Nurse Ryan: Did you do that with your will?

James O'Shea: Yes I did. I have left it between Cancer Research and the Alzheimer's Foundation. Don't worry there's a couple of bob for you.

Nurse Ryan: I don't want anything only for you to get better.

James O'Shea: Thanks but you can forget that. Listen, if any so-called relations call or phone, do me a favour and tell them I'm asleep. I'm bad enough without listening to them.

Nurse Ryan: All right. Are you warm, dear?

James O'Shea: Yes I am. Now, goodnight.

Nurse Ryan: Goodnight. Just press the button if you want me, ok.

James stays at the window looking at the lights of the city.

James O'Shea: I won't be seeing them for much longer. Ah well, it comes to us all at last. I will be with Louise, the twins and my parents. I gave the undertakers my instructions so at least all that's done.

James falls asleep. When he wakes up a young man and woman are looking at him.

James O'Shea: How did you get in? I told Nurse Ryan I wanted to be left alone. Who are you anyway?

Man and Woman: Friends.

James O'Shea: I don't know you!

Man and Woman: Yes you do.

James O'Shea: Listen you can tell your parents I've my will made out already. Now would you please leave.

Man and Woman: In a minute. Would you like to know why we came?

James O'Shea: I suppose your parents put you up to it, to soften me up. But I'm afraid it's too late.

The woman smiles.

James O'Shea: *(To himself.)* My God, she has the same smile as my Louise.

The Woman: You're a grumpy old man. You've been that way all your life, haven't you?

James laughs.

James O'Shea: Who told you that?

The Woman: You would be surprised. Are you afraid of death James?

James O'Shea: Well there's a question to ask someone who is dying.

The Woman: You still did not answer my question.

James O'Shea: Of course I am. There's so much left to do.

The Woman: Like what?

James O'Shea: Travelling the world, and spending money!

The Woman: But when you had your health all you did was work and make money.

James O'Shea: You seem to know a lot about me.

The Woman: I told you you'd be surprised.

James O'Shea: *(To himself).* She seems to know a lot about me but she is also making me laugh.

James O'Shea: What else do you know about me?

The Woman: Well, you married Louise Richardson. You loved her very much, you had twins, but they died half an hour after they were born.

James O'Shea: Please stop. I don't want to hear anymore.

The Woman: Why?

James O'Shea: Because it hurts too much. Now are you leaving or do I have to ring the bell and get you thrown out.

The Woman: I'm afraid Nurse Ryan is fast asleep.

James O'Shea: Well I won't be long waking her up, and by the way has he no tongue?

The Man: Yes I have. Do you want to ask me anything?

James O'Shea: What would I be asking you questions for?

The Man: Well are you curious who our parents are or which cousins they are? Maybe none of them is our parents, maybe we are not your cousins, maybe we broke into your house and maybe Nurse Ryan is tied up downstairs.

James O'Shea: There are a lot of maybes there.

The Man: Yes, but it's after putting you thinking.

James O'Shea: My dear boy, all the thinking for me will be soon be over. Between drugs and being unable to move it can't come quickly enough.

The Woman: You shouldn't be thinking like that. There's more to life than this planet.

James O'Shea: What do you mean? Like being from outer space? Or heaven or even hell. I'll tell you something—for the last twenty-five years I've been living my own hell, so when I leave this place it will be a blessing. And the sooner the better.

The Woman: Mam was right you are a very contrary old man.

James O'Shea: By the way I'm not that old.

The Woman: I know your age even the date of your birth.

James O'Shea: Tell me, do you know when I will die?

The Woman: Yes.

James O'Shea: When?

The Woman: Tonight. But don't be afraid Mam is waiting for you.

James O'Shea: Sweet Jesus, who are you?

The Woman: I am Louise and this is James. We are your children from long ago.

James O'Shea: Please don't play tricks on me I have suffered enough. How could you be so cruel? Please leave me alone.

The Woman: Dad you will never be alone again.

The Dark Horse Stories

James O'Shea: Will you please leave me alone, and I'm not your father.

The Woman: Yes you are. When we died we did not leave the room. We listened to you tell Mam you would have more children. That hurt us because we wanted to be with both of you and we knew in body we never could be. We also heard the doctor tell you Mam could have no more children. When we heard this we were glad. But then sad when we looked down on Mam. We also looked in on both of you at Christmas time but it was not a happy home. When Mam found us she was afraid for a while but now she has us, her parents, and tonight—you.

James feels as if he were going to have a heart attack.

James O'Shea: This is a dream, it's impossible, there's no such thing as the hereafter, no babies who die then come back as grown people. And yet, you're telling me things only my wife and the doctor could know. (Pause) Does she forgive me?

The Woman: Yes. She forgave you a long time ago but you never forgave yourself.

James O'Shea: How could she, the night she died I was not even with her. I was with another woman. May God forgive me.

The Woman: It's all water under the bridge now Dad. It's time. Give me your hand, we will be with you all the way.

James O'Shea: I'm frightened.

The Woman: There's no need to be, no more pain, no more loneliness. You'll be with the people who love you.

James feels himself leave his body and is at peace for the first time in a long time as he looked down on a sick body that was once him. Nurse Ryan wakens up.

Nurse Ryan: Christ! I must have fallen asleep.

Coming from the TV is a crackling noise and the screen is blank. She goes over, pulls out the plug, and looks at the clock.

Nurse Ryan: I've been asleep for the last three hours. Better go up and check on James. Here Blackie, where is that dog?

She heard whimpering from under the table.

Nurse Ryan: Here Blackie. What's wrong with you?

But Blackie does not come out. She puts her hand in to bring him out. He snaps at her.

Nurse Ryan: My God, what's wrong with that dog? Alright stay there.

She climbs the stairs.

Nurse Ryan: That was unusual for him. Usually he's the first one up the stairs.

She enters James' room.

Nurse Ryan: He must be asleep. I'll just see he's covered and leave him in the chair.

She pulls up the blanket and looks at James' face looking up at her with a look of contentment she has never seen before. She jumps back and screams.

Nurse Ryan: James can you hear me? James, answer me. Please, answer me.

She runs out the door, down the stairs, looks for the doctor's phone number. Her hands are still shaking. She drops the number, goes down on her knees to retrieve it and calls Doctor Moloney. Twenty minutes later the doctor comes through the door.

Dr. Moloney: All right nurse, where is he?

Nurse Ryan: Up in his room. It's up there, the second last one on your left.

Dr. Moloney: For God's sake woman, show me.

Nurse Ryan goes up the stairs with fear.

Dr. Moloney: Woman what's wrong with you?

Nurse Ryan: I don't know but when I went into the room I felt a chill.

Dr. Moloney: Surely you have seen bodies before.

Nurse Ryan: Yes but not like that. He was smiling at me. Maybe it was the medicine that did it to him.

Dr. Moloney goes over to James O'Shea and looks down at the body. James is smiling and his hands are posed as if he were reaching out to someone.

Dr. Moloney: Nurse Ryan, are you sure he had no visitors?

Nurse Ryan: Of course I'm sure. He hardly spoke to any of his relatives. And I had the doors locked because two houses had been broken into in the last couple of months, so I was taking no chances.

Dr. Moloney: I believe you. To look at him you would think someone was with him when he passed away. Ah well, call the ambulance. I'll sign the death certificate. Which undertakers are burying him?

Nurse Ryan: Philips's.

Dr. Moloney: All right, thank you.

Alone in the room Dr. Moloney is muttering to himself

Dr. Moloney: Nurse Ryan was right—there is an eerie feeling about this place. I'd better get out of here before I start thinking like her.

As he switched out the light he took one last look at James O'Shea and said a prayer.

Dr. Moloney: What a lonely way to die.

They danced the dance of death

Too many mouths to feed with no money coming in so you took the kings shilling and signed up in Tralee.

And with hopes high you and the rest of the new recruits set sail to fight the just war or so they said.

St Louis Missouri and a fine musician you are, played in the brass band back in your homeland.

Like the others you sailed for Uncle Sam and showed them how you played and marched to a brass band.

The end for you would be France and he the Dardanelles. Did you ever meet or pass one other on the street?

Both sent back photos as they stood proudly in their new uniforms. As the bulbs flashed and held them for all time.

Soon other flashes would put both in an early grave and the uniform would became their shroud.

The general sat back and said "Gentlemen its time for another attack."

"But sir can't. You understand we have lost to many. There must be another way."

"How dare you speak to me like that? Because it's going to be my way, do you understand?" "Yes, sir. "Good then behave like a man."

"There is a knighthood waiting for you, sir." "Yes, I know. But it's those amateur soldiers, afraid to show there head.

"And as for you, Captain, I am waiting for your answer." "I have none, your pride has blocked your way."

"Leave. Get out or I will have you Court Marshalled this very day."

When he was gone he turned to the others and said, "Make sure he is in the first attack." "Done, sir," they answered with delight.

The first assault, many fell; the second, you fell. As for the musician, the last sound he heard was the sound of hell.

In a music hall back home the manager came out on to the stage and said, "Gentlemen, please lift your glasses and join me in a toast to our gallant soldiers over there."

Then a lone voice came from the crowd and shouted back, "Better still lets drink to the slaughter that's happening right now over there."

"Who are you, sir?" "I am the voice of reason." "No, sir. You are the voice of a coward."

"I have been there and worn the shirt, have you?" as the crowd started to shout him down.

"A white feather to you," as the manager pointed him out. "And damnation to you."

Then the first bottle smashed off his head as they kicked him to the ground.

"Throw the coward out in to the gutter. That's where he belongs."

When it was done one put his hand in to his pocket and pulled out a cross for bravery.

"He must have bought it and I'll sell it," as he spit down on him and proudly walked back in to the cheers.

The guns roared, the ground exploded, as the general and his yes men ate their feast.

And up in the smoked fog bloody sky the four horsemen of the apocalypse looked down smiling with glee.

As the soldiers waited in the mud, and darkness became their last light, the orders came.

"Ready," the sergeant screamed out now. And as they climbed slowly out of the trenches and marched to the wire they began to pray, "Oh god please let me live," as they danced the dance of death.

Soul Train
A Black Comedy

One wet night after drinking too much, Scott May[1] got into his car, pushed it into first gear, and headed for the open road. His friends tried to take the keys off him, even to call a taxi. No way; it was new and he wanted to see what it could do. Now, he pushed it into top gear and was burning up the road when he hit a car driving on the opposite side and probably heading for home. Like a flash it was over for all of them.

When he awoke, Scott felt movements all around him; he saw a man and called him over to ask where he was or which hospital they were going to.

"Son," he said, "You're dead. I'm your conductor and I'm here to help you get through. Your problems are all over now; the rest is up to you. This train has been going since time began; I should know, I got on board a long time ago and I've see all sorts come and go"

"Christ, you can tell a good one."

"Do you think I'm funny? Just turn your head."

"Why?"

"I want to show you someone, that's why."

"Who am I supposed to be looking at?"

"See the young couple sitting by the exit door?"

"What about them?"

"They're the people you killed tonight. I don't know why they're sitting there—maybe they think this train is going to stop. Only passengers we take on are dead ones. I'd better go down and put their minds at ease."

"Do that." And as Scott May watched him walk back down and explain it to them, he thought [who jobbed him][2] now as he looked up and down the carriage. All the people in it were looking out of their windows with blank expressions on their faces.

"They're as bad as our friend the conductor. God, what kind of a mess have I got myself into now? There's no bones broken. I feel good. No police asking about the crash. Why? Maybe there were a lot of crashes tonight and they'll get to me later. But the conductor said the people in the other car were killed. Strange."

Now Scott May changed his seat so he could see the people he was supposed to have killed. Both were in their early twenties, just like him. As he looked more closely, he could see that drops of blood were falling from the girl's head. He pulled some tissues out of his pocket, got up, and walked down to them.

"Excuse me," he said to the girl. "You're bleeding."

"Am I? I wonder what caused it?"

Scott held out the tissues.

"I think it's a bit late for them, don't you?"

"What do you mean by that?" Scott asked her.

"What do you think I mean? We were going home, everything to live, for until you put a stop to it all—you and your drunken macho bullshit. Well you paid for it too, and I'm glad you'll never get the chance to drive another car or kill any more innocent people. Usually drivers like you walk away without a scratch. Well, my friend, your luck ran out as well tonight."

"Who told you to say this bullshit to me?"

"No one. There's a lot more I want to say to you but now I have all the time in the world so I'm going to drag it out and make you suffer like I did tonight."

"Woman, this is the last time you'll see me."

"Don't bet on it."

Scott May got up and went back to his seat. "What's going on here? Am I dreaming or what?"

"No, my friend, you aren't dreaming. This is the real thing. May I sit down?"

"Please do."

"Let me introduce myself; my name is Jeb and I'm the driver of this train—and I suppose head man now. What do you want to know? Ask anything. That's what I'm here for."

"Well for a start, your conductor."

"What about him?"

"Is he mad?"

"No, he isn't. He's just dead like the rest of us."

"What?"

"You heard me."

"If I'm dead, how come I don't feel it?"

"Because you don't have any feelings; they died with you."

"Why are those people looking out of the window?"

"Like you, they don't believe they're dead."

"Were they going to a costume party?"

"Not that I know of. Why?"

"Their clothes are all different."

"That's because they all came on board at different times. Some have been here a long time; others, like you, have just come on board. It still hasn't sunk in yet."

"What?"

"That you're dead. You should have listened to your friends, but you chose not to, so you reap what you sow."

"How did they get the souls on board before trains were invented?"[3]

"Ever hear of the headless coachman?"

"Yes."

"Well that was the coach used before this and the shuttle will be next.[4] Now I have to go and meet the rest of the new passengers and welcome them."

"One last question. The conductor said some have got off, not many. How did they get off?"

"Simple—they had served their time. Look at it like a halfway house or, as we used to call it, purgatory. When you're finished here, you either go one way or the other, and that's all up to you. And you, my friend, have started off on the wrong foot. It's all points here, so keep that in mind the next time you try to be smart. We've met your kind before.[5] Why don't you mix and meet your new neighbours and try to listen to what they have to say; it could stand to you down the line."

"I'll remember that."

"Good." And with that, he left.

"My mobile—I forgot about that. Time to make some calls. First, Eve, to let her know I'm alright." Scott dialled in her number. No answer. "I'll try again later. Parents next." After trying for some minutes, he put down his mobile. "What's going on? Surely someone must have heard it. Are they all gone deaf or what?"

"No. It's just that they can't hear it," a passenger from the opposite seat answered."

"But it's ringing, listen." He rang again.

"In here it's ringing, yes. But out there, no. You could be ringing for eternity and you'll still get no answer. That's the way it is in here; you get used to it after a while."

"How long did it take you?"

"I'll guess."

"Why?"

"Because you lose track of time when you've been on it so long. Eighty-six years? Could be wrong—maybe give or take a couple of years."

"What did you do when . . .?"

"I lived?"

"Yes"

"I killed a man."

"Why?"

"I wanted his money, that's why. And I wanted it fast. There are a lot of killers in this carriage. See that one fourth seat down?"

"Yes." As he looked, the man glared back at them.

"He says he's Jack the Ripper and why would he lie?"

As they watched, Jack turned to stare at the girl who had been killed earlier that night.

"Don't worry; it's all in his mind now."

"But why is she in here?"

"You mean with us killers?"

"Yes."

"They'll be gone before the night's out. There must have been a lot of murders and accidents down there tonight and the only space left was in here. And you're starting to come round."

"What do you mean by that?"

"Conscience. It hasn't left you yet."

"I wish I'd listened to my friends."

"And I wish I'd never killed, but it's too late for both of us."

"I had so many plans."

"So had the people you killed. Look."

Scott turned and watched as the couple now made for the exit. The girl turned and said, "Any parting words for us?"

"Well, I'm truly sorry. I wish it had been me."

"You can keep your apology. And, as for your wish, it's been granted. You're as dead as me. I knew as soon as I saw you coming over to our side of the road. Now we're getting off and you stay on.

"Why did you drive drunk tonight? Why? I was six months pregnant as well, but you finished that. I pray you never get off this train and if you do, that you rot in hell."

As she finished speaking, the conductor said "Time to get off. Ready?"

"Yes."

"Then follow me please." And they were gone.

When he came back in, the conductor walked up to Scott and said, "I wish I was doing that every night, but that's the first in years. I even forget the name of the last one."

"Marta Hari," said another passenger.

"What did you say?" he asked the stranger.

"I told you her name."

"Oh yes. I remember it now. And while we're on the subject, she used to sit next to you, am I right? Well, are you going to answer or what?"

"You're right."

"Good. Another second and I would have deducted points and you would have gone back to the night you came aboard screaming. Yes you did, I remember it well. How time flies when you're busy. And you, Scott May, how do you find time on board?"

"Very slow."

"Good." And he was gone.

"That man loves his job," Scott said. "Why was the other one taken off the train?"

"Because she got blamed for things she hadn't done and was executed for things she had done. And why did she do it? Money. It's the root of all evil, so they say, and that's what brought most of us here in the first placc. But she was beautiful. Jack couldn't keep his eyes off her. And she would walk up and down the corridor just to drive him mad. Take a look at him. He knows we're speaking about him."

Scott looked straight at him and as he did, Jack lifted his finger, brought it slowly across his neck, and then pointed at Scott, smiling.

"Don't mind him," the stranger said. "All he was good for was killing women, isn't that right, Jack? And poor defenceless ones at that, am I right or not?" With that, Jack was up and out of his seat and heading straight for the stranger when the conductor and driver appeared out of nowhere and stood in front of Jack, saying, "Get back in your seat now or it's hell for you. Am I right, driver?"

"Yes."

Jack's hands were now buried in opposite seats. "Take them out now or you're history here, just like you are on earth."

When he had sat back down, Jack said, "I'll never be forgotten, I made sure of that. Not like the rest of you."

"What did you say?"

"Nothing."

"Good. And keep it that way, understand?"

"Yes."

The conductor and driver were gone as quickly as they had come.

"Don't ask. They're dead as well. One of the others told me that, at one time, all of Jack's victims were in the next carriage and when they found out he was in here they tried every trick in the book to get at him."

"What happened?

"They let them go, just like the people you killed tonight."

"Mine was an accident."

"No, you're judged the same as Jack. You were drunk. Your friends tried to stop you, yet you carried on. So did Jack. You killed with a car, he with his knife. The end result was the same, death. That's why we're all in here, waiting and hoping it won't be hell for us. Even our friend Jack. He's afraid as well— he who terrorised Whitechapel."

"But I was never caught and hanged like you were," Jack screamed back. "And don't tell me you have a clear conscience, I've heard enough bullshit in here to last an eternity. Are you listening?"

"Yes, we were listening all the time."

"You mean ear drooping all the time."

The conductor was now standing alongside of Jack. "We've had enough of the two of you—one will be leaving in the next couple of minutes. Don't ask which; I don't even know. It's all in his hands now, so if you have anything to say, now is the time to say it, or, as they used to say, forever hold your peace. That's been a problem around here for some time, at least with the two of you, but it's all over now, boys. Which one will be history, you or Jack? The bets are on—just joking, Lord."

Then a bell rang. "Excuse me, boys, I'll be back in a minute with the answer. Now, don't go away, promise?"

"You're not very funny," Jack shouted after him. "It's a pity he wasn't walking around Whitechapel when I was doing my rounds; I'd have enjoyed meeting him in, say, Bucks Row. Yes, that would have been the ideal place to meet him. You've gone very quiet up there, has the cat got your tongue or what? You're worried it could be you going to hell and not me, aren't you? Well, I've been there in life and in death, so I don't give a damn. Satan will welcome me with open arms, but I don't know about you."

Just then, the conductor reappeared. "Well, boys, it's judgement day for one of you and, as you can see, no envelope. Ready?"

"Why don't you just get on with it? You're no comedian."

"But in life I was."

"Jack, I'm afraid you won't be leaving just yet—don't ask. Ours is not to reason why."

"Is that so?"

"Yes."

"Me, I killed only one man, which I will forever regret."

"Bullshit," Jack shouted. "You went there with a plan to rob and kill if you had to and you did that. Say hello to Satan for me, will you, there's a good boy. Now run along with the conductor and don't be boring the rest of us."

"He isn't going there either. Oh, he's leaving alright, Jack, but it's to freedom, not to hell."

"What?"

"You heard me. Stop shaking, boy, it's time. We have a lot of souls waiting to take your seat. Say goodbye and let's go."

He turned to Scott and said, "What's happening to you now was the same with nearly everyone in this carriage—with two exceptions. You've already met one." Just as Scott was about to ask who the other one was, the conductor said, "Enough of this, he doesn't like any hold ups and neither do I." And he was gone.

For a long time Scott went into a depression, if that's what a dead man would call it. All he did now was to look out the window like the rest of them until one day, or was it night, a voice asked, "May I sit down?"

Scott looked up and saw a face he had seen many times in the paper or on TV. But right now, he couldn't put a name to it. "Yes, of course, I must have been dreaming."

"You don't dream in here, you drift. And how are you getting along?"

"Bad."

"And you, Jack?"

"Very well, Adolph."

"Oh, God. Now I know who you are."

"You should have known straight away. If we were still alive, you would have been put on the train to Auschwitz on my orders, just like the rest. Are you a Jew? A Pole? No, you're Russian, am I right?"

"Your guess was like your life—shit. Now get away from me."

"How dare you speak to me like that?"

"I'll speak to you any way I like. I speak for the millions you murdered. Conductor, where are you?"

"Right here, listening to what you had to say to Mister Hitler."

"Conductor, I've told you countless times to address me as Herr Hitler, or Fuhrer, but not mister. Are you stupid or what?"

"Mind your own business.[7] Get back to your seat."

"Or what?"

"Or I'll send you to the carriage where a lot of your victims are and they're just dying to meet you. Do you get my drift, Mister Hitler?"

"Yes, but remember this, Conductor, the Third Reich will rise again."

"And so will Atlantis. Now move on."

When he got back to his seat, he was still shouting about what he could have done for Germany. "My mistake was I surrounded myself with fools, and weak ones at that."

"I'm telling you for the last time, shut up."

"Yes, Mister Conductor. I'll do that for now."

"Always has to get the last word in, that one. Now, as for you, Scott May, you seem to be attracting the wrong kind of people. Why's that?"

"How should I know? Why don't you ask them?"

"Maybe I will when they cool down—and with them we could be talking years. I'm glad I didn't know them when they were alive; it's bad enough having to listen to them in here."

"I heard every word you said," Jack shouted.

"I'll bet you did and does it worry me? No. Now I have a lot of carriages to check to make sure everything's in order and all I want from you lot is quietness. That's not asking too much, is it?"

"Yes," Adolph screamed down.

"That's it. You've lost your points. It's hell for you, Mister Hitler, the next time the train stops."

"Good. I always wanted to meet Satan; he was an angel after my own heart. And when will we be stopping next?"

"Very soon, hopefully."

"Good. Now I have something to look forward to."

"Good for you," Jack said.

"You never know, you could be going with him."

"Promises, that's all I get around here."

"Keep your head down, Scott May, and ignore those two—they're bad and mad, believe me."

"How dare you speak of me like that, you stupid conductor," Hitler screamed."

"And of me. I had respect and fear in Whitechapel, I'll have you know."

"I'm off," the conductor said. "Remember what I told you, Scott May." And before Scott could reply, he was gone.

"You seem to be getting bad advice from some quarters, don't you, Herr May?" As Hitler got up from his seat and started to walk back down, "Oh, God, help me please. I beg you," Scott prayed.

Suddenly, Hitler let out a scream, "He's put the barrier up now." As Scott turned and watched, Hitler was hitting out at something he couldn't see. Next Jack jumped up and said, "He's done the same to me. You're the cause of all this, Scott whatever-your-name-is." As their voices started to fade to nothing, both kept hitting out at something Scott still couldn't see. "Thank you, God," thought Scott.

"Not God. It was little old me," said the conductor as he sat down next to Scott. "I'd been meaning to do that for a long time and now that it's done, halleluiah."

"Amen to that," Scott replied.

"The people you killed, it was an accident. Whatever, they have forgiven you, although with the woman it took a long time. A very long time."

"What do you mean by that? At the most, I'd say a month is all the time I've been on this train. I mean, I haven't seen any souls—new ones—come in to this carriage."

"But then, you haven't seen any old ones get off, have you? It's taken a long time for you to accept what you did."

"But you asked me two or even three weeks ago how I was doing and I said 'slow' and your answer was 'good'."

"Yes, I remember. But when I answered you that day or night there had been a lot of trouble on the train. It had been selection time and those picked for Satan refused to go, so we had to help them on their way. I never liked doing that—not here or in life." "You were a prison guard?"

"Sort of."

"Where?"

"In Buchenwald. I was what you would call a kapo. My job was to get those chosen to die to undress as fast as they could, telling them they had to take a shower, and to keep their clothes tidy, and to remember where they left them, and then straight to the gas chamber. When they were all locked inside, one of the guards dropped the Zyklon-B crystals down into it and after fifteen to twenty minutes, it was all over. Then we, the kapos, would go back in and clear out the bodies, clean it out, and have it ready for the next lot."

"Why did you do it?"

"While I lived I asked myself that question a thousand times."

"And what was the answer?"

"Simple. I wanted to live."

"And did you?"

"What?"

"Live out the war?"

"Right up to the day the camp was liberated."

"And what happened?"

"The prisoners caught me and some other kapos and hanged us. Can you believe it? Me, who brought hundreds to their executions, ended up getting executed there myself. Maybe I deserved it, who knows?"

"Is that why Adolph could tell you what to do?"

"No. But the fear I had for him and his murderous friends in my lifetime follows me in death. I never thought it was possible to do what I did, but, you see, it was. When I was growing up—
"

"Where?"

"In Köln. I wanted to become a rabbi and help my fellow man. And what did I end up doing only help the killers kill them. Well, such is life.

"How long the barriers stay down is up to him. If I had the choice, they'd stay down for good but, like you, I'm awaiting my fate, whatever that may be. As for those two, it's the fear they spread, that's what we're afraid of, not them. And I should know, I lived through it. I wish it on no nation or race. Unfortunately, it will always be there—man's greed for power. It comes through closed doors; it even came in here. Even my people are at it now. Nothing changes except the country. Instead of Heil, it's now Shalom. Maybe I'm better off dead. Although if I had my choice, I would take the living." The bell rang.

"Sweet Jesus. He's been listening the whole time. How did I forget?" It rang again. "Patience, Lord, patience. You're always saying you gave it to everyone, you must have forgotten to give it to yourself." And as quickly as he had come, he left.

"He would have made a great rabbi. I would have gone to hear him myself. Not to change my religion, mind you, just to see the difference."

"What made me drive that night? I must have been mad as well as drunk. And now I'm paying for it. At least the people I killed are at peace now."

"Amen for that."

"No—thank God for that."

"And who is he?"

"You may well ask."

"I don't ask. I learned not to ask too many questions in here."

"Yet you do."

"No, I don't."

"How did you get past the barrier?"

"You're at it already—asking questions."[10]

"I'm asking you just one. Well, are you going to answer?"

"Maybe."

"What do you think of it in here?"

"Why?"

"Time and how you put it down. Is it slow or fast for you?"

"Minding my own business, that's how I do it."

"No you don't. You've fallen out with two of the souls in this carriage. I like to call them that, rather than passengers. It's nearer to . . ."

"What?"

"Well, he goes under many names, and it depends on what country you were born in."

"Is that right?"

"Yes."

"You were a very arrogant person when you lived—a bit of a show-off and a know-it-all. Not a nice person, in other words. Most of the girls who went out with you went because you had plenty of money. You would always ask them whether it was you or your money, and their answers were always the same— it was you. Money never entered their heads. I'll let you into a little secret—they were all lying. The whole lot of them. But you knew that as well. That's why you drank so much. You couldn't face it sober. Life is tough, so they say."

Scott answered, "Yes."

"As for the people you killed, they had a full life—whereas yours was empty. I see you have learned very little since you came on board. Now and then, the nice part of you comes out, but that's not enough. At least with Adolph and Jack you know where you stand, but not with you. You're like the weather, too many changes."

"Go to hell," Scott screamed at him.

"No, I will never go there, but you may. The jury's still out on you."

"Who are they?"

"Mind your own business. Conductor, the barriers go back up straight away and no buts about it. He's going soft, but not me. Maybe it's time for a new conductor. A clean sweep of old souls."

"Who in God's name are you?"

"I am he whom you just mentioned. You were very quick to take my name when you lived and not always in a good light. Or have you forgotten that too?"

"I've done my time here."

"And do you admit you are dead?"

"I realised that some time ago."

"Well, my friend, you're in the jury's hands now. I am the judge and it is I who will pass sentence, whatever that will be. They could be soft like our conductor is with you, or hard like me, but at least you're in with a chance. Which is more than you gave the people you killed. I know you didn't plan on doing it—what was it then? I know—it was fate. Perhaps it was their fault. You were drunk and they were driving on the right side of the road, am I right? Cat got your tongue? Then nod your head. Do as I say."

"Now he has disobeyed you, Lord," Jack shouted. "He should be put off the train immediately. What do you think, Adolph?"

"I agree with every word that you just said. Now, obey my orders and do what you're supposed to do."

"And what is that, Adolph?"

"Get rid of him."

"What kind of a judge are you?"

"A fair one."

"I don't think there were many of those in Germany when you were in power."

"Of course not. If there was even one, he slipped through my fingers, unfortunately. But you must admit any weak link that I knew of, I got rid of straight away. It used to drive Himmler mad and he blamed Goering. He made out he was telling me everything and so he was. But then again, so was Himmler. It kept them all on their toes and I loved it. But you must love it too, Lord, with the conductor."

"Not in the way you did."

"The end justifies the means, and near the end I could trust no one. Not even Eva."[11]

"But she committed suicide with you," God said.

"If you don't mind, I don't want to talk about that. That should never have happened. I still believe we could have won. I listened to the wrong people—like you, Lord, listening to the conductor about that piece of shit alongside of you."

"That's enough. I won't allow language like that to be used on this train."

"Then what would you call him?"

"A human being, like you once were."

"How dare you compare him to me? I, who nearly ruled the world—"

"But you never did and never would have. I personally would have seen to that. Now it's time you stopped talking and kept quiet for a while. And I mean that."

"Or else what?"

"Say what's on your mind."

"I always did."

"And where did it get you?"

"To the very top. And those who called me the little corporal behind my back, I soon quietened them."

"How?"

"You may ask. Don't interrupt me and I'll tell you. It was simple—I'd invite them over for dinner. Remember, I had one of the best chefs cooking for me. When the meal was finished, I'd sit with them on the balcony with the best of brandy or whatever they wanted to drink. If it was only one I had to deal with, I'd let him sit in my own chair and watch him think for a second he was me. I used to love doing that. And when they were at ease with the surroundings I would slowly say, rumour has it that you're saying bad things about me. With that, you could see the colour slowly leaving their faces and like a flash they'd be up on their feet screaming—'who would say such a thing, just give me his or their names and I'll deal with it personally.' I'd say nothing for a minute. If it was a group, I would stare them down. They'd look at everything—the sky, the pictures on the wall, pictures they never took notice of that suddenly became masters in their eyes. Then I would slowly start to answer them. 'Our friend Reinhard was telling me over a coffee just the other day about these malicious rumours being spread about me. He advised me to hand them over to him and that he would personally deal with them. What advice would you give me? I don't know what to do. Some of the names mentioned I thought were friends of mine—but now it seems they weren't.

"Then I would take out a sealed envelope, hold it up so they could see it, and ask them again, 'I'm waiting for your answer now.' They'd start to walk around muttering and scratching their balls or whatever bit of hair they had left on their heads."

"Adolph!"

"Sorry a slip of the tongue. Then I'd say, I believe it's a pack of lies in here—would you agree with me, gentlemen? Of course, they'd all agree with me, 'Are you not our Fuhrer?' 'Well, I don't know, am I?' You could hear their answers down at the main gate and that was a long way off.

"Now here's the best part. I'd let them think that I was finished and some of them would ask to be excused so that they could go to the toilet. 'How many of you want to go to the toilet? Hands up.' And nearly everyone would put up their hands. 'I have just one more thing to say on this subject and then you can go, is that alright?' 'Of course, My Fuhrer,' they'd shout back and I'd watch their faces as I moved among them. Some had their legs crossed already and I would go to them and ask were they all right, did they want to sit down. Their answer was always the same; they wouldn't dare sit down while I stood. The mention of Russia worked wonders around the place and when I got back to my desk and turned, those who had been standing at the front were suddenly now at the back, so I would continue as I've already said, slowly—but even more so. And I'd talk about rivers and lakes, asking them what it was they most liked about them.

"And as I waited for an answer, you could hear the first start to piss in his pants, and with that, it was as if a dam had opened up. They were all at it now, farting as well. So I would excuse myself, saying as I went, 'Please keep the windows locked I feel a cold coming on and, of course, the door will be closed too. My guards have been ordered to shoot anyone who tries to open them—especially when some of my own generals tried to blow me up. Maybe there's an assassin among you. Well, is there?' 'We love you,' they'd shout back. 'Of course you do—just like the people who tried to blow me up. I will never die. Remember, I'm watching you the whole time.' Then I'd close the door and gulp the air again."

"Tell me this," the Lord said.

"Yes. What? I can't read your mind. Ask"

"Did it ever enter your head about the millions of people that you sent to the gas chambers—how they held their last breath?"

"Of course it did. I even went so far as to ask Höss about it."

"And what was his answer?"

"It depended on where you stood. If you were in the middle, death came straight away; those standing by the door died last. Sometimes the last face they would see would be my colleague, Höss. That man took to his job like a duck takes to water. A great hard worker, that man was. Now you can answer my question.

"No, you can answer a question for me—where is he?"

"Who?"

"Höss. Guess and you could be joining him soon."

"Is that so?"

"And me?" Jack asked

"You as well."

"And our friend alongside of you?"

"As I've already said, the jury's still out on him."

"Why should that be? He killed two people with the car he was driving. He was there."

"What are you trying to say?" God asked Hitler.

"All I did was to sign the papers or give the orders, but I was never at the scene of the crime. Never."

"But you killed people in the other war," Jack said.

"Yes. I did, but that was kill or be killed. That was trench warfare."

"What kind of a war was that?"

"It was years after you disappeared from London, Jack."

"What makes you think I did that, Adolph, old bean? Maybe I just changed the situation."

"Well, if you were still alive when it started, you'd know what I was talking about. All you had to do was read the newspapers. That's if you could read. Could you, Jack, old bean?"

"Only when it was about myself, Adolph, old shit."

"What did you just call me, you snake in the grass? I'll have you know I nearly brought London to its knees."

"Well, as we used to say down at the club, nearly never did anything. And it seems to me that all you do is talk through your hole. And I should know because I've been listening to you all these years and I have to say that my patience has finally run out. The best thing you could do for me and the rest of the souls in here would be to—and this is a saying from the trench war—"

"And what is that, woman killer?" Adolph was now standing and pointing at Jack, screaming. "Afraid to say it?"

"Not at all. Ready? Go fuck off and take the conductor's piece of shit with you."

Now Scott was up and shouting, first at Jack and then at Hitler. While all that was going on, the conductor reappeared, shouting, "I am my own man."

"Soul," Hitler reminded him, screaming. And when you were in life, you were mine body *and* soul. But don't feel bad about it, so was the rest of the world."

"Wrong," the Lord shouted back. "You were beaten, or has it slipped your mind?"[12]

Scott May now stayed quiet and watched as it started to get out of hand. He thought of the God he'd grown up with; this was a cool, calm, and collected God, not the one he was listening to.

"Now, barriers, Conductor. Put them up now."

"But I've just put them back down—on your orders, I might add."

"Do it now. Don't have me repeat myself again or you and your job will be finished, understand?"

"Yes, Lord."

And in a second or two, maybe it was more, Adolph's and

Jack's voices started to fade.

"Peace at last. Who said that again, Conductor?"

"I think, Lord, it was Martin Luther King, but I could be wrong. Maybe it was yourself who said it. You're a great one for the quotes."

"Yes, you're right, I am."

"About my job . . ."

"What about it?"

"Do I still have it?"

"Of course you have it, why do you ask?"

"Oh, Lord, you know me—insecure. Must be the Jew in me."

"Well, it wasn't in your ancestors. They were quick enough to condemn me, I can tell you. They couldn't crucify me fast enough and all I wanted for them was a peaceful life and that's the thanks I got. Ungrateful shower of—"

"Lord, don't say it. Bite your tongue or you'll regret what you might say."

"Then again, I may not."

Then he turned to Scott and said, "Your surname, it's May, am I right?"

"Yes, you are Lord."

"Can't you get the joke?"

"What joke is that, Lord?"

"May—it's creeping up everywhere. So, never mind, to me right now you look like a lost soul."

"But I am lost, Lord; you above anyone should know that."[14]

"Yes, you're right. But at this moment I have so much on my mind—another war on earth which, if it gets out of hand, could destroy it; this train with its endless carriages; dealing with its passengers like right now and people not doing what they're supposed to do. That's why I'm angry—can you blame me? Well—answer."

"I don't know what to say."

"I find that hard to believe. You had all the answers when you lived and now—nothing. Trying to get back into my good books, are you? What do you say, Conductor?"

"About what, Lord?"

"The conversation your two ears have been listening to."

"I'm afraid I was too busy with the two gentlemen."

"So you heard nothing at all?"

"Not quite, Lord, but a bit here and there, that's all. I swear. As my mother's soul is in heaven with you, Lord."

"Tell me, what makes you think she's with me?"

"Well, she was such a humble and holy woman. And if she

couldn't do you a good turn, she'd be upset for the day—no, it'd be a week, as you well know, Lord. And for putting up with my father all those years, you should have made her a saint. Maybe you still can, as a favour to me."

"Am I right that you think I owe you something, Conductor, or am I wrong?"

"It's not that you owe me anything, Lord, but I do keep good order on this train, am I right?"

"Get to the point, I'm a busy man."

"You mean soul, don't you, Lord?"

"No, I mean what I say. I can be anything and go anywhere, that's why I'm called the Almighty. I have just come back from earth."

"And how is everything down there?"

"Not too good. But then, it was never good down there at any time. Now, if I remember, we were speaking about your mother and the hard life she had. Please continue."

"My father drank every penny he made—gone from home for months at a time, he'd come back for a day or two, and then he was gone again."

"Did it never enter your head to wonder why he stayed away from so long, Conductor?"

"So he could have a good time, that's why, Lord."

"And your beloved mother, she would stay in morning, noon, and night?"

"No, Lord. She worked at night in some factory; she couldn't tell us the name of it for security reasons. Spies were everywhere. We couldn't even speak to our neighbours."

"Who told you all of that?"

"My mother, of course, who else can we trust if not our own mother? Well, are you going to do it?"

"No."

"But why, Lord?"

"That's why."

"Is that all you have to say on it?"

"Yes. And now it's closed. Go and see whether everything is running smoothly on the rest of the train." And with that, the conductor was gone.

"You thing I'm cruel, Scott May, don't you? Answer me."

"Yes."

"What would you have done?"

"I'd have made her a saint."

"But you know nothing about her."

"That's true, but you do and one more saint wouldn't make

much of a difference."

"That's where you're wrong; it would make a very big difference. Every country down there on earth has someone it believes it should be a saint. Just suppose I made her one, the first thing each country would do is check up on her background and then all hell would break loose."

"Why?"

"Well, between you and me, it wasn't a factory she worked in, but a brothel and, going on the report we have on her, she excelled at her job, above and beyond the call of duty. If anyone should be made a saint, it's the father. He was a good man."

"Where is he now, Lord?"

"With me. And she's with Satan."[15]

"But if she was just a prostitute, why was she sent there?"

"Because behind the brothel she worked in was a river with a very strong current, and now and then bodies would be taken out of it."

"But there are bodies being taken out of rivers every night."

"True, but not like this one. There were more bodies taken out then fish—and a lot of people fished that river. I'd say most of the town were on its banks every night. The rest were in the brothel. Most got home, but some never did. That's how they were caught—they murdered the wrong man."

"Why?"

"Greed. They knew he was a prominent man and would be missed straight away, yet they killed him. But it wasn't the river for him—they buried him outside the town in an old barn. When they had finished, they had the cows go over it so as no one would be the wiser. Then they shared the spoils and went their separate ways."

"But the owner of the barn—surely he would have heard them."

"He was a she and the sister of the leader of the gang. And she got it into her head that he had more on him. So she got to work on her brother and one week later, both of them dug him up."

"And did they find anything?"

"No money, but they did find a beautiful watch hidden in a secret pocket. It had been presented to him when he first entered the council and had his name and the date engraved on it. The next day they took the train to the city and, through his contacts, soon had it sold—and a good price they got for it. But there's no honour among thieves and soon the talk was doing the rounds. The talk got to the ears of the police and they were arrested. They gave the names of everyone involved to save their own necks."

"And did it save their necks?"

"Believe it or not, it nearly did. They had a lot of dirt on some of the most prominent people in the town. But it was their own that got them. They told the police about a number of unsolved cases—murder, robbery, drug dealing—and who was responsible. A week before the trial the sister[16] was found dead in her cell and two days later, someone put a knife into him. The rest were found guilty and hanged—including his beloved mother. And you want me to canonise her? Just suppose I did that. The minute the world found out the truth about her we'd have had the biggest exodus the church has ever seen. You have to be very careful whom you make a saint. Back in the old days, you could have gotten away with it, but not now."

"Is that good or bad?" Scott May asked.

"Well, I'll put it this way. There are one or two saints here with me who would be better suited with Satan, but money spoke in those days and so I'm stuck with them. And you don't want to upset them, or their families—too many connections. You'd be surprised what a word in the right ear could do."

"And you went along with it?"

"Of course I did. How do you think we survived down through the centuries? By being nice and turning the other cheek? Forget it. We did it first with bow and arrow and then with steel—which is still used. Survival of the fittest, sink or swim and all that. You know what I mean."

"I don't, Lord," Scott May said.

"Oh, but you do—and if for one second I thought you were trying to make a fool of me, the next conversation you'll have will be with my old friend Satan. There'll be no answering back there. Even when he was an angel, he gave no quarter. If he had played his cards right, he'd be second to me now."

"I thought that he was."

"No, he wasn't. But he was near. His one weakness was lack of patience and that was his downfall. But that's all in the past. It's the present we have to deal with, starting with you, Scott May. What do we do with you? Is it heaven or hell waiting for you?"

"You told me the jury was still out on me, Lord."

"So they are—but me being the Almighty, I have the power to speed things up. And me being me, sometimes I do just that."

"Is that fair?" Scott May asked.

"It depends on who you ask. If the soul went up, they say it was great. But if the soul went down, forget it—you wouldn't believe the names I've been called."

"I wonder why."

"What did you just say?"

"It was nothing, Lord."

"It had to be something. Speak up. Get it off your soul. Can't say chest, can I?"

"No, Lord. Why are Hitler and Jack the Ripper still on this train after what they did back on earth?"

"Believe it or not, there are worse than them on this train."

"Like who?" Scott asked.

"You were good at history when you were at school. Who would you think I'm speaking about? Rattle your brain, as your old teacher used to say."

"It's impossible, Lord. The names going through my head . . ."

"No, it's not impossible. Nothing is impossible on this train."

"If that's the case, some are on this train since time began."

"Right. And some have been added since you got on. Remember, this is one long train that makes no sound and can't be seen and has never stopped taking on or dropping off souls. You could say we move with the speed of sound. No, faster."

"But these people, Lord, they murdered left, right, and centre without thinking of their victims."

"That's true, but you didn't think of them either. Well, did you?"

"Lord, if you don't mind me saying, I was drunk."

"So were they—you with drink, them with power. Same thing. Any more questions, Mister May?"

"Yes."

"Well, let's have it."

"What's the difference between a soul and a spirit?"

"Very good, Scott."

"No more 'mister', Lord?"

"Not at the moment Now, to your question. A soul gets here straight away. A spirit, well, he is a different kettle of fish."

"In what way, Lord?"

"In this way—he doesn't know whether he's coming or going. You know he's dead, but he won't lie down. Spirits go around the place giving the rest of us a bad name."

"Surely with your power you could do something about it?"

"Yes, I could. But catching them, that's another matter. They work between two worlds and the second that they think you're on to them, they're gone back into the other one. Those spirits, they can learn very fast sometimes. I wonder is it only fools and loudmouths come to me?"

"Thanks, Lord."

"Don't mention it. Time to move and stretch my legs—that's the great thing about being God—I can get off the train any time I want to. No one else can, so no one can spy on me. It's a great feeling. Hopefully, when I get back, a decision will have been made about you. You'll know you are going up or down—which way do you think it will be? It's all on the day—or is it night?" And then he was gone.

"Alone again. Stuck between two barriers. I wish I was dead.[17] If I could cry, I would."

"And if I could get my mother canonised, I would."

"You again," Scott said.

"Me again," the conductor answered.

"Don't feel bad about it. The Lord upset you."

"Yes, he's in a funny mood lately. Maybe the father is giving him a bit of stick. And between you and me, he deserves it."

"Why?"

"He's driving the whole place mad. There are a lot of souls on the train that should have been dispatched years ago. Excuse that word; I brought it with me from the camp. It was one of the last words I heard and to tell you the truth it's one I'm very fond of. The fear that it put into my fellow Jew had to be seen to be believed."

"And did it put fear into you when it was you that they were speaking about?"

"Of course, but that's life. And then death. And here I am now, doing the same job. I'm watching souls as they wait on their decision—is it up or down?"

"You were born for this job," Scott May said.

"Yes, I believe I was. Timing was everything. When we got a trainload, say from Hungary, we had to dispatch them straight away. You must remember that it was the end of the war and Eichmann was like a madman. Every train that he could get his hands on he used. The rest of the war meant nothing to him. Even when the Russians were in Hungary, he still sent the trains. And when they took most of the soldiers off him, what did he do? He used collaborators. That man was on a mission and nothing was going to stop him.

"If I do say so myself, I was the best kapo in any of the camps. Like Eichmann, I stuck to the plan and got the results the SS wanted. That's why I lived out the war, right up to the camp being liberated. And then my own hanged me. Ungrateful shower of bastards. I should have done away with the rest of them, but the guards all disappeared one night and the next morning I had them all ready for roll call when they started to whisper among themselves. Now, had they done that the day before, it was the gas chamber straight away. These were the work prisoners."

"What do you mean by that?" Scott May asked.

"They were picked out as the strongest when they got there first. It gave them three extra months."

"For what?"

"For living, that's what for. And Christ, did they work. Sorry, Lord."

"Why are you apologising now when you didn't a minute ago?"

"Just in case he's come back. You never know what he's going to do. He told me he paid a visit to my camp when it was is full swing and was very impressed by the speed I got things moving at. He called it above and beyond the call of duty. So when they hanged me, this job was waiting for me."

"And the conductor before you was put out to pasture."

"Just like I will, hopefully later rather than sooner. Survival, they call it, even among the dead. You're the same as me."

"I am not, and never will be," Scott May answered.

"Guess how many people like you I've met, in life and death? We have soldiers and generals on this train and guess what— their answer is always 'orders', and 'we were only doing our duty'. Their orders were to kill everything that walked, including women and children and they did it no matter what army they were in or in what century. And if the Lord came to you and said that this will be your new job and you'll start straight away, your answer would be the same as mine."

"No."

"Would you be worried where I might end up—even if it meant my paying a visit to Satan and staying there permanently? You've gone quiet, Scott May. Think what your answer will be. It's my job and what happened to anyone else would be out of my hands, that's what your answer would be. Passing the buck, they call it. Don't worry, I did it myself, even he does it to get out of things. That's why he's down on earth now—out of sight, out of mind. Sometimes I wish it would all end and then I could be with my mother up in heaven, finally at peace. That's all I have to look forward to, to tell you the truth. It's the only thing that keeps me going. And what have you to look forward to, Scott May? Nothing. But [you have like heaven over hell in here], 18 that's everything, believe me. And I should know. The stories I'm told—I couldn't repeat them. Then again, maybe I will. You can't beat a good story, my mother always used to say."

"You were close to your mother?"

"Yes, I was, and not afraid to say it."

"Why should you? And anyway it's no one's business but your own."

"To hell with them I say and maybe God will say it as well to some of them—and hopefully soon. Anyway, time to go."

Scott May never bothered to look and see if he was gone. Why should he? Nothing surprised him any more. How in God's name was he put in this carriage in the first place with killers? "Although in his eyes we're all equal, I'll never know how he came to that conclusion. But then, it's him has the final say, not me."

Time went slowly for Scott May. Now and then, he would wonder what year it was, even what month he was in and how long more he had to stay here. At least the barricades are still up. Adolph or Jack would run at them now and then just to see whether they were still up. And when they couldn't go any further, they started telling Scott with their hands what they would love to do to him. Adolph would become a hangman, Jack a butcher.

"Mind you, I have to give Adolph credit—he'd have made a great actor. How the other souls put up with him and Jack is beyond me, but then they never spoke to me either. They could be old friends who knew them when they lived. Who gives a fuck?"

"I do."

"Jesus!" Scott May screamed out.

"The one and only right here with news for you. The jury were out for a long time with your case and others. It's time to sweep the decks clean of the old souls and bring in the new. Our mutual friend, the conductor, is a very busy soul right now. I picked the right one when I picked him, if I do say so myself. Now, you want to know where you're bound for. Look, the exit sign is lighting up. Love to see that—it puts a glow in my heart—but not on Jack's or Adolph's face. They're like two lunatics."

"But that's what they were, Lord."

"I'll have no talk like that. We're all equal on this train."

"But, Lord, if you don't mind my saying so, how can you be the same as me when you're the judge and jury and you can come and go as you please. I've been here since I was killed."

"And whose fault is that only your own?"

"Yes, and every day I have suffered since and now I want it

over. I have suffered enough."

"So you say, Scott May."

"Lord, I can only speak for myself; the rest will have to do it for themselves. Live and let live."

"No, you're wrong. You mean die and let die, Scott May."

"Why do you call me by full name? Once you called me mister. Do you call everyone like that?"

"It depends on who I'm speaking to. If you were a king, or even a queen—and we have a couple of those on the train—they like to speak and for you to listen, so you have to show them straight away who the boss is.[19]"

"And what would their answer be?" Scott May asked.

"Not too good. They remind me just what they've done for the Mother Church and how much it cost to feed and keep an army—and especially my priests—when they start to eat you out of house and home and building monasteries on every hill they could lay their hands on."

"What about Popes?"

"You'll have the company of one very soon now."

The conductor was standing next to Jesus.

"Well, what's on your mind, Conductor?"

"Lord, I need help straight away. It's getting out of hand."

"And whose fault is that?"

"Yours or your fathers, Lord. I hope you don't mind me saying so. And please hold onto your temper, I have enough problems without you screaming at me."

"Tell me, Conductor, do I look angry?"

"No, Lord, but it's early yet."

"Another ass hole."

"Lord, say some prayers and you'll be alright, believe me."

"You aren't trying to take over my job by any chance, are you? Answer me or you'll be with the other lot that's about to go."

"No, Lord. I'm just trying to make it a safe passage for everyone."

"And you're leaving us as well, Scott May. You won't be sorry to see the back of us, will you?"

"It depends on where I'm going and who's going with me," Scott May said.

"Here come the others and it's time for you to join the queue."

"What, now?"

"Yes, right now."

"My legs are starting to shake."

"You'll be alright. Wish it was me that was going."

"You can take my place if you want," Scott May said.

"Afraid not. I'm here to stay," the conductor answered.

"How do you know that?"

"He's just after telling me."

"You mean right now?"

"Yes, that's exactly what I mean. This very moment."

"My good soul, he's the Almighty and he's here, there, and everywhere." Then the conductor let out a shout to the back of the queue. "You lot back there, behave yourselves and get back in line or you could be joining the other gang. Do I make myself clear? I want to hear an answer now."

"Sorry, Conductor, but it's been a long wait for us."

"And what about the rest? Do you think they came on board yesterday? Or me, for that matter."

"But you love your job."

"Who said that?

"I did," God answered. "Am I wrong in saying that?"

"No, Lord. Now it's time to begin. Right, Scott, fall in here before I go."

"What was your name on earth?"

"Fritz Canaries[20]—a pure German name. The only problem was, I was a Jew and, as you already know, they weren't too gone on us."

"Well, it was nice to have known you. Pity we didn't meet on earth."

"Well, had you lived in my time and we had met, we might have become friends, who knows? And of course, no war. But there will always be wars. Their leaders all want to be gods, am I right?"

"Who are you asking, me?" Scott May said.

"No, he's speaking to me. Am I right, Conductor?"

"You're on the ball, Lord."

"But I'm always on it. Have to be. Who else would do my job? Any ideas, Mister Conductor?"

"No, sir, none at all. And please stop trying to read my mind, you know it makes me nervous."

"Why should it do that?"

"How should I know, Lord?"

"If you have a clear conscience—that's *if* you have one—than you've nothing to worry about, have you?"

"No, Lord."

"Now, can we get on with the job?"

"You're in a bit of a funny mood tonight, if you don't mind my saying so."

"Not in the least. Should I mind?"

"Lord, you're standing in the souls' way and some might think you don't want them up there with you."

"Let them think what they like. They're not supposed to think. Neither are you, now we're on the subject."

"But we do, Lord. As your father once said, you can't beat a fertile mind."

"I don't remember him saying that."

"Maybe you weren't listening."

"I hear everything. Nothing passes me."

"Begging your pardon, Lord, it seems this did."

"Is that so? Is there anything else you know of that might have slipped my mind?"

"Right now, no. But if I think of something, you'll be the first to know. Now will that make you happy, Lord?"

"I'm always happy. And I know what answer you're about to give me, Conductor."

"Of course you do. You never play fair, Lord."

"I played fair when I walked the earth as a human and where did it get me?"

"You have to forget the past, it'll only eat you up."

"So a Jew says."

"Lord, you forget you were one also."

"Yes, and my own nailed me to a cross."

"And *my* own hanged me."

"Yes, they did. But you can't blame them—you brought enough of your own to their deaths."

"Under duress and under orders. And with a sad heart, I might add Lord."

"Are you joking me? Even Satan was impressed with your workload, and that says something.."

"I always tried to do an honest day's work. Keep the mind clear and get on with the job."

"Even at the cost of your fellow man?"

"That's the situation I was in and the only way out was up the chimney or, in my case, the rope. But you saw all of it yourself. Why didn't you stop it?"

"In what way could I have stopped it? You seem to have all the answers. If you were me, what would you have done? I'm waiting, Conductor."

"When we have all the souls off the train, I'll answer you. They've waited long enough. Let them go to heaven and be with your father and finally have their peace. It's the least we can do."

"Are you trying to blackmail me, Conductor?"

"No, Lord, I'm just trying to do my job."

"Like speaking to a medium and not telling anyone? Do I look like a fool to you? Answer me or no one gets off this train, and I don't ive a damn who hears me. I'm waiting."

"For God's sake, will you please answer him," Scott May pleaded.

"Yes, I have spoken to a medium—not once but a couple of times. And he asked me what it was like to be a kapo in a camp. Whether it was Auschwitz (which had a sign as you entered saying 'work makes you free'—but then that sign was up in most camps) or the one he had been sent to was all the same. Death was the final result."

"As you should know."

"Thank you, Lord, for reminding me. I don't know what I'd do without you."

"Just keep it up and you'll soon know, Conductor."

"Now Lord, had I been in your shoes or sandals—do you still want me to answer your question?"

"Of course. If I didn't I wouldn't have asked you, would I?"

"First, I would have paid a visit to the camp . . ."

"And which one would you recommend?"

"The one you did pay a visit to, Lord."

"And who, may I ask told you this?"

"That I can't remember. A touch of amnesia."

"I hope you didn't have that problem when you spoke to the medium."

"Not that I can remember, Lord. Then, when I had seen it with my own eyes, I would pay a visit to Churchill and Roosevelt—"

"What about Stalin?"

"No. I don't think you'd have got far with him."

"Why not?"

"He was as mad as Adolph—maybe even worse."

"A fellow passenger and you to speak of him like that!"

"I should have spoken like this when I lived. May I continue?"

"Please do."

"Failing that I would have put words into the head of bomber command."

"To do what?"

"To bomb every railway line that led to the camps. Even blow up the camps themselves."

"You mean kill the prisoners?"

"Why not? They were as good as dead already. At least that way you would have got the guards as well. But nothing was done, was it, Lord? Even you did nothing. You just sat back and watched it all. Not one finger did you lift. Nothing. You left a race of people—who had crucified you, which was wrong—to be nearly wiped off the face of the earth."

"How dare you speak to me like that?"

"You asked me to answer your question, and I answered truthfully. What more do you want me to say, Lord?"

"You're finished as a conductor on this train and that's all I have to say."

"And you've said enough. Now apologise to him."

"Father, I don't say I'm sorry to anyone, especially to him."

"You do and you will."

Scott May sat back down on his seat and couldn't believe what he was seeing and hearing.

"You've been getting out of hand for some time. I should have nailed it on the head sooner, but your mother said it was only a passing thing and that you'd soon get over it. Well, son, I'm finished listening to your mother where you're concerned. It's time, you grew up and got into the live and let live situation."

"Father, I hope you don't mind my saying this, but I've heard all this before."

"Of course you did, but did you listen? No. Well, son, I think it's time you went back to school and your teacher will be the conductor."

"Him?"

"That's right. Unless you know of another one on this train? Well, do you?"

"No, but—"

"No buts, understand? Conductor, I want this carriage emptied straight away. And in future, if you have a problem, call me right away. Now start. Son, you come with me. You're only in the way here."

"But this is part of my job, father."

"Not any more. I think it's time we as a family sat down and had a long talk. It's long overdue, don't you think?"

"Yes, father." And with that, both were gone.

"I think I have to sit down and get some feelings and air into me, if that's possible. If I hadn't seen it with my own eyes, I wouldn't have believed it. Would you, Scott May?"

"No. I'm still in shock."

"Well, at least you know where you're going now. I'd say you'll be bumping into the father a lot when you get up there."

"I don't mind. He seems like a nice person."

"So is the son, but he has a quick temper and lately boredom has set in. And what can the father do with him? Send him back down to earth for a couple of years. In to one of the hot spots. That'll keep him busy for some time. As for me, I'll carry on doing my job to the best of my ability and now it's show time, as they used to say in the clubs of Berlin: It's curtain-up time, ladies and gentlemen, and what a show we have for you tonight! And as for you, Scott May, we'll meet again. The big question is when, I suppose. Maybe when this train stops running and there's no more earth. Do you know the one thing I miss most?"

"Your wife?" Scott May answered.

"Do I look mad to you?"

"No."

"Good."

"Then what do you miss?"

"A good book. Laugh if you like."

"Maybe he'll put a library on the train if you ask him," Scott May answered.

"He will. And a cinema as well just in case we get bored. Now, to get the ball rolling. Who's down at the front?"

"I am."

"And who are you?"

"Henry the eighth, king of England and most of the world, that's who I am."

"Well, Henry, seeing as you were once a king, you can do the honours and lead the way." No reply.

"Christ, he's gone already. Talk about deserting the sinking ship."

The queue now started moving slowly towards the exit door.

"You'll have to get in line, Scott May."

"Ready I am, and able."

"Good man. I know what I'm saying. Sometimes it's nice to think of what we once were, even if it's only for a second. Don't you agree?"

"With all my heart," Scott replied. "Those people that I killed all those years ago—maybe now we can become friends. I hope so."

"Don't worry, Scott May. There are no enemies up there."

"Thank God for that."

"Were you a hippy when you lived?"

"Why?"

"Well, you'll be meeting a lot of them when you get up there. They wanted to get back to nature and they did—six feet under. And you don't get any closer then that, do you?"

"No."

"We're there. My family will meet and welcome you."

"Thanks. You never mentioned them to me before, only the wife.[21]

"Well, my parents, my wife, two children, and brothers and sisters will be there for you. Tell them I love them and will never forget them."

"How did you arrange that?" Scott May asked.

"I spoke to the Almighty."

"Then why didn't you get a message to them yourself?"

"They want nothing to do with me, that's why. You know I was a kapo?"

"Yes."

"And I would assemble the people according to who was to live and who was to die. Then it was the doctor and his thumb to decide their fate. Well, the fate of my family was death and, like Judas, I led them to it. As my father was being pushed into the gas chamber, he turned and spat in my face, calling every curse he could think of down on me. The Germans, who were watching, thought all of this was very funny. One of them handed me his stick, saying 'He has insulted you. Use it.' I tried to defend my father, saying, 'He spoke to me in Hebrew, how could you understand what he said?' He took out his gun and put it to my head. "Use it or die with the rest of this shit. It's up to you.[1]

and I did what he said, just to live another couple of weeks. My own father and family. What a son I turned out to be. And the hatred I had seen from the Germans toward the Jews was nothing to the hatred that came out of my father's eyes at that moment."

"And you want me to give him your love?" Scott May asked.

"Yes. And tell them I suffer every day and that one of his curses worked."

"Which one?"

"I don't know. Promise me, Scott May."

"I promise."

"That makes me very happy. That will help me through here. How long more I will be here is now up to the Almighty."

Then the door opened.

"Time to go through, Scott May."

As Scott looked out, he turned and said, "There's nothing but blackness out there."

"Have no fear. He is out there waiting with open arms. And peace is there too. Now go."

He felt a push and it was as if he were in a parachute, gliding towards heaven. Any doubts he had had were now gone. He felt at peace with himself for the first time in—how long?

Now he was in a tunnel. "Go with it. It has to finish soon.' As he came out of it, he saw people sitting down, other people walking around holding hands. "I wish there were someone whose hand I could hold."

He was starting to slow down and the cloud in front of him was beginning to clear. As he looked through it, he could see familiar faces, standing as if they were waiting for him. One looked like his grandmother, he had been only six when she died. But it felt just like yesterday that she used to play with his toes while he fell asleep. Now he began to recognise everyone in the group, "Thank God, I'm not alone any more." He felt a wave of happiness shoot through him. "I'm back with my family at last."

Between Peace and War

John Sims was born in the family home, just outside the town of Chesterfield in the year 1916. Some months later, the family moved back to their apartment in London, where he was looked after by a nanny. The next four years were a very happy time for him—people coming and going, parties in the house, everyone smiling—then suddenly, it was all gone.

Walking home on a foggy December night, his parents were killed by a hit and run driver. He remembered his cheeks being touched gently while he slept on the sofa after the funeral by a beautiful, feminine, scented hand with each nail painted a different colour, just like a rainbow.

Back in the family home with his grandfather he learnt the ways of the farm; "You're never too young to learn," he would say to him. But it was up in the skies he wanted to be, as he watched the pilots fly low over their land. Then in 1931 his grandfather was killed. The tractor he was driving overturned as he cleared a ditch.

As John stood by his coffin in the house, shaking hands with the neighbours and family friends, he felt himself getting faint and had to sit down. Between the people, the painted hand reached out and touched his hair. He knew the touch straight away and looked up, but all he saw was the back of its beautiful owner walking out the door.

The years passed fast; now it was 1938 and still he wanted to fly. So he left the farm in the hands of his foreman and joined up; dark clouds where gathering across Europe and he wanted to be ready. Some weeks later he had a dream. In it he was at war with Germany, shot down and was brought to their headquarters for interrogation and beaten. One of his interrogators said to get him a glass of water, then a finger touched him. He looked up and fainted.

But first to the beginning. The first day he flew his instructor asked him, "Were you up in many planes?"

"No," John replied. "Why?"

"Well, I didn't tell you to do anything, yet you're doing it perfectly. Strange."

When he had finished and become a pilot, Prime Minister Chamberlain told the country that they were at war, and so it came.

The first year was a disaster; the bombers came every night, not giving a damn where they dropped. John and his fellow pilots met them over London and loved it. He had never experienced anything like it. They were ready to die for one another, and a lot did, but they drove them back.

Six months later John was shot down over France and was captured two days later; he had gone to a house where he had been told he would be safe but he was betrayed.

On the road back to Paris the Gestapo man said, "They'd hang their own mother for money."

They locked John in the cell from where he could hear screams coming from a room he had passed on the way in. Then he heard someone being dragged out and, some minutes later, he heard shots coming from the courtyard.

That night they came for him, pushed him down on a chair, and started with their questions. How many planes had they; he answered truthfully that he didn't know. The first slap hit him. Next question: have you ever shot down a German plane? "No," he lied. Then they beat him with their belts; when he fell on to the floor, they started to kick him.

"Liar. We know you shot down two. Maybe they ran out of fuel and the holes in their cockpit were caused by a woodpecker. Answer me." He pulled John back on to the chair by his hair. "Get him a glass of water."

When he came to, he was back in the cell, covered in blood. His eyes were starting to close when the door opened and the woman came in.

"You don't look too good to me. How are they in Chesterfield?" she asked.

"Why don't you drop over and find out?" he whispered. "Who are you?"

"Your mother was my sister," she answered.

"And you became a traitor. I dreamed this would happen."

"I believe you. It's a gift; my father had it as well."

"Do you know how it will end?"

"No, do you? I'll let you into a family secret; I killed your parents and your grandfather, thinking that you would be handed over to me. But he was a cute old fox and put you in the care of the foreman. All my hard work went down the drain. I was going to drown you in the Riviera—not the Thames, too dirty. All that land and money left to you, it still makes me sick."

John kicked her in the legs; she fell back screaming on to the mattress. He jumped on top of her and started to strangle her.

Then he was hit on the head and collapsed back on to the bloody floor.

For the next month, they would beat him up, give him a chance to recover, and then start again. Then, one morning, he could only guess what day it was, they dragged him out past the room and in to the courtyard, dropping him down on the cobblestones by the main wall. One with a gun in his hand stood over him.

"I'm an officer, not a spy," he said.

"Is that so?" and he started to laugh.

In his last seconds, John looked up at the officers' window and there she was, smiling and waving down. Then he saw a rope appear over her head. "Thank you, God," as the bullet smashed in to his brain.

Four years later, wearing a civilian overcoat, she was caught by the resistance trying to flee France. First she tried to bribe them; then she said she was only doing her duty.

"Of course you were," the leader said as one of them threw a rope over the branch of a tree.

"I'd say it'll hold. There's not much weight on her. Ready?" the leader asked.

"You're not frightened, are you? I mean, you must have seen this many times. How does it feel now that it's you who'll be swinging?"

Then she threw herself down on to the ground and begged for mercy. "I'm too young to die," she screamed.

"So were my friends that you caught. Did you show them mercy? No. You reap what you sow."

They tied her hands behind her back. "Enough of this. Hang her."

"You can't, I'm English. Please listen to me."

"Put something in her mouth; she's starting to annoy me."

One took his dirty hanky out of his trousers' pocket and shoved it into her mouth.

As they where putting the rope around her neck, she saw John Simms standing and smiling behind them.

"Impossible."

They pulled her right up to the branch and, when she had stopped kicking, one asked the leader, "Do we cut her down or leave her hanging?"

"What do you think? Let's go. There's a lot of work to be done at the top of the hill."

The leader turned and looked back down, where he saw a young man in a dirty RAF uniform looking up at her body. He said nothing to the others, but blessed himself and started to pray.

The Rose Murders

Mary Ryan was rushing home after working late. She had not wanted to work late, but Mr. Long had said, "Either you work late or out you go." He always told her there were plenty of other girls out there looking for work.

As she rushed home, she didn't notice the stranger watching her.

"Damn, I'll take the short cut home and that will save me at least fifteen minutes," she thought as she started across the common. Half way across, she felt she was being watched. When she turned and looked behind her, there was nothing except shadows, and yet, she couldn't shake the feeling .

Then suddenly, from somewhere in the darkness, she heard a high pitched laugh.

"Who's out there?" she cried. "It's not funny, do you hear me?"

Back came a voice saying, "Just me and my knife."

Mary screamed, "Leave me alone," as she ran towards the light of a house. "Help me. Help me,' she gasped. A dog in the yard of the house started to bark.

"Thank god," she said. "He'll bring someone out."

Just as she came near the house, the knife struck for the first time. Mary felt no pain. All she was thinking about were her parents and her little brother, as the knife struck again and again.

It was a cold damp November the thirteenth. The killing had begun. Jennifer Blakeley was lying in bed and thinking back on her life. As a little girl she used to love watching her father walk his beat and seeing the respect people showed. But not now. How things have changed. Now there's no respect for the law. When she joined the police force her father had been as pleased as punch; but eighteen years on and now a detective inspector, she wondered whether she had done the right thing.

Just then, the phone rang.

"Hello, Inspector, its me," Peter Johnson's voice said. "I'm out at the common where a jogger has just found a woman's body. I'll tell, you some madman must have done this, because after cutting her up, he put her in a kneeling position, as if she was praying. And to top it all, he put a rose in her hand."

When he had finished, she said, "Give me twenty minutes and I'll be right over."

"See you then, ma'am."

The killer was very happy with his night's work. The fear in the girl's eyes, and her pleading with her hands had turned him on.

"And putting the rose in them was a brilliant idea. Next time, I'll have another rose so they'll know its me. But now I must clean up the inside of my car and burn some clothes."

As he was cleaning his car, a neighbour walked by and said, "Good morning. It's a beautiful day."

"Yes. It *is* a beautiful day." And he thought, "If only she knew."

She arrived at the common a little later than she had expected. Already a crowed had gathered. The body was closed off from the public and the pathologist was doing his work. Sergeant Johnson saw her coming and walked towards her.

"'Morning, ma'am."

"'Morning, Sergeant. Tell me, which one found the body?" He pointed to a man of about twenty five and called him over. The man told her, "I jog here every morning, and sometimes in the evening. As I was going around, I saw her. The morning dew was just rising and at first I thought she was meditating or something; but as I got closer I knew something was wrong. I shouted over 'Good morning,' but got no answer. I walked towards her and it was then I saw the blood on her face and her hands. They were holding a rose. I'm sorry for getting sick all over the place."

"That's okay," Inspector Blakeley said. "Please give one of the officers your address and phone number, just in case we want to get in touch with you. And thank you.

"Sergeant, find out how many entrances there are onto the common. And find out whether any of the people living around here saw or heard anything suspicious."

"Okay, ma'am."

Four weeks later, on the thirteenth of December, Joan Wright was doing her Christmas shopping. As she walked from one shop to another, she thought to her self, "Christ, I'm spending too much. But to hell with it, a nice bath, a glass of wine, and some soft music—what more could a girl want?"

He had been following her for the last half hour and was thinking to himself, "If only she knew. This will be her last Christmas." Inside one pocket was the rose and, in the other, the knife.

She crossed the road. He followed. She stopped to look at the shop assistants decorating the windows and thought to herself, "I just love Christmas and everything that goes with it."

As she turned around the corner to her new apartment, one of her bags started to break. "Oh God, I hope this holds together until I get in."

Joan lay down her bags at the doors of the lift. She didn't hear him coming up behind her. He grabbed her hair with one hand and, with the knife in the other, cut her throat. This time he put the rose in her mouth. "Easy. Too damned easy," he thought.

In between the murders, the police had gone from house to house, from estates to mansions, and all around the surrounding countryside asking questions. Now PC Ryan and PC James were coming into a cul-de-sac.

"Thank God," Ryan said to James, "this is the last. My feet are killing me. Twenty houses. Here, you take one half, I'll take the other."

So Ryan started at number one and James took number twenty. As they went from house to house, curtains were pulled back and eyes follow their every movement.

"Sweet Jesus," James said to himself. "Nothing gets missed here."

As they got nearer to one another, James knocks at number thirteen. No answer. Then an old lady from next door came out and said, "There's nobody at home, but would you like some tea and biscuits?"

"Thank you, madam, we'd be delighted. Anything to rest our feet."

As they sat down to tea, Miss Brophy told them about every neighbour; all about the fights and the divorces.

"And your next door neighbour, madam?"

"Poor Mr. Stanley is a lovely man. He loves his garden. He lives alone since his mother died. Loves going to shows and singing in the church choir. Only the day before last, a parcel of flowers were sent by the distributors, although their flower shop has been closed for some time. I suppose he brought them to his mother's grave. Between me and you, he's not been right since his mother died. You hear him coming and going at all times of the night. He used to work at the library, but he got into a fight with the manager and left. Sometimes you can hear him singing out loud."

After taking it all down James and Ryan thanked the old lady and, as they left the cul-de-sac, Ryan said to James, "And you thought it was lovely and quiet around here." They both laughed.

Back at the station they added their report to the thousands of others.

The maintenance man found Joan Wright. He couldn't believe what he was seeing. Just this morning they'd had a long chat about her job, her boy friend, and her singing in the shows. She'd told him one day she hoped to sing on a London stage. A beautiful girl—and for her life to end like this.

Panic started to set in as he rang the police. They arrived within minutes.

"Sergeant Johnson, you won't believe this, but the security cameras aren't working in this building. No one saw anything, no one heard a sound, and yet people were coming and going all the time. Maybe the cameras on the main street will tell us something later."

The Commissioner called a meeting. Everyone was told to be there. No excuses accepted for not attending. At the meeting, the Commissioner said to Detective Inspector Blakely, "We've done what you asked and said nothing about the rose. And yet the bastard could walk around the main street of this city, pick out a girl, follow her home and kill her, all in broad daylight."

Detective Inspector Blakeley stood up to address the meeting. "This is what we have so far. Information received tells us that both girls loved to sing. We were also informed that Joan Wright sang lead in one of the shows and there was a lot jealousy among the cast. Some of them said she did more then sing for the producer. We've put in long hours between house to house inquiries and following up any leads we've got and that's it. My God, four weeks on and still nothing. But from now on, and listen to me on this, no holidays, no going off sick. And I don't give a damn whose wife is expecting; she can have it on her own because this madman is just starting and I want him stopped before he kills again.

"That's it. Has anyone questions? Okay, meeting closed."

Outside the office the Commissioner called Jennifer Blakely over and asked her how her mother was. She told him that the last stroke nearly killed her and she'd had to put her into a home.

"Now all she does is look out of the window and wait to die."

"You know, Jenny, I don't think she ever got over your father's death. Your parents and I go back a long way and if there's anything I can do, just ask."

"I understand, Sir. And thank you."

"By the way—anything on what kind of knife he used?"

"Yes. It's an old one—about a hundred years old."

"That's all we need, a knife from Jack the Ripper's time. If the papers get hold of this, they'll nail me to the nearest tree."

Just then a photographer from the local paper took a photo of them.

"Thank you, ladies and gentlemen. See you on the front page, first thing tomorrow morning."

Trevor Stanley got up feeling great. It was Sunday, and every Sunday he sang in the church choir. Now it was time for a shower and breakfast.

He looked out the bathroom window and saw the lad from the shop delivering his newspaper. "Wonder if they'll be telling anyone about the last one? No satisfaction there. Too easy. But still, I could have been caught by one of her neighbours. I suppose they were too busy with Christmas coming."

After the shower, he went out to the hall to pick up the paper and, on the front page, he saw the people looking for him— Commissioner Daly and Inspector Blakely. "So these are the people who are calling me a madman. A Yorkshire Mick and a London bitch. I'll give them mad. Mind you, she's not a bad-looking woman. How would she feel if my knife went around her throat?" He started to laugh.

When his bell rang, he looked out. It's that old bag from next door, Miss Brophy.

"Good morning Miss Brophy, how can I help you?"

"Just dropped over to tell you two police men were here the other day. They were going from house to house asking questions like did we see anything suspicious."

"And what did you tell them, Miss Brophy?"

"Oh, not a thing. But you and the lady from number seven weren't in so they said they'd be back."

"All right, Miss Brophy, thank you. I have to rush now—church choir and a meeting after," he said as he closed the door.

"She said nothing. Nothing my arse. If I know her she'll have given them my family history and everyone else's in the place. I must be more careful from now on. I gave them enough clues with the number thirteen. I was born on the thirteenth, my house is number thirteen, the library was number thirteen. That's it. Next time I'll kill on the twenty-sixth and that'll keep them going for sometime.

"But I'll have to be careful about Miss Brophy. She watches everyone like a hawk. Time for church."

Between the killings one or two clues started to surface: first, that both women loved to sing, and second, that at one time they sang in groups. Joan Wright was excellent and was making good contacts with the show people in London.

"We also believe that he is between thirty and forty and must be a very strong willed man to keep his feelings bottled up for so long. As for the number thirteen we believe he is testing us. It could be his date of birth, it could be the day he left his job, or, more to the point, got sacked. But one thing is certain: he's going to and try and kill again, so if any one of you hear of a woman being threatened or attacked, report it immediately. We have pulled in every known sex offender, but this one we don't know anything about. So keep your eyes open and your nose to the ground.

"Just one thing more. The papers are saying maybe he's from London, Manchester, or even Leeds. Forget it. He's a local boy and maybe one of you has spoken to him already. So, no mention of the rose to anyone, especially the press, because the rose is his calling card."

"Thank you, Sergeant Johnson, for that report," Detective Inspector Susan Blakely said in the canteen after the meeting.

PC Ryan said to PC James, "Remember the house in the cul de sac? That was number thirteen. And the old woman said he'd had roses delivered to him. Do you think we should tell the sergeant?"

"Let's tell him later. Eat your breakfast before it gets cold."

Reverend Reeves was very pleased; the choir sang beautifully. Especially Trevor Stanley. His solos were just right.

After Mass, the Reverend approached the conductor, Mr. Jones, and said, "Your Christmas hymns were just beautiful. I was listening so much I nearly forgot I was saying Mass." They both laughed.

"Well, Reverend, a lot of hard work and a lot of hours went into it. And we have two extra hymns for Christmas Eve."

"Beautiful. And will Mister Stanley be singing solo on them?"

"I'm afraid not. These will have to be sung by our baritone, Mr. Llewellyn. I've just told Mr. Stanley. To tell you the truth, Reverend, he frightens me. When I tried to explain, he started screaming at me and calling me and Mr. Llewellyn, begging your pardon Reverend, Welsh bastards. And he also said he'd cut me up, 'But no rose for you, boyo, you're not worth it.'"

"I'll talk to him. But since his mother died, he's been a bit strange. I even heard him in the sanctuary, screaming to himself: 'So many were kneeling down, but too many roses.' I wonder what he meant by that?"

Later Reverend Reeves went up to Trevor Stanley and said, "Mr. Stanley, I think you owe both Mr. Jones and Mr. Llewellyn an apology."

"Fuck you. And fuck those two Welsh bastards. He wants a baritone, not a singer like me who everyone comes to hear. And fuck the rest of those pricks too. And as for you and your stupid sermons, you put everyone to sleep. You speak about the devil— what do you know about the devil? Me, yes me, I have walked with him. Have you, Reverend Stanley?" He started to laugh and the Reverend felt his body shaking. But he summoned up all his courage to tell Mr. Stanley, "In all my years as a vicar, I have never heard so much blasphemy inside the house of God. I'll ask you to leave. And, Mr. Stanley, don't come back until you feel better. I'll pray for you."

Stanley grabbed his coat and said, "Keep your prayers for yourself, Jones, and Llewellyn. You need then more then me." As he walked to the door, he turned to the Reverend, put his finger across his throat and then pointed at him. Then he started to laugh—a mad laugh.

That night the Reverend was wondering whether he should call the police and tell them about the threats. "Because truly Mr. Stanley is not well. No, I'll sleep on it. Maybe tomorrow I'll call them."

The days came and went[1] and every one breathed a sigh of relief. Some started to do their last minute Christmas shopping. Even Sergeant Johnson was caught on camera with the wife and kids.

"Great. Just great. It couldn't pick up a madman but it has me on it every minute. Nothing came from the footage of Joan Wright; two drunks fighting, kids fooling around, people rushing here and there, but not one suspect."

The days passed. The snow came and went. And yet they knew it was only a matter of time. Jennifer Blakely put up some Christmas decorations. "But for what? To be on my own? I'm off the cigarettes and the drink, my mother's gone senile, there's a lunatic walking around, and the press and the Commissioner are on my back."

Christmas Eve came. "Turkey ready. Food ready. Time for Midnight Mass. Funny how time changes a person. If my parents had asked me to go to Mass with them years ago, I'd have given them every excuse not to go. Now I'd give anything to have them with me."

After Mass, Jennifer Blakely went up to the Reverend to tell him how beautiful it was.

"Thank you, my dear. If I do say so myself, Mr. Johns has surpassed himself this year."

Just as he was about to tell her of Mr. Stanley's strange carry on, more people came over to congratulate him on the Mass. Jennifer Blakely grabbed his hand and said, "Got to rush. Merry Christmas to you."

"And a merry Christmas to you."

As she walked away he was saying to himself, "I must give that lady a ring."

"Twenty-sixth. Christmas is over. Christ, I hate Christmas. So how can I make my self feel good? Yes. I've got it—I'll kill someone. But who? Maybe that singer who was in the local Gilbert and Sullivan's Mikado. She murdered the musical, so I'll murder her." And he started to laugh. "Fair is fair," he said to himself.

Next door, Miss Brophy was getting worried about poor Mr. Stanley. He was getting stranger by the day. Only yesterday she had knocked on his door to ask him over for Christmas dinner. When he opened the door he told her, "Thank you, but no. I have left Christianity behind me. From now on, instead of looking for the good things in man, I'll look for the bad. But thank you, anyway."

Stanley got the car out of the garage. It was a 1960 Riley, as new as when it came off the assembly line.

"Now where does that bitch live? I know it's over by Merrill's Way, but where? She wasn't in the phone book; she must be ex-directory. Clever girl."

The car was cold, very cold. "It'll take time to warm up. Now, do I have everything? My beautiful knife and my rose. Can't buy any more. They must have gone to every flower shop in Yorkshire, looking and asking whether they knew anyone who bought them. The fools; if only they knew, Mother had a flower shop for thirty years and had contacts all over Holland and England. Now and then flowers are still sent to our house. Like the Dutch roses. They must have got my check by now. And my letter saying no more flowers.

"The shop has been closed since mother died. This will be the last rose. After that, I'll get a new flower. But which one is as beautiful as the rose?"

Jennifer Blakeley had a very quiet time over the festive season. On Christmas morning, she went and visited her mother. The doctor told her not to worry, "She's in safe hands and has the best of care."

Later on, back at home, after trying to eat a bit of dinner, she decided to go for a walk. As she walked she started to think of the murders. "Number one, they all sang. Both were cheerful and friendly. We went through all the people that they sang with, past and present, and not a thing. Both girls like to keep fit and loved a good book; we've done the keep-fit classes, so that leaves the library. But that's closed for the holidays. Must get Sergeant Johnson to check it out."

Stanley drove around without any luck. As he drove back to town, he thought, "I'll have to stop at some pub for a whiskey. These roads—all I can do is crawl with the frost." Up ahead he saw the Highway Inn and pulled in.

Inside it was nice and warm. "Whiskey, please." As he sipped his drink, his eyes started to take in the place. Some married couples and a lot of young people around a guitar player. Then he looked down at the end of the bar, and who was calling a drink but his ex-boss, Mr. Dunn from the Library.

"He must be out with his wife for a drink." Then he watched as Mr. Dunn sat down and put the drink down in front of a woman. He couldn't see her face, but he had seen that bracelet before.

He had another drink, then, "Time to go," he thought. "But first, got to go to the toilet."

As he passed Mr. Dunn, he looked at the woman and, lo and behold, who should it be only prim and proper Miss Jarvis.

"Well, Mr. Dunn, what have we here? Taking the staff out for an after-Christmas drink?"

"No, Mr. Stanley, you have it all wrong. I just happened to bump into Miss Jarvis and asked her in for a drink."

Stanley laughed and said, "I know the bumping you were doing. Now I know why Miss Jarvis here was getting away with murder. You're screwing her, aren't you?"

"How dare you make suggestions like that?" said Mr. Dunn. With that Miss Jarvis screamed at him, "How dare you? You fucking lunatic. You should have been locked up years ago— and your mother as well."

Then Stanley had her by the throat. As he did so, Mr. Dunn hit him, but it was no good. Some of the young people ran over and pulled Stanley off Miss Jarvis. At the same time, the barman was calling the police. "Get over here quick, there's a bloke going mad here."

They held Stanley down until the police arrived. When they came, one said, "All right, what's going on here?"

Mr. Dunn was the first to speak. "I bumped into my working colleague at the mall and invited her to have a drink, and so we came in here. Later that lunatic came over and started screaming at us. Next thing he had Miss Jarvis by the throat. The rest you know."

He looked at Miss Jarvis then at the other man. "All right, give me your side of the story. Your name first."

"My name is Trevor Stanley and I worked with these two people at the library. While I was working there, I had a disagreement with Miss Jarvis. She reported me to that prick; she also told a pack of lies. Dunn said he was suspending me for two weeks, so I told him what he could do with his job and he said 'Fine. Your sacked.' Now I know why—he was screwing Miss Jarvis."

"All right, we've had enough of that talk."

Then he went over to Miss Jarvis, who was still shaking and in shock. She said, "I started working at the library five years ago and at first I thought he was a nice lad. But after a couple of weeks, I became frightened of him. He was always staring at me and putting roses on my desk no matter what time of the year it was. They had a florist's shop. But when his mother died, it closed down. But even after that, the rose would still come and I told him to stop it. Even the other girls were frightened of him. After a while he used to follow me home. One day I told him at work that if he didn't stop giving me flowers or following me home, I would report him to the police. Then he started to call me every name in the book, so I reported him to Mr. Dunn. They had an argument and he was sacked."

PC Robins asked, "Do you want to press charges, Miss?

"No, no," she said. Mr. Dunn's wife might take it up the wrong way and so might our colleagues at work. All we are is just good friends."

Then went over to the barman. "Do you want to press charges?" he asked.

"No. Just get him out of here. I never want to see him in this place again."

"Mr. Stanley, how many drinks did you have?"

"Just a small whiskey."

"I'm letting you off with a caution. No one here wants to press charges against you, which is a pity. But if I ever hear of you going ncar Miss Jarvis or Mr. Dunn again, I'll see that you're locked up."

"So you believe that prostitute and that prick before me?"

"I'm telling you, Mr. Stanley, for the last time, keep your mouth shut and get out of here."

Stanley glared back at PC Robins. The policeman said, "Anything else on your mind, Mr. Stanley?"

"No," he answered and started to laugh as he walked away.

"I'll have to find more out about him. There's something wrong with him; something very wrong."

When Stanley had pulled into the car park two sets of eyes had been watching him. They belonged to Tony Harris and John Prichard, better known as Zak and Driver, two of the best-known car thieves in town. As they watched Stanley go into the bar, they made their move. Zak said, "This fuckin' car is too old. Let's go for the other one."

"No," said Driver. "We'll take it. We can rob any of the new ones any time, but when will you see a car like this again?"

They moved across the car park and in two seconds were driving away in it. Driver said, "Come on, check it out. See what*s in it.

"Not a thing only a rose and an old knife. Let's try Antiques Joe, maybe we might get a couple of quid for it. First let's have some fun."

As they drove the car up to Roundwood Estate, a police car was coming in the opposite direction.

"Cool it," said Driver. "I don't think it's us they're after. As the police car passed them, Driver said, "Come on, let's give them a wave," and both started to laugh. "Wonder where they're going to?"

When Stanley came out of the bar, he could not believe what was happening to him. His mother's beautiful car was gone. He ran back into the bar screaming, "My car's been robbed."

"Will you calm down, Sir," PC Robins said. "Calm down."

"Are you listening to me?" Stanley asked. "My beautiful car has been robbed." Everyone in the bar started to laugh.

"I'll sue the owner of this kip."

"All right. What make of car is it?"

"A nineteen sixty Riley, that's what it is."

PC Robins said, "That shouldn't be too hard to find; there aren't many of them going around. Was there anything inside the car? Anything valuable?"

"No. Just my mother's watch."

PC Robins went out to the patrol car and called in.

"Robins here. The disturbance I went out to—his car's just been robbed. It's a nineteen-sixty Riley, and his mother's watch is in the compartment. I'll bet anything it's now going around Roundwood Estate been driven by Messrs. Harris and Prichard. And you won't believe this—we passed it when we were coming here."

"Okay, John we'll get a car up there straightaway."

He went back into the bar and Stanley and Mr. Dunn were at it again.

"Its all your fault," Stanley was saying.

"You should be locked up, you raving lunatic," Mr. Dunn was roaring back at him.

"All right, Mr. Stanley, that's enough. We'll take you home."

As they drove Stanley home, Robins was watching him in the mirror.

"This guy is hiding something. I'd bet my week's wages on it." Suddenly Stanley caught him looking at him and started to laugh.

"Just around the corner, that'll do me fine. Don't want you dropping me at my front door—what would the neighbours think?"

As Stanley walked up to his house, he was thinking, "I should have kept the knife in my coat. Stupid, but so what? They'll burn the car and I suppose everything in it."

As he put the key into the front door, he looked over at Miss Brophy's house and saw the curtain moving.

"That old bitch. Nothing passes by her."

As the police car passed Zak and Driver, Zak said there must be trouble in the pub, or else someone else must have nicked a car. They started to laugh.

"First we go down to Antique Joe and sell him the knife. Then we go down to Luigi's fish shop and have something to eat. I'm fed up of fuckin' turkey; give me fish and chips anytime."

As they came in to Cherrywood Drive, Zak said, "I hope he's there."

"Are you joking me?" They pulled up outside number six. Driver went in and knocked at the door as he waited for it to be opened, he heard from inside, "Get the door."

"Will you look who's here? Bonnie and—where's fuckin Clyde—of Yorkshire."

"Mabel, my love, I see you've lost about a pound."

"Are you trying to be funny?"

"Certainly not. May I speak to Joe, please?"

"Joe, there's that bloke who can't leave a car alone out here looking for you."

"All right."

Joe comes out. Well, Driver. What have you this time?"

"Zak, bring in the knife and the rose."

Zak gives the knife to Joe. "It's worth at least a hundred pound."

"Well, I'll tell you what you can do: take it away and if you get thirty you'll be lucky."

Zak said, "Are you joking me? This knife is years old."

"It is," says Joe. "But it came from a set that are fairly common around here. Now, if you had the whole set, that would be something else. Also, the knife's been used recently and whichever one of you tried to clean it did a bad job."

Driver said, "Not us. We just found it in the car out there after we nicked it. Both of these were in it."

Joe looked and saw the Riley. "If you had brought that car in, then honestly, we'd be talking money," he said

"Never mind the car. How much are you giving us for the knife?"

"Twenty pound. Take it or leave."

"Give it to us," Driver said. "And here's a lovely rose for your mother or your wife or girl friend."

"Very funny," said Joe. He gave them the money and, as he closed the door, said, "And a merry Christmas to you."

"Fuck you too," says Zak.

As they were getting into the car, Zak says, "Honest Joe? Antique Joe? Joe the robber would be more like it."

Joe put the knife in the dresser in the sitting room.

"Must clean it before I sell it. And he went into the kitchen. "Here," he said, "the boys gave me a rose to give you."

She says, "I wonder who the poor bastard is they robbed it from."

"God only knows," said Joe as she put the rose into a vase.

Zak saw the police car coming up the road and shouted at Driver, "Here they come, and here we go." As he did a quick reverse, the car started to skid in the frost.

"Turn the fuckin' thing around fast, or we've had it."

A gang of young teenagers were watching this nightly ritual. Among them was Mary Banks, whose little sister Jane and her friend had been killed six months ago. No one could prove who had done it, but she believed it was Driver and Zak; they didn't even stop after knocking them down. And they were seen burning the car later that night.

As the teenagers screamed on Zak and Driver, Mary prayed that the car would go out of control and the two bastards in it would get killed. But no such luck; they turned the car around and headed for the main road.

When PC Black and PC Neville saw the car reverse and then go into a skid, they thought they had them.

"Shit, they're after straightening it out. Look, they're making a break for the main road. Calling all cars. Nineteen-sixty Riley, green, coming out of Roundwood Estate."

As Zak tried to make it to the main road, the car went into a skid again. Zak had lost control.

"It hit a wall first and then straight into the back of a parked lorry," Neville was saying through the radio. "All cars, the stolen car has just crashed into the back of a lorry. Send an ambulance. I've a feeling we'll need one."

Inside the car, Driver was screaming. "My legs, my legs, they're caught."

"Shut fuckin up will you," said Zak as he got out. "I'm off. Don't give them my name, do you hear me?"

"Zak, don't leave me; don't leave me, Zak." But Zak was already gone.

"You lousy prick. I'll nail you for this."

PCs Black and Neville came upon the stolen car. As they did, a man jumped out and ran across the waste ground. Picking up his radio, he said, "Calling all cars. Man running across waste ground opposite Roundwood Estate. Suspect believed to be Tony Harris, better known as Zak."

Inside the car, Driver was screaming, "Help me. Help me."

"Well, well. If it's not Mr. Prichard. What's wrong?"

"Call an ambulance, please. My legs are killing me and I'm caught in here."

"Tell me, Prichard, did you call an ambulance for the two little girls you knocked down and killed? No. You just left them with every bone in their bodies broken."

"It wasn't me. I only heard about it the next morning."

"Pull the other one, Prichard," as they waited for the ambulance to arrive.

The young teenagers came down to see what was happening. One said, " Listen to that prick screaming in there. Hard man my arse. He's worse then an old woman."

After some minutes, the ambulance crew arrived and got him out. As they were taking him away, Mary Banks walked over to the back of the ambulance and called in, "I hope you die screaming. Remember me? Remember my little sister? You and that other coward Harris left her by the side of the road." And she spat at Prichard. "You scumbag."

"All right, love. He'll be stealing no more cars for a long time."

"But it was him that killed her."

"I know that love but we have no proof."

Hours later Zak was picked up. He was screaming, "I'm innocent."

Trevor Stanley knew time was running out. If they get the car back in one piece, they'll find the knife and the rose. The driver would not put any meaning into the rose because the police did not publish it. "If they burn it, I'm in the clear; but I can't take the chance. So what to do now? Too late for a train or a bus. No car. And if I got a taxi down to Whitby, he could radio back to tell the base where he's going. No. I've got to think of something fast. Wait a minute—Miss Brophy. She has a car. If I borrowed it and the police came she would tell them everything. No, I'll have to kill her."

He knocked on Miss Brophy's door. She opened the door slightly, leaving the chain on.

"It's you, Mr. Stanley."

"Yes, it is. I'm here with your Christmas present."

"Thank you, Mr. Stanley, but couldn't it wait until the morning?"

"I'm so sorry. I'll come back in the morning."

"No, no. That's all right. If you can't trust your next door neighbour, who can you trust?"

He came into the sitting room and said, "It's been a long time since I've been in here and it still looks the same."

"Cup of tea, Mr. Stanley?"

"No, thank you. What I came over for was your car."

Miss Brophy started to laugh and said,

"Mr. Stanley, you love your little joke."

"No joke, Miss Brophy."

Now she started to get frightened and said, "Mr. Stanley, please leave."

As she moved to the door, Stanley hit her with the poker.

"Your Christmas present, Miss Brophy. And now, my dear, the keys."

No answer came back. She was dead.

Stanley went into the kitchen where he knew all the keys were kept he spotted the car keys and her handbag. He opened it and found two hundred pounds.

"Now, what to do with her? Ah, I know. I'll put her in the armchair and if anyone looks through the window they'll think she's sleeping."

Stanley lifted up the body, making sure no blood got on him. After putting her in the chair, he put a rug around her. But her hair was splattered with blood.

"I'll have to get one of her hats. That'll cover it up."

After fixing her up, he stood back and admired his work.

"Christ, I should have been a make-up artist. I'd have been brilliant." He dimmed the sitting room lights and closed the door. It was starting to snow.

"That's all I need. That'll add another hour to the journey."

He got into the car and switched on the engine.

"Good, the tank is full. Lights on, and away we go."

As he pulled out of Miss Brophy's driveway, number seven was getting a bit of air. He had been down at the Rugby club all day and the wife was giving him hell.

"Wonder what that creep's doing with Miss Brophy's car?" he thought as he watched him drive out of the cul de sac. He went back into his house and said to the wife, "Listen, it was all an accident. I just went down for one pint when all of the boys came in and they would not let me go home."

"Is that right?" she said. "Did they put a gun to your head or did they chain you to the bar?"

"Very funny. You know that bloke that lives in number thirteen? He's just driven away in Miss Brophy's car."

"Maybe she gave him a loan of it."

"Maybe. But she's very touchy about things like that. Anyway, it's none of our business. And they've been neighbours for years."

"So, tell me, were any of the wives or girlfriends at the club, or did you all keep the secret?"

"What secret?" But he knew that no matter what he said, she would not believe him. But what a day. The best booze up I've had in a long time."

PCs Black and Neville followed the ambulance to the hospital. When they got there, they could still hear Driver screaming, "My legs. Will they be all right?"

Black said to Neville. "I just wish the kids who think he's a god could hear him now. Pity his neck isn't broken." They started to laugh.

The porters came, with one of them saying, "OK, son. You'll be all right. We're going to fix you up in no time."

After the doctor had fixed Driver up, PC Black went into him and said, "I'm charging you with stealing a vehicle, damage to private and public property, and the theft of an antique watch belonging to the owner of the car of that you stole—you and your good pal, whom we believe is none other than Tony Harris, alias Zak. We picked him up a couple of minutes ago and he's now saying that you must have been on your own."

"My pal! My pal, my arse. First he leaves me, then he puts a watch in his pocket and says nothing to me. Well, I'll tell you something, the only thing I found in the car was an old knife. That's all I swear, no watch, nothing. And a rose."

PC Black felt a chill going down his back.

"What's that you said?"

"Are you going deaf too? I said a knife, no watch, and a flower, which was a rose, all right?"

PC Black's hands were shaking as he got through to headquarters.

"This is PC Black over at St. Jude's hospital. I think I know who the rose murderer is."

"Hold it one second; I'll put you through to the murder division."

"Sergeant Peter Johnson here."

After hearing what PC Black said, the sergeant said, "Don't move or leave any of Prichard's relations alone with him. We're coming straight over.

"Get Inspector Blakely on the phone straight away and tell her where we're going."

Susan Blakely was taking a shower. "I'll be right over."

As she got dressed, she was thinking to herself, "Thank God. If he had the knife and rose with him, he was about to do another killing tonight."

Sitting on the bed in the hospital, Prichard saw the murder squad coming towards him. He thought, "Zak must have stolen another car and hit someone. Well, that's nothing got to do with me."

Susan Blakely and Sergeant Johnson went straight up to Prichard. Blakely said, "What did you do with the knife? No bullshit, Mr. Prichard, straight talk."

"I want my solicitor here. I'm not saying anything."

"Mr. Prichard, I don't know if you're aware, but your friend Mr. Harris is in custody right now. If you don't tell us what we want to know, I promise you that when you go down, you'll go down for a long time."

"Hold it a minute, will you—you didn't tell me what you want to know."

"All right Mr. Prichard, what did you do with the knife and the rose?"

"I sold it to antique Joe."

"That's Joe Brady in number six Cherrywood Drive. Thank you."

And as fast as they came in, they went out. Inspector Blakely was on her mobile phone.

"Get two cars over to Ash Drive. It's a cul de sac; close it off and watch number thirteen for any movements, but that's it until we get there."

Joe Brady couldn't believe what was happening to him. His wife had told him not to deal with those pricks.

"Look," Joe was saying, "all I did was buy a knife off them. I did not know it was stolen."

"Mr. Brady, all I want to know is where the knife is."

"it's here in the sitting room."

"I know you've already touched it, but just point it out to us and we'll do the rest. And the rose? Where is it?"

He brought her into the back kitchen.

"Where?"

"It's in a vase over on the fridge."

"Same kind. We have him now."

As they pulled out of Cherrywood drive, Inspector Blakely asked what back up they had.

"Four of our men are armed, so they'll go in first."

"Good. The others will be back up."

James Dwan knew he was in trouble. His wife had just been talking to Myra, the mouth of the rugby club. Anything that happens or that's going to happen, she knows about it.

"Do you know what she was just saying to me?"

"No. Was she wishing you a merry Christmas?"

"Very funny. Very fuckin' funny."

"While I'm slaving here, you're watching a strip tease by none other then Miss Tits. You and the rest of the rugby team and, lo and behold, the only woman in the place is Miss Tits herself."

"Listen, you're not going to believe this. While that was going on in the lounge, I was having a quiet drink with John Holland."

"I'm telling you now, this is the last straw with the club. Brian you married me, not the rugby team. You play a rugby match and you come back legless. That team can't even play without getting drunk. A shower of alcoholics—and that includes you. If that manager had any decency, he'd have the lot of you committed to an asylum. Twenty six years of age and we're up to our necks with the mortgage. We're living from week to week, but all that matters to you is the fucking rugby team and how you played and what position you're in in the league. I've had it. I'm telling you, you're not a little boy any more—now grow fuckin up."

James went up stairs and started to look up at the sky. Beautiful." He was looking at the houses around him, thinking, "All right, so we have a mortgage, but who hasn't? This is a lovely place and most of the neighbours are lovely people. And the price of the house has gone up by ten thousand. But you can't please everyone. If its not one thing, its another. I should have stayed with my mother." As he looked out the window, he saw movements in the snow. "Sweet Jesus, what's happening here?" The Police were moving from garden to garden.

"Rachel, come up here, quick."

"You can forget it. Call up Miss Tits. She'll come and give you a hand."

"Rachel, turn off the lights and look out the window."

"Christ what's wrong with him?" Rachel thought, as she pulled back the curtain. A face was looking at her then another. She knew it was the police. She screamed up at her husband, "What did you do at the club? The house is surrounded. I'm leaving you and never coming back."

Just then, there was a knock at the door. She opened it.

"Please keep quiet. We're the police."

"He's up stairs, Officer."

"Who's up stairs?"

"My husband. Himself and the fuckin' rugby club can go to hell."

The policeman started to laugh. "It's not him we're looking for. It's number thirteen, Mr. Stanley.

"But he's gone. My husband saw him drive away in Miss Brophy's car." He got on to the radio.

"This is Ferguson in number seven. Check out number twelve, they saw the suspect drive off in the car belong to the lady that lives in number twelve."

"Okay."

They knocked at the window. No reply. "Christ, she's a sound sleeper." They knocked again. Still no reply.

"There's something wrong here. We'll have to break the door to get in."

They hit the door together. One moved down the hall to the kitchen; the other went into the sitting room.

"Miss Brophy, don't be alarmed. "We're the police." Still no reply. He went over and started to shake her. As he did, he felt his hand getting sticky on her shoulder.

"Come in here quick," he roared. "And turn the lights on."

When they had turned on the lights, Miss Brophy's blank stare was looking back at them. There was blood all over the place and half of her head was stuck to the chair.

"Call Blakely and Johnson over here fast. And don't move anything."

"Jesus Christ, what did he hit her with?"

"The poker, Ma'am. There it is."

"Get Meehan to check it for fingerprints, just to be sure. Though I'll bet they belong to Mr. Stanley. "What about number thirteen?"

"We got the address of the retailer who was sending the flower samples to Mr. Stanley. Seems he did a lot of business with the mother and was hoping the son would open the business again. And one of the neighbours saw him drive away in Miss Brophy's car."

"What neighbour?"

"Number seven."

"Okay. We'll be over there, if you want us."

As they headed over to number seven, Johnson said, "He must have killed her for the car. And he was at her handbag. I'm guessing, with her Christmas pension, there must have been a nice couple of bob in it."

As they entered number seven, they could hear the wife having a go at her husband.

"This is the worst Christmas I've ever had. "First, you've been drunk for the last week, then Miss Tits did a free show, and now the police are all over my house. If this gets out, I'll have to pack up and move to another town—all over you."

"Listen," the husband said. "Don't wait. I'll pack them for you, right?"

"No, I'll pack yours now."

"This house is mine and if anyone's moving it's you."

"Excuse me, I'm Inspector Blakely, and this is Sergeant Johnson, can we ask you some questions, please?"

"Yes, of course."

"We've just found Miss Brophy's body. She's been murdered, we believe, by Mr. Stanley."

"Oh God. I don't believe it!"

"I'm afraid so. Can you tell us anything about Miss Brophy or Mr. Stanley?"

"To tell you the truth, I did not like Mr. Stanley. He gave me the creeps. I always got the feeling he was watching me."

"How is it you never told me this?"

"What for? All you were in interested in was your rugby club— and if you had enough money for drink."

"That's lies."

"Is it?"

"If you don't mind—Miss Brophy?"

"Dear old lady. Loved to talk. And when the cold came, she'd sit by her window, and, if you waved a hand, would wave back. That bastard Stanley—how could he do a thing like that? Between him and that other murderer of the two girls . . . "

Blakely and Johnson looked at one other but said nothing.

"Mr. Dwan, what kind of car did Miss Brophy own?"

"It was a Ford Escort; the colour was black, but I don't know the number."

"Do you know where he might be going to?"

"Afraid not. I never spoke to him, didn't like him one little bit."

"Hold it a minute," his wife Rachel said. "One day, I was having tea with Miss Brophy and Stanley came in with his mother. She said that Mrs. Stanley had been left a beautiful house by her brother a couple of years ago. I forget Mrs. Stanley's maiden name, but she said the house was in Whitby, and that if you look out the window you can see the old ruins and the graveyard."

"Thank you, Mrs. Dwan, we don't know how to thank you."

"Well, you could thank me by checking the rugby club's license and what time they're supposed to close at—and about having a license for a strip club."

"Inspector, please don't take any notice of my wife. I can assure you they're the strictest club in Yorkshire."

"We believe you, for now."

"He's a liar," his wife said. "If the truth stood up and gave him a kick in the balls, he wouldn't know it."

"Well, a merry Christmas to both of you. And thank you again."

As they left they could hear the husband saying, "If any of the committee heard what you just said, you'd get me expelled from the club."

"Good, I hope they do. As a matter of fact, I'll tell them myself.

"This is Inspector Blakely here. Get Whitby station on the radio, now."

"Whitby here. A suspect in three murders is coming your way. His name is Trevor Stanley. He's aged about thirty four, and he is very dangerous. If you find him approach him with caution. We're on our way. Get a patrol car on the main road, straightaway."

"On it's way, Ma'am. Calling car One, where are you?"

"We're at Moors Crossing."

"Listen, forget the drunk drivers and get out to the main road straightaway. Be on the look out for a black Ford Escort, reg number unknown. If this car comes into view, just follow suspect. Do not approach. He's wanted in connection with three murders. The head brass will be here soon and they'll handle it. Over and out."

"Were you listening to all that?"

"Yes. Never a dull a moment. One minute we're looking for drunk drivers, the next minute we're on the trail of a serial killer. Bet anything he's the bloke that killed those two girls. Must have killed another one tonight. Let's go."

As they turned to get on the main road, the car went into a skid and straight into a ditch. "Jesus Christ, we're stuck. I don't believe this. Get out and we'll try and push it back on to the road.

"After some minutes of trying to get it back on to the road, they gave up. You better phone the Sergeant and tell him what's after happening."

"Why don't you tell him; you're his pet."

"Very funny."

As they were calling in, some cars passed and one was the Ford Escort with Trevor Stanley in it. He'd seen the police car in the ditch and he smiled to himself.

"If only they knew who was passing them. Now onto the house. Maybe mother told Miss Brophy, but she won't be talking." He laughed. He had decided to take the back way to Whitby; fewer cops this way.

Now, as he stopped on the hill over looking Whitby, the snow was starting to fall.

"There'll be no food in the house," he thought to himself. "I'll have to stop and get some food. I'd better not forget to get candles; the electricity will have been turned off."

As he entered Jackson's shop, Maria looked up and said, "Can I help you?"

"I just need to pick up a few things, love. You're open very late."

"Who are you telling? My friends are all gone to the disco and I'm stuck here. But another couple of minutes and I'll be gone."

"Nobody saw me come in. I'll tell her I'll bring her up to the hotel. Once I get her into the car, I'll hit her with the hammer that's under the seat. Then I'll take her up to the house and play with her for awhile, and then kill her."

Just as he about to ask her, the door opened and Maria's father walked in.

"Okay, love. It's time to lock up."

"I'll just finish off this customer and be with you in a jiffy."

Paul Jackson looked over at the customer and thought, "He's no local. Could be a tourist. On a night like this, he must have a holiday home here and he's checking up on it."

"That will be eight pounds, please. And a happy New Year to you."

"Thank you."

As he got back into the car, Paul Jackson was saying, I didn't like the look of him."

"Dad, you don't like the look of anyone that speaks to me, never mind him. Come on, you and Lady can walk me up to the hotel."

After leaving his daughter, Paul decided to have a walk down by the quay. But the snow was falling faster.

"That's it, Lady, no more walk for you. Time for a brandy and into a warm bed. As he walked up the hill to his house, he looked down a side street and saw the car parked.

"Wonder why he didn't park out in the front? And I wonder which house he's in. True for Marie, I'm a frustrated police man."

Inspector Blakely and Sergeant Jackson were driving through the snow to Whitby.

"The snow seems to be stopping, Ma'am."

"I hope so. And I hope he's gone to Whitby. Because if not, we're up shit creek without a paddle."

"Where else could he go? Every main road, every camera, and every station for miles around are on the lookout for him."

"I know but he's a devious bastard. And so far, he's had the luck of the devil."

Just then the radio came on. "Inspector Blakely here."

"This is Sergeant Scanlon here. The house they own is number four, Wellington Terrace. Her maiden name was Morrison and, believe it or not, her brother who owned the house died in Broadmoor, a raving lunatic.

'Years ago, five women were attacked in Sheffield and he was the main suspect, but before we could do anything, his sister had him committed and everything signed over to her including, wait for it, a flower shop."

"Could he have got through, Sergeant, if he took the back road?"

"Yes. One of our cars ploughed into a field and some cars passed. But we don't know right now whether he was one of them. Two cars are on their way to Wellington Terrace."

"Good. Tell them to wait until we get there, because if he's there, he's armed and dangerous. Make sure you tell them to keep their distance. We'll be there soon."

"Okay, Ma'am. See you then."

"I hope to Jesus none of them is looking for a quick promotion and decide to go in alone."

"Not when you gave an order, Ma'am."

"I hope you're right. But I have a bad feeling about this one—a bad feeling."

After getting the car out of the field and an earful from the

Sergeant, they were told to follow the two cars that were already there. Keep out of the way and wait for the big guns to arrive."

As they drove to Wellington Terrace, PC Steven Brolin said, "You know, there's a promotion here."

"What are you talking about?"

"Suppose he's in there? All we have to do is, I'll go in the front door and you go in the back or I'll go in the back door and you go in the front door."

"Are you mad or are you deaf? Did you hear what the Inspector said? Do you want to get me thrown out of the police force as well as your self. This bloke is a killer and he might think nothing of killing again."

"Will you give me a break. He's only a coward. He killed two or three defenceless women; you're six foot one, I'm six three, and we'll be ready for him."

"No. You can fuck yourself. I love my job and I love Whitby and I have no ambitions."

"Well, I have and if he's in there, I'm going in and fuck the big guns. I'll nail him myself."

PC Sean Maloney said no more. He knew he was wasting his time. Steven had his mind made up and nothing would change it.

As they pulled into a side street adjacent to Wellington Terrace, they saw the other police cars and, right out side number four, was the Black Escort.

"He's there. The bastard's in there. Sean you go in the front, I'll go in the back."

"Is there, anything I can say to make you change your mind?"

"No, not a thing. This only happens once in a lifetime and its happening now, and I'm ready for it. When this is over, we'll go over to Ireland and have good piss up. How's that?"

"I hope we won't be having a piss up and no jobs."

"Will you think positive, for fuck sake. They'll be patting us on the back and telling the press what good policeman we are. Right, let's go."

When the two moved into Wellington Terrace, the police in the other cars couldn't believe what they were seeing."

"I don't believe what Brolin and Maloney are doing. They're going in alone. Radio the Sergeant fast. Jesus Christ, they should be locked up with the lunatic inside the house. Sergeant, is that you?"

"No. This is Santa Clause. Who the fuck do you think it is? What do you want? He's still in the house, isn't he?"

"Yes he is, but two policemen are going in after him."

"I don't believe this. The murder squad will be here in a couple of minutes. They must have heard the order to hold back over the radio. Let me guess who they might be—would it be Mr. Brolin and Mr. Maloney?"

"I think so, Sergeant."

"Listen, don't follow them in, just keep an eye on them. We'll have him soon" He called Inspector Blakely. "This is Sergeant Higgins here. It seems two of my men must not have heard my orders and they're moving into Wellington Terrace now."

"Sergeant have you any control over your men?"

"Yes Ma'am, I have. These are two good police men who are just doing their job. Suppose he left the house tonight, Ma'am, there's a disco on in the hotel and some girls will be walking home alone. You must remember, we never had anything like this here before. All they do here is get drunk."

"All right, Sergeant, I get your point. We'll be in Whitby soon, but when the disco is over, let none of the people near Wellington Terrace. Do you hear me?"

"Yes, Ma'am."

After putting the radio down, Sergeant Higgins was wondering what to do about the two of them. "I'll put them on nights for the rest of their careers. I'll think of something—but, fair play to them, at least they doing it and not talking about it."

Maloney and Brolin had separated one from the other. In the back, Trevor Stanley had been watching them for some time. So they found me—but now they have to catch me. I think I'll leave one of my calling cards. Stanley went into the kitchen, got a knife and unlocked the back door. And he thought to himself, "Uncle John would be proud of me. Yes, very proud," as he stepped back into the comer and waited.

PC Brolin was making his way to the back door, thinking to himself, "This is my ticket out of here. Hello, London. Yes, London. It would have to be big. He kicked over one of the chairs as he entered the kitchen. "Shit, should have brought my lamp with me. Maybe he's asleep now." As he got to the centre of the kitchen, he saw him coming, but too late to get out the way.

PC Brolin tried to hit him with his truncheon, but the knife had already found its mark.

"Die, pig, die." Stanley was screaming as he stabbed him again and again.

PC Maloney heard the screams, "Sean, help me. He stabbed me." Maloney kicked in the kitchen door and switched on the lights. "No lights. He's gone out the back door." Maloney knelt down to help Steven Brolin and knew there was nothing he could do. "I should have listened to you. He came at me too fast. Sean, will I be all right."

"Of course, you'll be in the hospital in no time. But while we're waiting, let's say some prayers."

"It's a doctor I need, not prayers. I'm frightened, Sean. Oh God, I'm frightened."

"Steven, say after me, 'Oh my God, I am heartily sorry for all my sins because they offend you who are so good.' Steven, answer me." But PC Brolin would never answer anyone again. When the other policemen came in the door, PC Maloney was still praying into PC Brolin's ear. One of them raced out the back door and looked up to the top of the steps, and there was Trevor Stanley, holding up the knife and screaming, "Come and get me you bastard. I'm not finished yet." He gave a mad laugh and ran towards the old ruins.

At the same time at the other end of town, Maria Jackson stormed out of the disco. Her boy friend, Tony James, ran out after her.

"Look I'm sorry, but all I did was dance with her, that's all."

"How dare you. When I came in you were whispering into Louise Moran's ear and holding her hand, for God sake."

"I was shouting into her ear because the music was too loud. And, as for holding her hand, that was because we were getting pushed all over the place."

"Tell that to the fish."

"Maria, I love you. But your father could have looked after the shop. It's Christmas, you know, and you're only young once."

"Well, if that's the way you feel, you can go back in the door you just came out of. It's me you were supposed to be with, not the bike of Whitby."

"Look, I was with no one and I don't want any one only you. Look at the snow and look down on Whitby. I did it years ago with my mother and I never forgot it was beautiful—just like you. I love you."

"Tell me, did you kiss the Blarney Stone, because, if any one has the gift of the gab, its you. But I'm telling you, don't ever let me catch you speaking to her again. Do you hear me?"

"Yes and so does all of Whitby. Now tell me you love me."

He grabbed Maria and kissed her and they started to walk up the steps just behind the Hotel.

"By the way, how many drinks did you have?"

"As God is my judge, I only had two."

"Pull the other one, you lying bastard."

"In a minute, darling." And both started to laugh.

Trevor Stanley knew time was running out for him, with the women's murders and now the policeman's.

"That's if he is dead. But," he thought, "I'll be famous. If they catch me I'll get one of those do-good barristers who'll blame it on my family history or something. Wouldn't it be a laugh if I was caught, and while he was doing my defence, I killed him? I'd be more famous than Jack the Ripper.

"But I must get to the other side of Whitby."

As he went through the graveyard, he spotted the couple courting. Well, if it isn't our shop assistant, burning the midnight oil. It's as if I was meant to kill her—and that prick with her. But I'll have to move fast. Maybe I'll kill him fast and play with her for a while."

"Slowly does it," Marie said to Tony. "Did you hear something over there?"

"Are you crazy? There's no one here only us. Look around you."

"I tell you, I heard something like a laugh."

"That's only a wave or an owl. Never mind that, what about me and you?"

"Tony, stop it. I'm getting out of here—I'm afraid. You can stay here if you like, but I'm getting out."

"All right, all right, I'm coming."

As they walked back to the steps they saw people coming towards them.

"Oh Jesus, it's the police—and they're carrying guns."

Marie said, "Were you net fishing again?"

"No, I wasn't, I swear it. What are they doing up here?"

As the police marksmen moved towards them, one said, "Miss, is he with you or is he holding you hostage?"

"No, no; he's my boyfriend, honestly."

As they stopped more police came out of the shadows. One was a woman, "Tell me, did anyone pass you in the time you've been in here or did you see anyone acting strange?"

"No," Marie said, "but I felt we were being watched and 1 could have sworn I heard a kind of laugh."

"Where? Over by the old tomb."

"Which one?"

"That one down by the walk."

"Thank you. One of the police officers will see both of you home."

"OK, lets go."

"And remember, he's a killer and he has nothing to lose. If any one feels that their life is in danger, shoot. But be careful, other police officers are coming in from the other side.

"All right, spread out. Hopefully his footprints are still in the snow."

As they moved slowly through the graveyard, Sergeant Johnson was saying to himself, "All I need now is for Peter Cushing to appear. If someone had told me a month ago that I'd be looking for a lunatic in Dracula County, I'd have told them they were mad."

As he moved towards the tomb, he saw the footprints.

"Ma'am, over here."

Jennifer Blakeley came over, looked down at the footprints and said, "The girl was right. He was coming towards them and he must have been following them. He stopped here so he must have seen us coming. Look, here's where he turned back. He must be trying to get back into Whitby."

"There's no way he can get back, Ma'am. Every step, every corner is blocked off."

"Make sure the hotel steps are blocked off, because he could get lost in the disco crowd."

"Yes, Ma'am."

Trevor Stanley had seen them and watched them stop the girl and her boy friend. And he saw Inspector Blakeley.

"So it's the bitch from the TV. The place must be crawling with police."

He also saw that they were carrying guns.

"I must get out of here fast, but the snow is leaving my footprints everywhere. I'll have to try and get back into Whitby and break in to one of the summer houses. But how to get back? I've got it, I have a jacket with a hood on it, and some of the police don't know what I look like, so all I have do is wait for them to come to me and I'll pretend I'm one of them." So he waited and soon they were around him. He called out, "You two over there, move down by the wall, do you hear me?"

"Yes, Sir."

As they watched him go back, one said, "Who the fuck is he?"

"Must be another wanker from head office."

"If he is, what's he going that way for?"

"I don't know and I don't give a damn."

Trevor Stanley could not believe it. Here he was surrounded by police and not one making a move towards him. Now, as he moved back, he looked over at the ruins and there was the Blakeley bitch.

"I could I kill her here. Yes I could. All I'd have to do is get behind her. There's no one with her. All she's doing is giving orders in to her mobile."

And so, like a panther, he made his way towards Jennifer Blakeley. "Slowly does it. Must make no noise—no stepping on pebbles, just the snow."

Now he was right behind her with the knife in his hand. "Merry Christmas, Inspector Blakeley ." As he raised the knife, a shot rang out, and then another. Trevor Stanley was dead before he hit the ground.

Jennifer Blakely let out a scream and, just as she turned around, blood spilled out across her face. Trevor Stanley was lying just yards from her. She felt as though she were going to faint; her legs were giving out from under her when Sergeant Johnson grabbed her.

"Are you all right, Ma'am?"

"What happened?" she said.

"He tried to double back into Whitby but we were watching him the whole time. We were going to take him at the steps, but he must have seen you."

"Christ, he must have wanted to kill me to."

"Ma'am, he was a mad dog; he wanted to kill every one. Are you sure you're all right?"

"Yes. Thank God it's all over."

The next day it was all over the front pages. Trevor Stanley had got his wish; he had become famous. It was all about his childhood and his family's past, and some do-gooders were saying that if they had got to him in time, he could have lived a normal life.

"Bullshit if he had got to them in time, they would be dead now."

Jennifer Blakeley was sitting in the kitchen when the phone rang. It was the Commissioner.

"Well done. A great job; take some time off. Are you all right?

"Yes, I'm fine."

"Well, I hope I'll see you again soon. Merry Christmas."

"And the same to you, Sir."

As she was making another cup of coffee, the phone rang again.

"Christ, not the Commissioner."

"I'm looking for Miss Jennifer Blakeley."

"Yes, speaking."

"This is Matron Dean. I'm afraid I have bad news for you. Your mum has just past away very peacefully. She wasn't alone. Her Vicar was with her and she had made her peace with God."

"Thank you, Matron. I'll will be right over."

That night, alone in her house, she was thinking, "At least now she is with my father."

The Vicar made all the arrangements with the undertaker and informed all the relations.

Jennifer Blakeley looked over at the dresser. Inside it was a bottle of whiskey and a packet of cigarettes. She had given up some months ago. She went in to the kitchen; got herself a glass and a lighter, came back in, poured herself a double, and lit a cigarette.

"Fuck it. I could be dead tomorrow."

Later that night, after finishing most of the bottle and smoking all of the cigarettes, she lay down on the bed and thought of her parents and her childhood, and sobbed.

"What a fucking Christmas. Thank God this year is nearly over. I never want another one like it again." And as she drifted into sleep, she thought, "Today's headlines, tomorrow's fish and chips paper."

The log book from the doomed ship Mermaid

It was an eerie early morning with the mist moving slowly, just above the water, like a ghost. The Mermaid waited for its cargo; the night before the owner, James Boyd, had said to the captain, John Hughes, "One third of the profit will be yours so pack them in well. Every inch is more money."
"What if they run out of food?" he asked.
"That's their problem, not ours. And if any die, throw them overboard. Instead of looking for food, they'll be food for the fishes," he said, as he started to laugh.
"Where are your Christian beliefs?" he wanted to ask him.
"Now some punch to wish you a good and profitable voyage."
When they had finished and Mr. Boyd was about to leave the ship, he turned and said, "Remember what I told—you pack them in. The more the merrier. I'll see you and the log book in ten months' time. God go with you."
Later, standing on the deck, he saw them coming out of the morning mist down the quay, looking like the walking dead. They were all in rags; most had no shoes. The children were cold yet smiling; the fathers knew what lay ahead; and the mothers prayed that they would get to the new world alive.
They came aboard whispering to one other in Irish; the first mate grabbed the nearest man and said, "We speak only English on this ship. Not Gaelic. Understand?"
"I don't think he does," Captain John Hughes said. Let them speak what ever language they like."
"Aye, Captain. This way then," and the deckhands started to push and manhandle them.
"Stop it. There will be none of that on this trip," Captain Hughes shouted at them.
"But Mister Boyd said—"
"I don't care what he said. I'm the captain, and what I say goes—unless you think you know better. Do you?"
"No, Captain," the deck hand replied sarcastically.
"Good. Now show them their quarters."
When they where all aboard, he thought, "If we get rough seas and delays that hold will be a mortuary for most of them. Now, we wait for the tide."
He looked at the port town of Queenstown. The year: 1841. The country: Ireland. And why the population was leaving: famine.

The first mate, Joseph Ryan, came up the steps and said, "Everything is ready captain."

"Good. Cut loose the ropes and point the bow to the open sea and the new world," he replied.

"Aye, Captain," the first mate answered.

For the first four days, everything was fine. The captain wrote in his log book:

Some are sea sick and, in all my years of sailing, I have never seen anything like it: nothing comes up. I have ordered the first mate to give them bread and cheese and to have the hold cleaned out. He told me that there is a foul smell coming from it.

A baby girl was born and they named her Maud, so they're happy. Some are singing. As I listened from my cabin it became more like a wailing—as if it was the banshee. It gave me such a fright that I ran back up on deck to ask the watch man whether he had heard it.

"What, Captain?" he asked me.

"A woman singing."

"No. But the men were. That's just the wind coming down the sails, Captain, nothing more," he replied.

"Yes, you're right. A good sleep is what I need. Goodnight to you."

"And the same to you, Captain."

The ship is now making good headway. Strong winds fill the sails.

A father of a girl—I'd say ten years of age, but to look at her you'd think she was older—came and pleaded with me to ask the doctor to examine her, so I got him to look at her and he tells me she is dying. "Put her in to sickbay," I said.

"Yes but that will only prolong it; her stomach has closed. But there is one thing you could do."

"Ask," I said.

"She wants to see the flying fish,"

"What kind of fish are they?" I asked him.

"Dolphins."

And from dawn to dusk, all she did was to look at them. Now the men think they know and are doing tricks just for her. On her last day an albatross landed beside her. As the news spread through the ship, all my men gathered around to see it

The only people it would allow near her were her parents. But how would a bird know who they were? And just before she died, she reached out to the bird; he bent his head gracefully, and laid it gently in her hand. After some minutes, the tiny hand fell back on to the deck and, at that very moment, the albatross spread its massive wings, looked up to heaven, and let out a screech.

Superstition and fear raced through my body, as everyone on the deck started to pray.

"This is a dead ship," one of my men said.

Doctor Samuel Johnson walked slowly over to the parents and, as he bent down to the girl, he looked up at the bird, knowing his beak could cut out his eyes in a second. But again it was as if it knew what he was there for. Had I not seen it I never would have believed it.

Then he got up and went down below. After some minutes, he came back up with a shawl and a bible. He wrapped the shawl around her body and told some men to bring the cooks table out. When they had done so, he said, "He won't touch you."

But, still afraid, they moved over slowly. All the time, he kept guard. They lifted her body and put her on the table. As they moved back, a sound came from the albatross. It was as if he was crying.

Now the doctor started the prayers in English and they answered him in Gaelic. When he came to "ashes to ashes", it bent its head and moaned, even as the doctor prayed. With all of his education and the books that he had read, he had never come across what was happening now.

They lifted the table and her body slipped in to the sea. The bird watched and the second it hit the water, flung itself down after it, diving into the waves at the spot where the body had gone in. Then it came back out with a piece of the shawl in its mouth. It stopped in mid air, looked straight at me, flew once around the ship and then up in to the clear blue sky. As we all watched, suddenly it was gone.

Later the doctor explained how this had happened. We had all watched it for too long and the sun was too strong for our eyes. We had to turn away and when we looked back up, it was gone. "Pure and simple," he said.

I said nothing, but I did not believe him. I don't think he even believes it himself.

The next month went fast. We had some more deaths, but nothing like what happened with the girl. I found out that her name was Molly O Callahan. One night, as I did my nightly rounds, one of the crewmen told me that the bird was really the banshee and that it follows certain families.

"Who told you this?" I asked him.

"Her father," he answered.

"But I thought his English was bad," I said.

"It is, Captain, and so is my Gaelic, but he knew what I was asking and I knew what he was answering. Remember the night you thought you heard a woman singing?"

"Yes."

"Well you did and it was her."

"Then how come you didn't hear her?" I asked him.

"Not everyone does. She could be right along side me now, screaming her head off and, if I did not see her, I'd never know she was there. And you could be at the other end of the ship, hear her, and it could bust your eardrums"

"Have you ever met anyone that this has happened to?" I asked him.

"No, but I never met the banshee either," as he blessed himself. " Nor do I want to," he replied.

Back in my cabin, I wondered whether it were possible. I had heard these stories as a boy but had put them down to old folk tales. The men have all gone quiet since Molly's death. I can't put my finger on it, but it's as if everyone is waiting for something to happen. It's as if doom has come on board. And it has.

The wind has deserted us and the sails are dead. Some of the men say that they have seen Molly. And the dolphins have returned.

I asked where Molly had been seen, and each gave a different part of the ship. She has even been seen up in the look out. I had the first mate bring her parents to my cabin. The unfortunate people went down on their knees when they brought them in. I asked crewman Ford, who had come in with them, why they were doing that.

"They think that you are going to throw them overboard, Captain. They know she has been seen."

"Ask them have they seen her," I said. He spoke to them. Then he turned to me and said "If they answer you truthfully, can they stay on board?"

"Of course," I answered. "Well, they say she is now right outside your door." I rushed to the door, opened it, and gave a sigh of relief. Nothing. I looked up and down the corridor. The same. Then something made me look down at the floor and, just at my door, was a pool of water. Nowhere else, just there. A coldness shot through me. Is it possible that these people, who can't even write down their own name, know more about life or death then the teachers who taught me?

"What will I do with them, Captain," crewman Ford asked me.

"Let them go back."

As they passed me the mother stopped, looked straight in to my

eyes and I into hers. I felt I was looking at a walking corpse.
When they had left and crewman Ford returned, I told him what
I thought.
"You know why that is, Captain," he said to me.
"No, tell me," I said.
"Because that is the first time you've done it. Me, I see them
most of the days when they come up, and they all have that
same look."
"But I have seen them many times," I answered.
"Yes, Captain, but from a distance—not like awhile ago when
she was right in front of you," he said
"Why did she do that?" I asked him.
"Because she was trying to read your mind. Don't worry, she
speaks well of you."
"She told you this?" I asked
"Yes."
That night, I slept soundly. The cook even had to waken me. And
as he put the breakfast in front of me, he said, "Good news,
Captain."
"Thank god. What is it?" I asked him.
"The wind has come back with a vengeance, haven't you
noticed?" he asked me.
"No my mind is miles away," I replied.
"Well, with the speed we're going, we should be there in no
time," he said.
"I hope you're right," I answered.
After finishing breakfast and cleaning myself, I went up on deck.
"The sails are full, but the sea looks a bit rough," I said to the
watch man
"Yes," he answered slowly.
"Is something bothering you?" I asked him.
"Well, I don't know, Captain. One minute not a puff, and now
this," and he pointed to the sails.
"Can't make head or tails of it."
"Don't," I answered. Just thank God it has come back."
It was as if we were flying over the water. But, seamen being
what they are, they said it was an ill omen. And the next day
they where proven right. The smell of sickness from the hold
was unbearable. I had words with Doctor Johnson, telling him
they were his responsibility and that, if he had done his job
right, it would never have happened.
"I did do it right. I checked them once a week, ask any of the
men," he said.
Then came a knock on my door, "Yes, who is it?" I shouted out.

"Me, Captain," Crewman Ford answered. "You'd better come up on deck fast."

"Why? What is it?" But he was gone.

"We'll continue with this later," I said to the doctor, as I put on my captain's hat and went straight up.

What I then saw was like something out of Dante's hell.

The hold people, as the crewmen called them, were all huddled together with red sores over there faces and bodies, with puss coming out of the open wounds. They pointed to the hold, and then I saw them. The leader came out first, looking cautiously, then turning and looking back down, giving a nod of his head. And then they came out: rats. They started to run in every direction and in to every hold.

"How could so many have hidden without anyone noticing," I asked Crewman Ford. We saw some, but where they're after coming out of I don't know." So I asked some more of the crew and they said the same.

The sails started to creak as the sea and the wind started to push us from side to side. During the next couple of days, it never stopped. We lost one crewman and some of the hold people—how many, God only knows. And some of the rats started to attack the sick as they lay in their hammocks. So, from now on, while one sleeps, another watches. Then the fog came back and, with it, calm.

We are near land. I can hear seagulls but not see them. We have reached our destination, and I have ordered that all the lamps be lit. We have to be careful or we could end up on the rock.

We sent signals and, after some hours, they answered that we were to come in at the bay. Hallelujah. God be praised. Strange that we can read their light clearly, yet it took some time for them to read ours.

Suddenly, the ship's rudder broke and we began to make speed it's as if an invisible hand was now steering the ship. Then the fog lifted and, just ahead of us, were giant rocks. We had been led in to a trap. The ship smashed straight in to them. God have mercy on us.

Some time later, its sinking with no survivors was reported in all of the papers. The insurance company paid up; the owner, Boyd, made a very good profit.

Then rumours started going around the town that the ship was never sea worthy and that he had paid some men to scuttle it. No one will ever know; his body was found in his garden a week after receiving the money. There was a look of horror on his face, and he was soaked, with seaweed all over him. Yet that night had been one of the driest nights we had that year.

Twenty five years later, the captain of a timber ship was having a drink in the Cove saloon when a man came up and asked him to buy him a drink.

"Why should I buy you one," he asked the stranger.

"Maybe it will loosen my tongue," he replied.

"I'd say it's well loosened. But here, have one. Better than drinking alone.

After some more he asked whether had the captain ever heard of the Mermaid, the ship that went down out there," as he pointed out with a shaky hand.

"Yes," he replied.

"Would you like to buy the logbook from it," he whispered to him.

Captain Saul Rodgers was suddenly all ears, having heard so many different stories about it.

"Where did you get it from?" he asked.

"From a sailor who went mad," again, he was whispering

"Was he part of the wreckers?"

"Yes."

"Were you?" the captain asked him.

Sweat started to pour down his face; then he turned to look around.

"What's wrong with you, man? Just answer the question."

"No I wasn't in on it, I swear on my soul. But I think someone is following me."

"Where is it?" the captain asked him.

"Behind the bar," he answered.

"How much blood money do you want for it," the captain asked him.

"As much as I can get. Now, do you want it or not?"

When the price had been agreed on, and the money handed over, he went back to the bar and said something to the owner, who handed it to him. He came back.

"Here," he said. "And good riddance to it."

"You're not trying to make a fool out of me?" the captain asked him.

"No."

"That's all right."

"He was mad you know," he said.

"Who?"

"The captain," he replied.

"How do you make that out," Captain Rodgers asked him.

"When you've read it, you'll understand. Now I'll leave you."

And he made for the back door, opening it and looking out cautiously, as if someone was waiting for him. Then he was gone.

After finishing his drink, the captain picked up the log book and started to walk back to his ship. Suddenly he heard a scream that put the shivers through him. Then another. Then quietness. "They're starting early tonight," he thought.

The Ghost of Plassey

On the Black Bridge at Plassey, the story is often told of a boat being seen with a man trying to get to shore. They whisper his name, afraid that he might hear. Didn't Tim Ryan look down from this very same spot one night and there he was holding onto one of the beams.

Yes they'd heard that story and then one man said he had also seen it. "Tell us where."

"I was fishing one evening up by the Falls when I looked across to the rocky side and saw it moving with the tide. It went through the boats, making not a ripple or a sound, he even put out his hand to try and grab hold of the keel. I swear he turned and looked straight back at me as it went into the middle and continued down with the stream. The swans took no notice; it was as if it were not there. Yet they moved away from their feeding as it passed their way."

"What happened then?" one asked.

"It went straight to the island and just disappeared. Now, as you know, some say it was him, others say it was a bargeman or even a sand cot man. But they can say what they like; I saw it and I swear it was him."

He'd had a fight in the pub that night and left his friend badly beaten on the floor. He came back across the bridge and then down by the garrison wall where he met Tom Flynn and told him what he had just done.

"My temper got the better of me," he said. "I'll have to go back and apologise even if it's the last thing I do."

"It's too dark to walk back now," Tom said.

"My boat is just over there and it will be faster to row across. Anyway the light from the pub will guide me." With that he was gone.

Later some said that they heard a cry for help saying, 'For God's sake, someone help me to get back to the shore," and then it faded away. They thought it was someone acting the fool, so they ignored it.

He was never found, and neither was the boat. But a courting couple some weeks later saw it for the first time. Since then, it can be seen coming up to each anniversary of his disappearance. It is now seen more often at the bend just at the top of the river. Mostly those who have seen it say he just sits and waits.

The pub is long gone. Those who knew him when he lived are also gone.

Some also say on a clear night if you look from the bridge to the cut, you might see him, still trying to get to the opposite side.

Scent

On our last night together, she told me she would find me, no matter where I was. As the years went by, I thought of what she had said to me now and then, but it was the aroma of her perfume that I remember the most. Then, one afternoon and many miles from home, I thought I smelled it in the kitchen. But the same perfume was still being sold all over the world; maybe Mia had bought a bottle of it when she went into town.

Misty, my dog, seemed very upset. "What's wrong with you?" 1 asked, but all she did was lie down in front of me.

"I tell you what, I'll take you for a walk, that'll cheer you up."

With that she was up straight away. As I was putting my coat on, I heard the rain starting to pour down.

"Come out to the kitchen for some food; the rain should clear up soon."

Walking towards the hall, I smelled it again. This was starting to get on my nerves, so I went up to Mia's room to see whether she had dropped a bottle of it—just in case it was leaking down through the floor boards. No, not a thing.

Then I went over to where she keeps all her perfume; there were all kinds in it, but the not the one I smelling now.

As I was coming back down the stairs, I could hear Misty howling.

"What's the matter now?" I asked. Then I realised that the smell was getting stronger, and that parts of the carpet were now wet. It couldn't have been from my shoes, I hadn't been out. Looking up at the ceiling, I prayed it wasn't the water tank; the ceiling was dry.

"Where's it coming from I wonder?" Misty was now moaning. I went over to her, knelt down, and put my hand on her head to stop her shaking. Then I felt the dampness on her and suddenly I got a strange feeling that I was being watched. I turned, picked up the poker from the fireplace, and walked slowly back into the hall. Again, nothing.

Then I looked down at the tiles. It was as if someone had taken a bucket of water and thrown it on them. Christ, what's happening here?

"All right, who's in here? I have a poker in my hand and I'm prepared to use it."

As I looked up the stairs, I thought I saw the shadow of a

woman on the landing.

"Mia is that you?" I called, running up the stairs. But I could see nobody. When I opened the guest room door, the smell and the dampness were there, but not a sign of anyone. I tried all the rooms, including the attic, but they were all the same.

As I walked into my room my mobile rang. "Hello, who is this?"

"It's me, Peter."

"Well, what's the news from home?"

"Remember the girl you went out with years ago?" Peter asked.

"Which one?"

"Joan Ryan."

"Yes. What about her?"

"She was taken out of the river this morning. Don't ask me what happened, but you know this place—everyone has their own story. Tony, are you still there?"

"Yes."

"I always knew you had a soft spot for her. If there's any more news, I'll give you a call."

Tony Prendergast sat on the bed and put his head in his hands. When the smell started to overpower him, he looked into the mirror and could see Joan Ryan standing behind him saying, "I told you I'd find you, Tony".

The end